ECHO'S REVENGE: THE ULTIMATE GAME

THE ONGOING INVESTIGATION OF SEAN AUSTIN

BOOK 1 V 1.0

SEAN AUSTIN

REALITY GAMES

This is a work of fiction. All of the characters, organizations, and events portrayed in this novel are either products of the author's imagination or are used fictitiously.

Echo's Revenge: The Ultimate Game
The Ongoing Investigation of Sean Austin
Book 1 V1.0

Published by AAA Reality Games LLC
11693 San Vicente Boulevard, Suite 498
Los Angeles, California 90049

www.aaarealitygames.com
Library of Congress Control Number : 2012932642
ISBN 978-0-9837264-0-1

AAA Reality Games LLC is a company dedicated to exploring the art of reality games through robotic engineering.

www.aaarealitygames.com

This Is An Ongoing Investigation

Look. It doesn't matter if you believe this account or not. At any given time there are so many unbelievable things going on, hidden right in front of us, that hardly anyone even knows about...it doesn't matter to me what you believe. I'm just reporting what I found. For the record. For the whole team at AAA Reality Games.

The following report was acquired through extensive interviews after the fact. I could not fully understand or describe the psychological effects ECHO-7 had on ECHO gamers, how it bent its victims' wills into submission to its incomprehensible schemes, but everything I found is included in this report. I will update this version if I find any more information, so if you want to know anything more, don't ask me, and don't try to find me. I don't have much time left, and there are other things I have to do now.

Everything that follows is recorded from actual observations and interviews. To protect my sources, I had to change some names of people, locations, and other items, except my own name: my name is Sean Austin, and I was there.

Sean Austin
May 15, 2012
Pasadena, California

P.S. And don't forget, this is an investigative report, not a "storybook." These are just the cold, hard facts and as much information as I could uncover. Despite the insistence of certain AAARG team members that I release this report immediately, this investigation is ongoing at echohunt.com. So, AAARG team members, if I left anything out, let me know for the next version of this report. You can always email me at seanaustin@echohunt.com, and I'll follow up on any leads.

PROLOGUE

"Fog! It's so foggy, I can't see a thing," Reggie whispers as he peers around the cold granite corner of the County Courthouse. It is cold, and getting darker, perceptibly darker each minute. The streets have been abandoned by almost all humans, due to some unnatural series of events.

"Jeremy, it's breaking. Watch our flank."

POUND, POUND, POUND...deep, earth shaking footsteps.

"Shhhh!" whispers Jeremy, "It's ECHO. He's here."

"Wait. There's a break in the fog. I can see something."

More fog...then another break...

A pulse blast hits Reggie in the back. He crouches in pain, grasping his SAW (Squad Automatic Weapon) tighter, as someone runs by.

"Hey, losers! I told you to back off! This one's mine!"

"It's just Masterson," says Jeremy.

"What a jerk! He hit me in the back."

They look back down the street.

"Something's different, Jeremy. I can't tell what, but something's different. Part of that building...it's gone!"

"Sh-sh-sh-sh-"

"It's so close I can feel it."

Zip-zip. A tiny vehicle covered with electronics appears on the sidewalk behind them. They spin around.

"SPYBOT!"

Reggie raises his SAW and it blazes with a deafening explosion. A smoking hole is all that's left in the asphalt.

"It saw us. We are so dead!" whispers Jeremy.

Reggie can't argue. He doesn't know what to say.

"Can we get some help here?" Jeremy whispers into his walkie-talkie, but no one answers. "No one can hear us."

"At least we'll die together, little bro."

Something new. The crystal-clear music of an ice cream truck, moving down the street, coming closer.

"Huh?"

The fog lifts, but they notice the shadow of an armored mechanized ghoul looming behind them on the granite wall. Although it is robotic, a machine, it appears angry, and its cold eyes indicate only a calculating cruelty.

The instant they turn, the mech blasts Jeremy to smithereens.

"JEM!!"

Now the mech's gun is on Reggie.

"Where are the others?" demands the mech-ghoul in a cold, synthetic voice. Its shock-red troll-like hair stands out in brilliant contrast to the neutral, washed-out greys and blacks of the foggy, ruined surroundings. The bright, glistening color is surreal and distracting.

Reggie rips a high-tech device off his vest.

"Eat this, mech-head."

The mech-ghoul freezes.

"That's right! EMP grenade with your name on it!"

EMP as in Electromagnetic Pulse, the most feared weapon known to mechs. If it explodes, it'll fry the mech's processors and kill it, but the powerful pulse would also transform Reggie's brain to Jell-O.

The ghoul knows this.

It mechanically clicks forward one centimeter at a time. Reggie realizes he is being tested the way only mechs can test humans. When Reggie fails to detonate the grenade, it's obvious that the mech knows that he isn't ready to sacrifice himself to kill a mere machine. The mech is going to charge. Reggie knows he's doomed.

As quick as a mech, Reggie activates the grenade. The ghoul freezes–this situation does not compute–and Reggie throws the grenade up in the air and dives behind the granite corner. He hears the explosion, and feels his tooth fillings tingle from the radiation of the EMP blast as the building trembles. He peers around the corner and sees the crumpled mech.

Then he looks behind the metallic corpse. The fog has cleared and there are another hundred and sixteen mech-ghouls flat on the asphalt–all dead from the EM pulse. He had no idea they were even there.

1. HOME SWEET HOME

"Whoah. Smokin'!" said Jeremy, who was watching the computer screen from over Reggie's shoulder. Reggie was playing "ECHO's Revenge." He was very good at it–no, make that great.

The version was ECHO-6, and ECHO, a 35-foot tall extreme predator clad in impenetrable body armor, was hot on Reggie's trail. Reggie knew the killing machine was there somewhere, but couldn't figure out exactly where. The problem was that the creature was cloaked, so it was virtually invisible. At times like this, Reggie was stressed to the max, searching every detail of the scene in front of him for any mirage-like distortion that would give away ECHO's position.

E-6 suddenly de-cloaked and materialized, its head protected by a helmet, its face hidden behind a visor shield. It appeared out of nowhere–like a nightmare of shiny, sharp, shifting, glass-like scales and armor–solidifying in thin air.

The visor retracted, revealing green, menacing eyes and a mass of razor sharp teeth forever grinding, mechanically, inside a cavernous, snarling mouth. ECHO was a perpetually traveling eating machine that was programmed to stalk and consume an endless supply of on-line gamers.

Reggie realized that ECHO-6 had been disguising itself as part of a building connected to the post office. ECHO could easily camouflage itself as a part of just about any building because it could easily shape itself to fit into any box-like form. It could also do rocks. What it couldn't do was turn itself into flowers or leaves because they were much harder to replicate, especially when it was moving.

Eight-inch steel claws extended from ECHO's hands as it moved forward. Its feet left an odd pattern of triangular imprints in the asphalt as it headed straight for Reggie, followed by a blurry, dispersed swarm, also apparently under some kind of invisible cloak. At first barely visible, another squad of armored ghouls now materialized out of the swarm.

"Blow the Ghouls away!" yelled Jeremy, "Then you gotta warn the other guys that ECHO's here!"

But telling the other gamers wouldn't help Reggie right now. More vicious, marauding ghouls were materializing like demons out of buildings and alleys everywhere. The ghouls wore less armor, and more of their scaly bodies were exposed as they had no helmets or armor below their waists. Reggie quickly analyzed his options.

"Hmmm..." he said, as if he knew all along the ghouls were going to come. He waited for the perfect moment...

From downstairs, a deep, hoarse voice suddenly exploded. It was their mom's boyfriend, aka "partner," Asa.

"I TOLD YOU TWO TO SHUT UP. I CAN'T THINK WHEN YOU'RE PLAYING THOSE STUPID INTERNET GAMES!"

"Yeah yeah..." said Reggie, under his breath, "we heard ya..."

"Get 'em now!" said Jeremy.

"No, wait..."

Reggie was 14 years old, and Jeremy was 11. Reggie had been playing "ECHO's Revenge" for five years, so he knew the game inside and out and had developed special techniques for playing the game. One technique was to hide and wait until the last second to blow his enemies away. None of the other players around the country, or even around the world, ever had a chance. Not the Russian kids who tried to reprogram the game. Not the Koreans who formed impenetrable gangs to execute their strategies. Not even the programmers who made the game. He blew them all away. When it came to playing ECHO's Revenge, Reggie was merciless.

At the last possible second he finally fired another EMP grenade and blew a large squad of charging ghouls into oblivion.

"Objective Complete," flashed the screen, "Final Objective: Take Out ECHO!"

"Watch out...it's changing," said Jeremy, as the giant ECHO morphed into a tank and advanced, aiming its huge cannon directly at them.

"Hit it before it cloaks!" said Jeremy.

Reggie fired and one of the tank's treads blew apart, immobilizing the tank and freezing its turret, now safely pointing away from them.

But just as Reggie was about to advance, the screen suddenly froze. A flat, animated black cartoon drawing of a pair of black glasses and a big mouth full of sharp teeth appeared.

"No! It's HAkr!" cried Jeremy.

"Man, I hate that guy!" said Reggie, "He's always messin' with me."

"It's because you got him that time with Rhino."

The cartoon mouth split open with a big laugh and the face traveled across the screen eating everything like some sort of nerdy Pac Man as it shouted "How ya doin' Reggieee? Ha Haaa..."

"Man that guy's a pain," said Jeremy. "How does he get into the system?"

"And when will he stop messing with me?"

As suddenly as the face appeared, it disappeared. But the action in the game had not stopped. ECHO was right in front of them, and about to devour Reggie.

"RPG!" yelled Jeremy.

"I'm loading!" said Reggie.

As the creature's cavernous mouth plunged downward, Reggie fired the rocket propelled grenade straight into its throat. ECHO immediately reared and gagged. Then its head exploded.

"Waiting For You Survives!" flashed the screen, "Final Objective Accomplished!"

"Waiting For You" was Reggie's avatar name.

"Try to call the other E-6 players," said Jeremy, "so they can attack the rest of the ghouls! Surround and Capture!"

"Wow!" said Reggie, excitedly reading another message on the screen. "Huh? Hey, guess what? I made it! I'm one of the top 3 players!"

"You kicked ECHO's butt!!!"

Then a final message appeared, so briefly, maybe less than a second, that Reggie wondered if it had really been there. He thought it said *I'm Watching You Now*. Was it another threat from HAkr?

"QUIET, Dammit!" screamed the voice downstairs.

"Sounds like he's drinking again," said Reggie. "We better watch it."

Jeremy panicked.

"We gotta get outta here."

It was too late. Heavy footsteps were stomping up the stairs.

Reggie ran to the window of their second story bedroom and tried to open it. It was frozen shut. He scanned the room to find something to loosen the window with and spotted his black pocket knife. He grabbed it, cut out a chunk of ice between the window and window frame, and pulled up on the window.

The window popped open and Reggie dropped the knife outside just as Asa stormed into their room.

"Quick!" said Reggie. "Go!"

But it was too late. As Jeremy jumped out the window, Asa, his face bright red and the veins in his neck bulging out, hurled a bottle at Reggie. The bottle shattered on the wall.

"I TOLD YOU TO SHUT UP!"

Jeremy landed hard in the snow and barely missed a big rock. Reggie was right behind him. Fortunately, there was about five feet of fresh snow on the ground. When the rest of Reggie's body landed on top of Jeremy, they both just sank deeper into the powdery soft snow.

The window slammed shut.

"Man, I smacked my head," said Reggie, holding his hand up to his ringing ear. He felt dizzy and began to black out.

Jeremy was holding his own injured hand. He had put it between Reggie's head and the rock just before Reggie hit it to cushion the blow.

Reggie heard a rushing sound, then a weird sort of mechanical purring hum, and then he thought he saw…was that ECHO peering at him through the trees?

"Reggie!" screamed Jeremy. "Reggie, are you okay? Wake up!"

Reggie shook his head and looked into the forest where ECHO had been. All he could see were tree branches.

"Home Sweet Home," said Reggie.

They both laughed.

Reggie picked up his knife out of the snow and dusted it off on his pants. As they brushed the snow off themselves, a dirty, mud-covered Jeep Cherokee pulled into the driveway.

"Hey, look! Mom's here," said Jeremy, sounding surprised to see her.

A short, plump, disheveled 45-year-old woman with shoulder length, bushy black hair got out of the jeep. She gathered up a pile of disorganized papers. It was Reggie's and Jeremy's mom, Jennifer Edna, or Jeda, a name she had been called since she was a little girl.

"Hello, my bunnies!! How was your day today?" she asked in the same sugary, over-excited voice you would use with a couple of babies.

"Okay mom."

Reggie was always embarrassed when his mom spoke to him this way in front of other people. Part of the reason was that his mother looked like a plump Raggedy-Ann doll with slightly psychotic eyes. She always wore frumpy clothes, the type an old fashioned librarian would wear. The other reason was that instead of treating them like they were grown up kids, she always babied them like they were still two.

"What are you two doing out here with no coats on?" she asked.

"Asa threw us out of the house again," said Jeremy.

"Ooooh," said Jeda. "Well then, get your jackets out of the garage and just stay out of his way."

Jeda noticed Reggie putting his knife away.

"WHAT is THAT!?" she asked.

"Just a knife. Dad gave it to me," said Reggie.

"That's VERY dangerous!" she said, rushing over and grabbing the knife from Jeremy. "And your father's CRAZY to give you such a thing! First he abandons us, then he gives you a knife!?"

"Mom, it's no big deal. It's just a tool."

"Well, I'm going to hold onto this," she said as she headed inside. "Your father's head is stuck in the clouds. This is very dangerous!"

"The only thing dangerous around here is Asa."

"Honey, you just don't understand him. If he's upset, you must have done something," said Jeda as she went into the house.

The broken screen door closed behind her.

"Man, why doesn't she ever get it?" asked Jeremy.

"I know, she gets everything totally wrong. Girls are whacked."

"I just hope he leaves her alone," said Jeremy.

"Don't worry. He'll be nice. Mom got paid today."

"Partners" is what Jeda and Asa called themselves. Jeda worked as a social worker and Asa took care of the house and the kids when they came home from school. Jeda was always late–to pick them up or take them to school–and often completely forgot to pick them up, or get them to appointments, or even school.

Asa was like a grumpy babysitter with a powder-keg temper. He didn't like fixing things that broke or leaked, so things were always broken and leaking around the house. He didn't like watching the guys or cooking dinner for them, and he didn't like making sure they did their homework or got to school on time.

Since Jeda and Asa were not married and were often fighting, there was never any peace and quiet or predictability. Reggie and Jeremy never knew when Asa would explode, or if Jeda would even show up at home before they went to sleep every night.

Reggie put his arm around Jeremy as they headed to the garage. As crazy as their two "partners" were, at least Reggie and Jeremy had each other. When Jeda forgot to pick them up, or Asa tried to beat them up, they could always depend on each other. Whenever they were left alone, they kept each other company, mostly by playing video games on-line. Reggie often wondered–who was more difficult to fight–ECHO on-line, or Asa for real?

Reggie and Jeremy constantly wondered what it would be like to be in a normal family in a normal home, where two normal parents were married and didn't just call each other "partner." Where things didn't always leak or break, and where no one ever screamed, threw anything, or hit anyone.

"I'm sure glad you're here, Reg. I don't know what would happen if it was just me alone with those two."

Reggie didn't want to imagine what it would be like.

"Well, at least you'd have Dad, too," said Reggie.

"Yeah, but he's long gone. We'll probably never see him again."

Their dad, Aaron King, was a mystery. He seemed like a nice guy, but they hardly ever saw him. Their parents divorced when they were little, so they never got the real story. All they knew was they had to live with their mom, which seemed weird, because their dad seemed normal and had a job at the Jet Propulsion Lab in California. He was some kind of rocket scientist.

Reggie didn't say anything. It didn't make sense to him. Jeda was always saying their dad had abandoned them, but he called for Reggie and Jeremy every week, even though Jeda made a point of not picking up the phone. And when they did talk to him, they couldn't discuss any real problems because it would cause their mom and dad to fight.

Reggie felt bad about Jeremy's hand. He noticed Jeremy was holding it like it was a broken bird. Things were so out of control that Reggie was always feeling guilty about something Asa or Jeda had done or caused. It was so unfair. So out of balance.

They put their jackets on in the garage. The jackets were the old style, big and puffy, not made of thin, modern Gore-Tex like everyone wore. There were two full backpacks embroidered with thunderbolt logos hanging on the wall, looking like they were just waiting there, ready to be used for a camping trip.

Outside, they noticed that the sun had dropped behind the trees and everything was growing darker. The valley and imposing mountains surrounding them were muted by the same cold, dreary, blue light of every other winter day in Meadowbrook. Meadowbrook, King County, Washington State, U.S. of A., Planet Earth, Milky Way Galaxy.

Reggie's head was still throbbing and he was still light-headed. Even though it was getting colder and darker, they knew they couldn't go inside until Asa had his cooling off period. It was like the day would never end.

As they walked and slid down the icy road, Reggie suddenly felt a painful "thwack" on the back of his thick coat. He rubbed his back and noticed red liquid on his hand. Was he bleeding? Then he saw a paint ball shell in the snow. He looked into the dark recess of the open door of the house in front of them.

"Knock it off, Masterson!" Reggie yelled.

Chuck Masterson, a beefy 12-year-old with short, spiky blond hair, emerged from the doorway holding a massive paint ball gun.

"Hey, freakazoids. Nice marshmallow costumes! Did your parents wear those too when they were kids?"

"Ha ha, Masterson," said Jeremy. "Butthead!"

Chuck shot at a squirrel with his gun, but missed.

"You look like big, walking, butts with heads! Ha, ha! Losers..."

"Knock it off with the paint balls, Masterson!" yelled Reggie.

"Yeah, yeah, weirdos," said Chuck, as he continued firing at the squirrel while it scampered across the snow behind them.

Reggie and Jeremy continued down the road as the paint balls zinged by.

"So, have you figured out a name for your avatar yet?" asked Reggie.

"Still workin' on it. I just can't find anything that's me. I don't want to use 'Cougar,' or something."

"Yeah, that's stupid," laughed Reggie.

"Or 'Crusher'," said Jeremy, as they both laughed.

"Spike..."

As they faded into two small, distant dark figures at the end of the icy road, a salt truck's red brake lights flashed briefly and it slowed down. It was a mechanic they knew who worked at a gas station in town and scraped the roads when it snowed. Reggie and Jeremy were always getting rides with the mechanic or other people they knew from town.

"Hop in," he nodded.

They jumped into the back of the truck and headed into town, to a burger place where they always ate when Asa was in one of his moods.

Later, they'd hitch a ride home, when Asa was sure to be asleep.

2. THE LETTER

When school ended the next day, Reggie and Jeremy walked home across an ice-covered field. As usual, Asa had forgotten to pick them up. It was cold, really cold, and by the time they got home, their ears, toes, and fingers were numb. As they walked in the front door, Asa emerged from the living room.

"Hey, where were you?" said Jeremy. "We waited for an hour."

"I was busy. You guys wanna help me make a fire?"

"Sure," they said.

"Okay, bring in some firewood from the garage and we'll start one."

"Cool."

They dropped their backpacks and headed to the garage.

"Wonder why he's in such a good mood," said Jeremy.

"Who knows? With Asa you never know what's going to happen."

As Reggie lit the fire, Asa brought the boys some hot chocolate. Jeremy was surprised–Asa usually wasn't this nice. He wondered what was up. After a few minutes of warming themselves at the fire, Reggie and Jeremy could feel their feet again. Before anything else weird could happen, they went to their room to do their homework.

After the time when Jeda was supposed to have come home, but once again hadn't, they ate dinner and watched a video. Asa believed that television, like fast food, soda, amusement parks, and everything that was fun, was 'consumer brainwashing,' so they were never allowed to watch TV. Instead, they rented videos. Tonight's video was "Dirty Harry," starring tough-guy Clint Eastwood. Asa sat in his special chair–the Stratolounger–the chair no one else was ever allowed to sit in, and they watched the movie. When the movie ended, Asa was still lying back in the big vinyl chair.

"Now that's a real movie," said Asa, "not like all the stupid computer graphics stuff today." Then he pulled on something that was bugging him, something he was sitting on. It was a letter.

"Oh here," he said to Reggie, "this came for you."

He handed Reggie the letter.

"What is it?" asked Jeremy.

"It's from AAA Reality Games!" said Reggie.

Reggie opened it and read it aloud, excitedly:

Dear Mr. King, aka 'Waiting For You,'

It has come to our attention that your latest game scores indicate that you have attained the Master level of *ECHO's Revenge* on-line game. We would be very excited to meet you, and would like you to participate in a focus group for our newest game, something we believe you would enjoy.

If you would like to do this, please come to our lab located at the address below at 2pm, Saturday, February 16th. It's going to be great fun and you will get to meet the other Master Gamers who play at your level.

Please note that we will pay for your travel costs.

This letter must be signed below by your parent or authorized guardian, and must be brought with you to authorize your participation.

Sincerely,
Luca Esposito
Lead Designer, AAA Reality Games LLC

"That's tomorrow! Cool, can I go too?" asked Jeremy.

"Who said Reggie should go?" said Asa.

"I'm not doing anything tomorrow. It's Saturday," said Reggie.

"No go, showboat. You're not doing anything for free for some billion dollar game company. If they want to pay you for your time, too, fine. Otherwise, no way. Besides, this gaming stuff is stupid–really stupid–a total waste of time."

"But there's no time to find out if they would pay me. You just gave me the letter and it came...a week ago!"

"Why should those corporate bloodsuckers get free labor? They pay–or no go," replied Asa.

He took the letter, crumpled it up, and threw it into the fire.

"You're staying home. Besides, they don't wanna hear what you have to say anyway. They just wanna sell you, and every other kid in the world, something you can't afford. Why don't you try reading a book for a change? Or spend some time doing something with your family?"

Asa got up and headed for the kitchen, but Reggie wouldn't let him get away with refusing to let him go.

"You can't do this! You're not my father! And we're not a family!" said Reggie, angrily.

"Oh really? Well ask yourself, are you feelin' lucky, punk?"

Asa's impression of Clint Eastwood was ridiculous, but he out-weighed Reggie by almost a hundred pounds. Reggie backed down.

"That's what I thought."

As Asa headed to the kitchen for another beer, he yelled out, "And Jeremy, clean the dishes, or else!"

What a joke, thought Reggie as he crept over to the blazing fireplace. The letter had landed in the back of the fireplace and one of the edges had caught on fire. He grabbed it, burning the hair on his arm, blew out the flames, and stuffed it in his pocket.

"Good save!" said Jeremy.

But Reggie was too angry to say anything. He left the room and stomped upstairs. He knew it was useless to argue with Asa, and he was furious that Asa always threw the things he cared about into the fire.

At exactly 8p.m. their father called, as he had done Tuesday and Thursday for as long as they could remember. That was the deal–two calls a week. Sometimes they would miss the call because Jeda had unplugged the phone to keep them from telling his father something, like the time when Asa had punched Reggie in the jaw. Or she would pretend not to hear the call. And sometimes she would intentionally be on the phone at that time and claim that "she forgot."

Reggie usually did all the talking, because Jeremy sometimes let the cat out of the bag and then everyone would get in trouble.

"So how's it going, Reg?" asked Reggie's dad.

"Good," said Reggie.

Asa stuck his head into Reggie's room, listening in on his call. His expression told Reggie that he couldn't mention being thrown out the second floor window, or made to stay home, or anything else unless he wanted to face more of Asa's infinite anger.

"Everything's great!" said Reggie cheerfully, for Asa's benefit. Asa faded back into the darkness.

"How's it really going there?" asked Reggie's dad, "Everything okay?"

"Well, the snow's starting to melt."

"You be careful with the ice and everything, Reg," his father said. "Winter's not over till it's over, and I don't want you falling through any ice, so stay off the river and lake."

This was the typical conversation Reggie had with his dad. His dad was always telling him to be careful and take care of himself. Reggie wouldn't say much because he was afraid that if he said the wrong thing, his father would make Jeremy talk and then have a big fight with his mother. Then his mother would scream at him. Asa would get pulled into the fight, and then Asa would get mad at Reggie for getting him into trouble. The last time it happened, Jeda had to agree to have a counselor come see the family every week for a year just because Asa had screamed at Reggie too much. From that point on, Jeda never spoke to Reggie's dad again.

Like a lot of people living in Meadowbrook, Asa had a problem with his temper. He was broke and couldn't find a job. Reggie thought that his mom had it hard enough already since Asa screamed at her too, and even made her cry sometimes. Reggie figured it wouldn't help anything to make it worse, so he always told his father that things were "good" to keep her out of trouble with Asa.

After the call with his dad, Jeremy said a quick "hi," and Reggie hung up, flipped off the light, and they got into bed.

Soon Jeda poked her head into their room and said in her baby voice, "Good night my bunnies!"

"Good night Mom," said Reggie.

"Good night Mom," said Jeremy.

As they lay in the dark, Reggie whispered to Jeremy, "Cover for me tomorrow, okay? If they ask, I'm cross-country skiing."

"Okay..." said Jeremy, wondering what Reggie was up to.

"And one more thing," whispered Reggie, rustling out of bed and climbing over to Jeremy with a small flashlight, "I need you to tell me if it looks like I faked Asa's signature on this letter."

"Are you crazy?" whispered Jeremy, looking terrified. "No way! He'll break every one of your fingers if he finds out you forged his name!"

"He'll never find out! Come on, you're good at art and stuff. Do you think this'll work?"

"You're cracked! He's gonna kill you!"

"Hey," said Reggie, "don't I always bail you out when you need my help? Come on man, we're brothers! You cover me, I cover you. That's what normal brothers do."

Jeremy thought about it for a second. All he wanted was to be normal, and he always did want to cover Reggie's back. He leaned over and looked at the crumpled, charred letter.

"Yeah, it looks okay–you might smudge the signature a little since the rest of the letter got burned."

"Excellent. I owe you," said Reggie. "I owe you..."

Reggie lay under his covers listening to the clock tick as he thought about Jeremy, and wondered if he had pushed too hard. It didn't take much to get Jeremy to help him. Reggie knew that ultimately he could always depend on Jeremy. But when it came to Asa and Jeda, nothing they did ever made sense to him. It was an endless circle of lies and confusion.

The wind howled outside and something tap-tap-tapped sharply on the window. As tired as Reggie was, the noise kept him from falling asleep. He glanced over and saw a branch tapping in the cold blue light. He was so tired that it looked as if something was distorting the blue light filtering through the window. He got up and stood in front of the window, looking up at the bright white crescent moon in the deep black sky.

As he watched the clouds pass in front of the moon, his vision momentarily blurred and he felt dizzy. A morbid feeling of dread seemed to envelop him. His view of the cold blue winter landscape somehow shifted, splintered. *Am I so tired I can't see straight, or am I going mental or something?* He couldn't figure it out, but the overwhelming feeling was a new combination of dread, depression and claustrophobia.

It's Asa – he's driving me crazy. No – I'm tired, so tired...it's just my life. It sucks. I'd be crazy not to be depressed.

He tried, but couldn't remember the time when things were simple, when everything made sense, and when his mom, his dad–not Asa–and he and Jeremy were together. He looked at a crumpled old picture of the street he used to live on, in Pasadena where his father still lived, and tried to remember. He missed those warm summer nights in California. What the heck had happened? He collapsed back onto the bed, overcome with misery. He was so tired. To sleep would end the depression...

In what seemed to be a moment later, he was suddenly outside in the cold, armed with a heavy SAW and several EMP grenades. For the last few months, Reggie often couldn't tell if he was in a dream or in another reality when he tried to fall asleep, but he craved sleep as relief from his life.

He was crouching in the woods, barely able to make out his bedroom window, where a tree branch was tap-tap-tapping on the window pane in the icy breeze. He knew he had to get Jeremy out fast, because something was stalking them.

"Rhino, where are you?" he whispered into his radio.

No answer.

Reggie looked around, hoping to find some good cover, and spotted a thick tree line he could walk behind.

"Flanking right," he whispered, as he quickly approached the right side of the house in a crouched position, staying hidden in the woods.

But as the predator approached the house, Reggie noticed that the woods he was walking through ended, and there was nothing but empty black space. He poked his rifle into the void but there was simply nothing there. It was like a glitch in a video game, where the code ended and there was a broken boundary of nothing. As he leaned over he could almost see something under him, under the ground, and when he leaned further, trying to see more, he tumbled down into the dark space.

As he fell, he instinctively lifted his weapon and looked up. He noticed that the ground was transparent and he could see the foundation and all the walls in his house, the road, the tree roots in the woods, and all the other houses in the neighborhood.

He shivered, not from the cold, but because he saw Jeremy sleeping in his bed while ECHO scanned inside the bedroom window.

3. THE FOCUS GROUP

Reggie got up at 6 a.m. He was toasty warm under the covers and hated getting out of bed, but he got dressed quickly as Jeremy slept.

In less than five minutes, he got to the garage, put on his cross-country skis and set out through the woods. Reggie had often gone out on long trips in the forest, returning home only after sunset, so he knew Jeremy wouldn't get into trouble if he told Asa that he was out cross country skiing all day.

After a short, bitter-cold trek across some fields, Reggie hid his gear in a storm drain under the highway. Twenty minutes later, he was traveling out of town on a grimy bus. He videotaped a sign that read "Interstate 5" and "Now Leaving Meadowbrook, Washington." It was an odd feeling, leaving town. He was escaping, and it felt good.

When the bus finally stopped in Longview, Oregon a couple of hours later, Reggie got out and followed his printed directions to an office complex, which was deserted for the weekend. When he entered the dark, foreboding complex, the cold, empty industrial park evoked a feeling of dread in him. Reggie wondered if AAA Reality Games would be as severe, but as he entered the company's lobby he saw that it was the opposite: sleek and bright, like a super-modern laboratory. The receptionist, a young woman wearing a T-shirt and jeans named Charlotte, greeted him warmly.

"Hi there. Focus group?" she asked.

"Yes," said Reggie.

"Got your signed letter?"

"Uh, yeah."

"Okay then. Take it down the hall and turn right. Look into the lock and it'll scan your eye and let you in. That way we'll have a record of your "eyeprint," so when you come to other events you can go straight in."

"Thanks."

Reggie walked down the hall and turned right. The door to the lab was on the right and locked. There was a small lens that said simply, "Lock." He tried the door but it wouldn't budge, so he peered into the lens scanner. His eye was immediately filled with beautiful flashing kaleidoscopic light patterns. The light suddenly turned green and the door hissed open like a pressure sealed vault.

Weird that they would scan our eyes for ID, thought Reggie, feeling kind of creeped out, like someone had taken something permanent from him like a fingerprint at a police station. He had committed no crime, at least he couldn't think of any.

But as soon as he looked inside he forgot about it, because he immediately noticed a bunch of guys around his age sitting at a table inside the large open space. An adult with a laptop sat at a small table at the far right side of the lab and watched the boys. Reggie also thought he saw, or maybe only sensed, an odd sparkling effect in the room–a sort of glistening, flitting effect. Maybe he was tired, or maybe it was the after-effect of the beams scanning his retina.

As he walked into the lab he pulled his video camera out of his pack, stuck it under his arm, and turned it on, all in one smooth motion so no one would notice.

"Hey..." said a boy as Reggie approached the table.

Seven other guys and a girl were seated. Place cards said:

Dexter Spano, aka "SpanDex," San Diego

Jimmy Kwan, aka "Chainsaw," Ventura

George Johnson, aka "Snake," Medford

Jorge Sanchez, aka "Rhino," San Francisco

Isaac Podansky, aka " IPod," Redondo Beach

Claire Hamilton, aka "Scratch," Los Angeles

Vincent Morano, aka "Power," Sacramento

Abdullah Khan, aka "Flame," New York

and finally, by the only empty seat,

Reggie King, aka "Waiting For You," Meadowbrook.

Since Reggie was the last one to get there, everyone knew who he was. As he walked in, IPod hit a switch on his iPod and music from the movie "Predator" played loudly and ominously. Everyone laughed.

"Hey Reggie, so we finally meet. You kill me!" said Chainsaw.

Everyone laughed again. Reggie had killed them all so many times they couldn't count them. Whenever anyone who knew anything entered the ECHO-6 on-line game, they would always try to get on Reggie's team because they knew that

Reggie was their absolute best chance of staying in the game longer. They knew that they wouldn't get killed as quickly with Reggie on their side instead of fighting against them.

Seeing all these guys in real life was so freaky it made Reggie smile.

"Hey, Waiting For You," said SpanDex in an Asian accent. "Is that an Indian name or something? Like 'Dances With Wolves?' You don't look Indian to me."

Abdullah tapped his fist against Reggie's as Reggie sat down.

Everyone laughed happily again, except Jorge, aka "Rhino," who glared at Reggie, and then at Abdullah.

Suddenly there was a dramatic change of mood.

"Hey! what are you laughing at, Abdullah?" asked Jorge. "All you do is camp in a corner with your noobtube, coward."

The room went silent. As Jorge spoke, Reggie thought he saw more sparkling around the guys and wondered if his eyes had been wrecked by the scanner. He squeezed his eyes shut to try to clear the effect. It seemed to work.

Abdullah's face darkened even more than its natural color and then turned red. His temples pulsed and everyone thought he was about to explode. They were right. His head was heating up under his short, fez-like cap.

Everyone froze, looking at each other, waiting for Abdullah to explode, but instead, Abdullah cooly regained his self-control. He calmly looked into Rhino's eyes and said,

"Camp? Reggie's the camper! You're just agro 'cause Reggie pwns you every day!"

Everyone exploded with laughter, except Jorge, who was so stunned that he froze in disbelief with his jaw hanging open.

Then, from somewhere, Jorge heard Abdullah say, "Scrub!"

Everyone who was laughing froze.

"What did you just say!?" said Jorge.

"I didn't say anything!!"

And no one did see Abdullah say anything. It almost seemed like he had spoken without moving his lips. But they were so confused that no one knew what to say.

Before anyone could blink, Jorge lunged at Abdullah, knocking down some chairs. They went at it on the floor, rolling and punching each other furiously. Everyone cheered except Claire.

"Brilliant," she muttered to herself. "Noob vs. Scrub."

Abdullah had his right arm wrapped around Jorge's neck and was squeezing as hard as he could. They were already sweating and breathing hard as they rolled around on the concrete floor in mutual headlocks. Jorge started pounding Abdullah's back as hard as he could with his fist. Abdullah smelled like wool and sweat; it was a strange, alien scent to Jorge. It revolted him.

"RHINO!"

When Claire yelled his name, Rhino froze. He even seemed a little embarrassed and confused as he snapped out of it. Reggie was surprised that Rhino responded to Scratch. The two boys sat up on the floor, not knowing what to do next, but before anyone could say anything a short old guy with steely, intense eyes entered the room, bringing with him the powerful aroma of fresh, steaming hot pizza. Everyone's sights zeroed in on the pizza boxes.

"Pizza! Yes!"

“Sweet!”

“Hello everyone,” said the man, “Sorry for the delay. I’m Luca Esposito. Thanks for coming today. Please, dig in!”

Jorge and Abdullah got up and everyone started eating. The room went silent and all they could hear were the contented groans of chewing noises. Suddenly everyone was the best of friends.

Luca loved the effect that pizza always had on people. It was like a slice of heaven. He ate a piece too, then picked up the phone.

“Hey, Charlotte...looks like we’ll need more pizza!”

“Yes!” said Snake, pumping his fist in the air.

Then Luca turned to the focus group as they all ate.

“Everyone get their letter signed by a parent?”

Everyone mumbled “yeah” with pizza in their mouths and handed their letters down to Luca while they continued to chew and pop open cans of soda. When Reggie’s burnt letter got to Luca, he held it by his fingertips and glanced skeptically at Reggie.

“Okay. Thanks for your help today. AAARG has been working on a new game, a hunting game, for ECHO. We want to give gamers the greatest game of all time–The Ultimate Game, the ‘Game of Games,’ as it’s actually been known through the ages, but new. Very different. So we wanted to get some feedback from the best gamers. That’s why we asked you to come, those who reached the “Master” level. Are there any questions before we begin?”

Everyone continued eating, focused on the pizza, not hearing a word he said. Someone burped. They laughed.

“Okay, it’s still top secret...” continued Luca.

They started to listen.

"...but what I can tell you is that we've added another dimension, what we call the fourth, extremely realistic dimension: Fear. Fear was the missing ingredient from our on-line games. If you died, nothing bad happened."

"Except you probably went back to doing your homework," said SpanDex, getting a good laugh out of everyone.

"Homework can be scary," said Luca, "but we're adding something much scarier, and that's what I wanted to ask you about without giving away exactly what the game really is. I just wanted to ask you all one question."

There was silence again as everyone stopped eating and listened.

"What are you really, really afraid of?"

The eating and burping resumed.

"Not knowing," said Rhino. "Not knowing what's going to happen, or what's around the corner, or what ECHO might do." Then, turning to Reggie, he said, "and not hearing from someone who's seen the enemy, so you get no warning, just because you aren't on the same team and someone might think they'll get a few extra points without you around."

"Yeah, and not knowing if someone is going to be a traitor and get you killed," said Power. "Sometimes you think you're on a team together, and then someone like Snake turns on you and you're suddenly dead and he's laughing."

"Ha!" laughed Snake, gleefully.

"Yeah, not seeing something dangerous until the last second," said Flame, "and you find yourself trapped, with no time left, and before you know it you're dead."

"Also not knowing how many of something there is, like ghouls. You never know how many will be coming at you or where they'll come from," said Power. "The Unknown."

"Ooooooooo," said several boys eerily, laughing at their own joke.

"Okay, but what makes you afraid in real life? In the real world."

Up until now, Scratch had been silent. Even though she was quiet, she stuck out. She was the only girl in the group, and despite her sleek jeans, perfectly form-fitted t-shirt, long dark hair, bright icy-blue eyes, and her tanned, blemish-free face, she looked tough enough to pound anyone there. The guys, on the other hand, were complete slobs.

"Being made to do something you don't want to do, by someone who has power over you, but doesn't even really know or care about you," said Claire.

It was funny. Claire's clear feminine voice was like a fresh, cool breeze in a fart-filled room.

The guys stared blankly or glanced sideways to each other like they didn't know what she was talking about. Everyone except Reggie and Luca, who both listened intently.

"That's interesting, Claire," said Luca.

"It can be," said Claire. "Sometimes life has to be a game so you can survive. Then you can think clearly, break a problem down, and manage it. Research, find the right code, the right approach, the "cheat code." That's how you find the answer and that's how you solve the problem.

Reggie thought about his bedroom window, his escape hatch, about avoiding Asa when he had been drinking. He nodded in agreement. But then he noticed that the rest of the guys didn't get Scratch at all. They were raising their eyebrows like she was nuts. So he stopped nodding. He didn't want them to think he was nuts too.

"Sometimes the life you get really stinks, but if you make a game out of it, you can win. You just have to be realistic about your situation. Start with the real facts."

"Yeah," said Luca. "Play the cards you're dealt, but decode the problem and determine what to do. Excellent!"

All the boys nodded in solid agreement now.

"Anything else about the fear part, though? On being made to do something you don't want to do, or think is bad for you? What's really terrifying?"

"Getting cornered, and knowing it's just a matter time before you get killed," said Chainsaw, getting back to the game, "and you can't escape."

Luca listened, but they weren't quite answering his question again. *Why can't I control the direction of this session*, he thought.

"But in real life," he said.

"Or lost," said Flame, ignoring Luca.

"Or when your team doesn't follow your instructions well enough," said Power.

"Yeah, like when you got us all wiped out at Hamburger Hill?" said SpanDex.

Everyone laughed.

"Or if your team leaves you behind and you lose them," said Chainsaw. "There's nothing funny about that!"

"What about you, Reggie?" said Luca. "But in real life, not just games."

"Being hunted in a confined space, alone, without any help, and you know if you get caught something really physically painful will happen to you, so you have to think very carefully about what you're going to do next. Because there will be consequences for any decision."

Back on track. Finally. Luca liked Reggie's answer. *This is useful stuff. Thank you, Reggie, for getting us back on track. At least this focus group won't be a complete waste of time.*

"If you were alone, being hunted in a confined space, what would your very worst fear be, Reggie?"

Reggie thought for a second. As he looked up he noticed more of the sparkling, and closed each eye to see if he was going blind. *What IS that?* thought Reggie, *throwing me off track, confusing...what was I thinking.* Everyone laughed for a second because Reggie seemed so confused. The sparkling stopped. *It's gone now, everything's clear.*

"That the enemy knew HOW I thought, what my next move would be. Maybe– because they had followed my movements– that they knew what my next move would be even before I knew."

"From a tactical point of view," said Luca.

"No–like you said–not as a game. Sort of like chess, but for real," said Reggie. "The more it knew about you, psychologically. Your personal thought patterns..."

"Your behavior patterns," interrupted Claire.

"Exactly–the scarier it would be. You'd have to change the way you think. Like if it had known you your whole life, and, for example, knew how to make you mad. Confuse you."

"*That* would be a real game," said Claire, electrified with excitement.

"Whoaaaa, *Waiting,* you're so intense. It's just a game," said SpanDex.

The group laughed with relief.

"I get that sometimes real life can be played like a game," said Reggie as he looked at Scratch, "but sometimes real life isn't a game. It's much scarier because there are actual consequences that can really hurt, especially when you're being watched and don't even know it. You can give something away about yourself without realizing it."

"That's EXACTLY what we're doing." said Luca, happy with Reggie's response. "We're making it much more like real life. The GAME becomes REAL. Confusing. With HARD consequences. Anyone else?"

No one could imagine what Luca meant and no one else had anything nearly as smart to say as what Reggie or Claire had said.

"The only thing confusing is that sometimes HAkr hacks into our game." said Claire. Several of the boys agreed.

"HAkr's a nuisance," said Luca. "He's an annoyance we're trying to eliminate from the game, but we haven't been able to find him yet..."

Reggie's concentration wandered off Luca's words to wondering about Claire. She looked too pretty, too clean, and too perfect to have gone through anything hard in her life. Yet she was so serious. It didn't make sense. Something was puzzling and he couldn't quite put his finger on it. Was it just that she was so pretty, or was it something else? What did she know? He got a strange, unfamiliar feeling in his stomach every time he looked at her. Twisting. On fire. It was an alien feeling which prevented him from thinking clearly. Talk about confusion! It was all the more irritating because Reggie didn't know why he felt this way about her. Maybe he was going crazy.

He thought she looked like the pretty girls on T.V., but even prettier, maybe because this was real life. He wondered if she had a secret too, or if there might be some way to figure out who she really was.

SpanDex and Rhino threw some pizza at each other and it felt like the group was falling apart, so Luca decided it was time to end the focus group.

"Okay, before we finish, is there anything else you guys like to do, other than on-line games?" he asked as Charlotte brought in some donuts.

Flame and Chainsaw responded at the exact same time.

"Radio Controlled Cars!"

"Yeah, RC's are cool," said several other guys.

"Yeah, Racer Balls."

Racer Balls were a product invented by AAARG Products Division. They were balls which you could throw or roll and they'd transform into RC cars when they hit anything. Then you'd steer them with the remote control in a race with other Racer Balls.

"Do you all use RC's?" asked Luca. "Everyone who does, raise your hand."

Everyone raised their hands. Some of the guys gave Claire a funny look when she raised her hand too.

"Anything else you like a lot?" asked Luca.

"Yeah, these Krispy Kreme Donuts," said SpanDex, belching.

Everyone laughed again. The meeting was over.

Across the lab, the guy at the computer terminal kept watching the gamers and glancing above and around them, like there was something invisible to everyone except him. He was especially observant when they talked about strategies, and seemed almost to get excited when the gamers revealed how they couldn't depend on each other. He had taken it all in and had entered everything into his laptop.

Especially what made them afraid.

4. REAL LIFE IS NOT A GAME

On the way out of AAA Reality Games, something weird happened to Reggie. First, a wiry adult with black glasses bumped into him, stunning and disorienting him for a second. It was as if the guy purposely slammed into Reggie. His AAARG name tag said Marshall somebody. He looked right at Reggie as he passed him and said, "How ya doin' Reggieeee? Ha Ha Ha Haaa..."

Something about the man seemed familiar. Where had Reggie heard that voice before and why did it irritate him so much? How could the guy know his name, and why did he slam into him?

Before he knew it the guy was gone and a strange-looking guy was talking to him. The guy had bright icy-green eyes and shockingly white hair. His name tag read "Sean Austin, AAARG Narrative Development."

"Don't listen to that guy," said Sean, intensely. "He's just in a foul mood because he messed something up. You're Reggie, right?"

"How'd you know?"

"Never mind. I'm going to give you a password that'll freeze the new game if you ever play it. You'd want that, wouldn't you? An edge against the others?"

"Sure!" said Reggie.

Sean looked into Reggie's eyes with an intensity that made Reggie feel uncomfortable, like Sean was trying to control him or something, but Sean only wanted to make up for his co-worker being a jerk.

"Listen up," he said. He whispered the word to Reggie. Then he repeated it to make sure Reggie got it right.

"I *pray* you never need it."

And then, just like that, Sean was gone.

Reggie thought about following him, but he had a bus to catch. Across the street the 1:33 was about to leave in twelve minutes, and it was the last bus home. If he missed it, he knew he would be in big trouble when he got back. He wanted to play it safe and get in before it got to be too late, so that he wouldn't suffer the wrath of Asa the Barbarian.

Reggie caught the bus just in time. He would make it home by 3:30 pm. While bouncing down the highway, he opened a package Luca had given him just before he had left. In it was Luca's business card and a brand new AAA Reality Games jacket. Luca had told him that he appreciated everything Reggie had said, and that he valued Reggie's ideas, so he had also given Reggie a small 24 carat gold pin of ECHO's head, cast in fine detail. It was spectacular.

"Call me if you ever need to," Luca had said. It had seemed a strange and unusual offer to Reggie.

Reggie remembered the words as he took the gold ECHO pin out of the tiny box and looked at it. It felt unusually heavy for its size in his hand. He pinned it on his new jacket sleeve so he could get a good look at it.

As he thought about the focus group at AAARG, the voice of the guy who had bumped into him still bugged him. *How did he know my name*, Reggie kept thinking. Then he looked down at his jacket. His name tag was still on. "Reggie King, 'Waiting For You,' Meadowbrook, Washington" was printed on it in big black letters. He laughed and ripped it off. *Space-out. What a dork.* No more mystery. He could forget about the weird guy now. But what was that password again? *I need to write it down ASAP. As soon as I get home!*

Reggie liked the jacket and decided to make sure it stayed clean. He thought about Luca again. Luca was different, an adult who really listened and made sense. He wished he knew other adults who would talk to him the way Luca did, who were really interested in what he thought even though he didn't know anything about designing games. Reggie was curious and anxious about the new game and wished he could find out more about it before the others did. Maybe he could find out something about the game's design, and gain another advantage like the code word Sean had given him.

When he finally got home, Reggie hung his AAARG jacket in the garage, figuring he'd wear it to school the next day. He wore his old jacket inside so that Jeda and Asa wouldn't notice anything out of the ordinary. As he walked into the house, Jeda was just leaving.

"Hi Mom," said Reggie, as he slipped through the kitchen pretending nothing had happened.

"Hi sweetie," she said. "There's some lentil soup that's ready, and some pesto in the fridge. I'll be right back."

"Okay Mom," said Reggie, knowing she probably wouldn't be back for hours.

To Reggie's relief, no one seemed to notice that he had been gone all day. He walked into the small dark living room where Asa was watching T.V. Several empty beer cans littered the area around the Stratolounger. The news was covering federal budget issues, and an economist was protesting the President's spending on "incentives."

"Idiot," Asa mumbled to himself, half asleep.

Reggie headed toward the stairs, figuring Asa wouldn't notice him, but Asa bellowed at him before Reggie's foot hit the second step.

"Where you been all day?"

"I went skiing," said Reggie, which, technically, was not a lie, just an incomplete answer.

"Bring in some wood for the fire."

"Okay," said Reggie, exhausted. "Just a sec."

He headed upstairs to his bedroom, where Jeremy was online playing ECHO-6. Jeremy was wearing his headset talking to his team, directing a SAK operation against ECHO. "SAK" stood for Surround and Kill.

"Hey, I'm about to blow away ECHO," whispered Jeremy. "Josh, get out of the way, I have a clear shot!"

But ECHO was ahead of them. Just as the guys circled the creature, ECHO's ghouls appeared from behind several buildings and surrounded them. Now they were about to be SAKed.

"I'm bailing out," said Tom.

"Me too," said Josh.

"Tom! Josh! Come on guys, I'm open," said Jeremy as a large pulse blasted him.

"Die, human!" flashed on the screen.

Jeremy was dead.

"Thanks a lot you guys!"

Jeremy took off his headset and turned to Reggie. "So what happened?"

"It was really cool," said Reggie as he laid down on his bed. "They asked us all kinds of questions in a secret lab, but it was pretty much empty. I didn't get to see anything, but the new game sounds really scary. I got my eye scanned, too."

"Cool!" said Jeremy, "but it can't be that scary. It's just a game. How bad could it possibly be?" Jeremy chuckled.

"Yeah, and guess what? Crazy SpanDex was there, and Snake and Chainsaw and a bunch of other guys, even Scratch, and get this...he's a SHE!"

"No way!"

"Yes way! And she looks like a model. Can you believe it? But she's really intense. I can't figure her out...Rhino's STILL mad at me about that one lousy game, and SpanDex is a total joker."

"Wow, everyone sounds so different from their avatar," said Jeremy. "I can't believe all the ECHO master gamers were there. All the top generals and enemies, in the same room...it must have been weird!"

"REGGIE!!" yelled Asa up the stairs, "GET YOUR SKINNY BUTT DOWN HERE! WOOD! FIRE!"

"JUST A SECOND!" yelled Reggie back down at him. "No," continued Reggie, "it was cool. Like, we all sort of knew the same things, so we compared notes. The game designer is brilliant. He actually listened to what we had to say, gave me his business card to keep in touch with him."

"Awesome!" said Jeremy. "Maybe I can go too next time."

"*And* I got a back door code for the new game..."

Asa headed out the door, complaining, "Worthless punks..."

The screen door slammed behind him.

Reggie heard the door slam and sat up. His eyes got as big as ping pong balls as he strained to listen.

"Oh no!" he said as he ran to the window and opened it as quickly as he could.

"ASA – I'LL GET IT! I'LL GET IT!!" he yelled in panic, but Asa was busy muttering to himself and didn't hear him. He disappeared into the garage.

"What's the big...!?" said Jeremy.

"I'm dead, I am soo dead. I should have hidden it better!" said Reggie, hoping that Asa would be too dazed to see his new jacket. They hid by the window waiting to gauge Asa's mood. They waited. A moment later Asa stormed out of the garage waving Reggie's jacket angrily in his clenched meaty fist.

"Quick!" whispered Reggie. "Closet walk!"

They bolted to the closet. It was narrow–only about 4 feet deep.

"Go! Go!" said Reggie, and they climbed up the walls of the closet by bracing their backs against one wall, pushing their legs against the other wall, and shimmying up to the ceiling.

But it was too late. Asa had stormed up the stairs and into their room. As he stood there, seething in rage, he heard something and immediately ripped open the door. Asa stood beneath them, scanning the tiny space, furiously wondering where they had disappeared to. Reggie and Jeremy tried not to breath, but Jeremy couldn't hold his breath forever and finally let out a tiny gasp.

"Get down here, you idiots!" said Asa, pulling one of each of their legs so they fell to the floor. Reggie bolted to the window as Asa picked Jeremy up by the back of his shirt and pants, and threw him onto his bed. Then he turned to Reggie.

Reggie was already hanging outside the window, about to drop down to the ground, but the snow had melted and the ground was still frozen. He wondered for a second if he would hit the ground too hard and break an ankle. Just as he let go he felt something like a pair of vice grips clamp around his wrists. Asa was pulling him back inside.

"THIS IS NOT ONE OF YOUR STUPID GAMES!"

Asa held Reggie up in the air by his collar with one hand. He wasn't screaming this time, but he was so angry that his voice cut through every wall in the house. As he spoke, his voice got gradually louder and his face turned beet red. At the same time Reggie smelled something odd burning. It was a weird, sharp smoky smell that he didn't recognize.

"Didn't I say not to go there? But you did, and you lied to me. You gave a billion dollar company free advice when I told you not to! You're a corporate stooge! Just what we need–a corporate stooge, in our own house! No wonder your dad left you and your mom. You're useless. You're an idiot!"

Reggie grabbed Asa's wrist and Asa became angrier and started pounding him against the wall. There was nothing Reggie could do about it, he was being pounded against the wall like a door knocker as Asa became angrier and angrier, losing his temper. And even worse, Reggie couldn't yell for help because his throat was squeezed shut.

"STOP IT ASA, YOU'RE HURTING HIM!" yelled Jeremy, pulling on Asa's arm.

"Shut up, you little brat!"

Asa shoved Jeremy across the room with his free hand and Jeremy hit the floor with a sickening thud. Jeremy lifted his head up off the floor and rubbed the new lump that was rapidly forming on his face. His eyes began to well up, but he was too angry to cry.

Asa had turned back to Reggie, who was now a shade of blue and dizzy.

"Think you're so smart that you don't have to listen to a word I say? What? You don't have anything to say for yourself now, big shot?"

In his barely contained rage, Asa spun Reggie headfirst as if he was about to launch him through the window twenty feet straight down to the hard ground, but instead, suddenly turned and threw him onto his bed.

"Don't you EVER disobey me again. Tomorrow you're going to pay for this. And you mention a word of this to "mummy" and you'll never see the light of day. The river's still covered with ice, punk, and it won't melt for a long, long time! Corporate stooge. The two stooges!"

Asa turned and shot Jeremy a final glare before leaving the room.

Jeremy ran over to Reggie, who was almost crying, but couldn't because he was still gasping, trying to catch his breath.

"Are you alright?"

"One day," said Reggie, barely audibly, "I AM gonna kill him." Then, seeing Jeremy's cheek, he asked, "Are you okay?"

"Yeah, but I think it's going to be a big one. I hope dad doesn't find out this time." Jeremy held his cheek. "We'll all have to go back to therapy forever."

"Asa will kill us if we tell dad."

There was a drop of blood on Jeremy's face, but that wasn't a problem. You could wash blood off. The problem would be the lump and bruise that he knew would follow. That would hurt for a long time.

"You know what this means," said Reggie, suddenly resolved.

"What?"

Reggie carefully considered his words.

"Operation Thunderbolt."

"Operation Thunderbolt? Seriously?"

"At 0600 hours. Tomorrow."

"Awesome! Are we gonna take Mom?"

Reggie turned to Jeremy with the patient look he always used when his younger brother didn't get something. He knew he had to get Jeremy out of there, away from Asa, but he knew Jeremy always tried to protect everyone and would try to do the same for Jeda.

"Jeremy, how many times have I told you? Mom doesn't go with us on Operation Thunderbolt. She'll never leave, no matter what I say. She never gets it about Asa. And it's her house. She owns it. She pays all the bills. Plus, have you ever seen Asa do anything to her?? She's his meal ticket. And she's hardly ever here anyway! But us, he'll kill, and there's nothing she can do about it. We have to get out of here. It's just a fact."

Jeremy paused and gave it some serious thought. It was true–he *had* never seen Asa hit or throw Jeda around. He heard them argue and heard her cry sometimes, but Asa only fought with them when Jeda was gone, so that Jeda would never believe them because she never saw it for herself. Or maybe she pretended not to know. He wasn't sure. Like Reggie, he could never be sure what was real with Jeda. She always saw things in a strange way that never made sense. It was so confusing when she was around. It was like she was there, except she really wasn't. Or like her mind wasn't there, even when she was talking to him. Her body was there, seeing things, but her mind was processing everything wrong. Maybe something else entirely was going on in her head, and she had no connection at all with what really happened in front of her.

Jeremy hesitated. It was too much to think about.

"I don't know...it's so confusing."

"Jeremy, remember the letter opener?"

Jeremy shuddered. He remembered the letter opener. How could he have forgotten? He was alone with Asa that dark, bitter cold day. Asa had asked him to open a letter with his long shiny letter opener, the one that looked like a sharp-pointed knife. Jeremy opened the letter, but had somehow cut it in half. It was a check. Asa went crazy, grabbed the letter opener and threatened Jeremy with it while he screamed, "LOOK WHAT YOU DID! LOOK WHAT YOU DID! HOW COULD YOU RUIN THIS? IT'S A CHECK!!"

Jeremy had been so frightened that he ran from the house and hid outside in the woods in the dirty, ice-covered bushes until Jeda came home hours later, hours after she was supposed to have gotten home. It had seemed like forever. Asa stared at him all that night, giving him the hard look, so Jeremy never said a word about it to his mom.

Jeremy's eyes welled up with anger again.

"I don't know about you, but I want to live through the summer," said Reggie, "preferably in a normal family."

"Roger that! Operation Thunderbolt. 0600 hours. Heard, Understood, Acknowledged!"

For a moment, each of the boys thought about what they were doing.

"What's our objective?" asked Jeremy.

"Destination: Pasadena, California–Dad's house."

"HUA!" said Jeremy. "Wait. Didn't he abandon us in the first place? That's what Mom always says. Won't he just kick us out?"

"He wouldn't do that."

"How do you know?"

Reggie took a gamble, and decided to reassure Jeremy despite his own doubts.

"He wouldn't do that, once we tell him everything. And anyway, it doesn't matter. At least we'll be out of here. No matter what happens to us, we'll be better off than 'under the ice.'"

"What if he sends us back here?"

"He won't. If we BOTH tell him about Asa, say the same things, the truth, it'll all be over. We just have to get there without anyone knowing where we're going. Trust me. You cannot *ever* tell dad where we are. Okay?"

"HUA."

"Mom would call it kidnapping."

"You're right, but it's not kidnapping if we kidnap ourselves," said Jeremy. They both smiled.

That night Reggie waited for his mother to come say goodnight to him. He already missed her and they hadn't even left yet. He wanted to say good night to her one last time since he knew he might not see her for a long time.

He waited for a while and then grew restless, so he got up and looked out the window toward the woods. The moon was out again, but it felt like there was film over his eyes distorting the bright crescent, making it shimmer. The deep, dark blue-black woods blurred momentarily, and for a second he could have sworn he saw the shimmering effect which he experienced in the focus group lab. He was drowsy, and the cumulative effect felt like a dreadful, suffocating, hypnotic blanket surrounding him, making him terrified of the future. Once again he felt like a complete loser, a helpless victim of his pathetic circumstance. The closest word he could think of to describe the feeling was "depression," but it really didn't cover the intensity of what he felt.

He shook himself free of the morbid effect and got back in bed, convinced he was just tired, as usual, and waited for his mother as long as he could stay awake.

But she never came.

5. ON THE ROAD

Six a.m. came a lot quicker than Reggie thought it would. He was sore and exhausted when he woke up. When he peered over to the bed next to his he saw that Jeremy's cheek had swollen up into a black bruise. The ugly damage resulting from the impact with the floor made a sharp contrast with the rest of Jeremy's soft, pale face. Reggie was amazed that even with the injury, Jeremy still looked like a delicate angel when he was sleeping–perfect, sweet, and kind. Jeremy was still so young. Too young.

Reggie suddenly realized that he couldn't take Jeremy with him to California. It would be far too dangerous. What if something bad happened? What if someone beat them up on the way and Jeremy was permanently injured? It was going to be a long trip, and probably dangerous. They would be relying on the kindness of strangers, and it was hard enough to find any "kindness of their own family" as it was.

Jeremy was in such a deep sleep that at first he didn't hear Reggie, but he slowly came to and saw Reggie leaving the room. Realizing that Reggie was sneaking out without him, fear and the sickening feeling of betrayal plunged through Jeremy's heart.

"What are you doing?" he asked, almost crying.

"Change of plans," said Reggie.

"What? You traitor! I'm not staying here!"

"Shhh! Look, I thought about it. It's not fair to you. This isn't your fight. You could get really hurt. I can't be responsible for anything bad happening to you. Besides, Asa never gets mad at you anymore except when I'm around. I'm the one who gets you in trouble."

"No, no, no–I'm going," said Jeremy, "If you think I'm staying here alone with these two"–Jeremy thought furiously for a second–"I'll scream and wake them up!"

Jeremy's determined expression told Reggie he had no choice. If Jeremy screamed, Operation Thunderbolt would be over before it began. At first angry, Reggie suddenly saw a powerful bargaining opportunity.

"I'm the boss then," said Reggie, "completely your boss."

"Right, Chief!" Jeremy saluted.

"Get moving before I change my mind."

Jeremy got dressed as Reggie went downstairs, then grabbed a small compass and headed down too. Jeremy peered into every room as he passed though the house, taking in each for what was possibly the last time. He expected he might never see home again. When he got to the living room, he saw Reggie crouched in front of the fireplace. The AAARG jacket was burnt to ash, and only part of a sleeve remained, but way in the back of the fireplace something glimmered. Reggie pulled out the sleeve and discovered that the gold pin was still attached. He grabbed the pin, and the sleeve disintegrated into the burnt out ash flakes.

"Nice save, again!" whispered Jeremy happily.

Reggie said nothing, but threw the ashes back into the fireplace and stuck the pin in his pocket.

In the garage, their thunderbolt packs hung ready.

"Excalibur operational?" asked Jeremy.

Reggie got the packs down and opened his. He pulled out a notebook computer and turned it on. The power level read full.

"Excalibur is fully powered."

"Roger that," said Jeremy.

Next, Reggie checked a vid-cam.

"Video is operational."

"HUA." said Jeremy.

Reggie re-packed his notebook and vid-cam. They slipped their packs on in complete silence, but just as Reggie attached the gold ECHO pin to his pack, Jeremy suddenly turned and ran back to the house.

"What are you doing!?" asked Reggie, regretting his decision about bringing Jeremy. "Don't go back in! You'll wake 'em up!"

It was too late. Jeremy was already inside. First, he grabbed a box in the kitchen, and then crept to Asa's and Jeda's bedroom. He looked in, made sure they were asleep, and scanned the rest of the room. His eyes came to rest on Reggie's pocket knife, which was sitting on the dresser. He wanted to grab it, but Asa snorted in a dream, and rolled over to face him.

A moment later Jeremy emerged outside, holding up a box of chemical hand warmers.

"It's still cold. You never know when you might need 'em," said Jeremy.

"You risked everything for hand warmers!!?"

Jeremy shrugged.

"Don't do that again. Remember, I'm the boss."

Within a minute they were out on the road walking past Chuck Masterson's house.

"Operation Thunderbolt has commenced. Confidence is high, little bro," said Reggie.

"At least Masterson's not out yet," said Jeremy. "Where to? Can we go to IHOP first?"

"First we get to Interstate 5, the I-5 runs all the way to LA, and no, no IHOP. That's why we have our protein bars, remember? We only have so much money, so we have to conserve it. First Objective: Get across the state line!"

"Roger that," said Jeremy, as they trudged through the snow and dark blue shadows of the foreboding mountains.

"Wait up," said Jeremy. "You're walking too fast."

"Check."

Reggie fell back.

"Have you ever noticed how squeaky fresh snow is when you walk on it?" said Jeremy.

"Huh?"

"The shadows in the snow are so blue...like water."

Reggie turned around and faced their house.

"What?" asked Jeremy, wondering why they had suddenly stopped.

"So long, House of Hell," said Reggie bitterly.

Jeremy smiled at the joke, but he knew it was true, and this time he couldn't laugh.

Minutes later, Reggie pulled out binoculars from his pack and watched the sparse pre-dawn traffic approaching. He spotted an old 18 wheeler coming their way.

"Exit crazy town...enter normal wooootld..." Reggie paused for dramatic effect. "NOW! Follow me!"

Reggie led Jeremy to the side of the freeway and stuck out his thumb. Jeremy watched and copied the thumb thing. Reggie had been careful to choose a big rig because he figured a bigger truck would be going further south. His logic would soon be proven right.

The truck pulled over and the door opened amid the hissing of air brakes. The grey truck was an eighteen wheeler, about ten years old, fairly clean, and had D.O.T. license stickers as well as stickers from Canada, San Diego, and Mexico. A big guy with long black hair invited them inside, gesturing *come up!* while yelling "¡Rapido! ¡Rapido!"

The cab was up high, and Reggie had to help Jeremy make the climb up the ladder because their backpacks were so heavy. After pulling him inside, Reggie noticed a small statue of the Virgin Mary, a C.B. radio, and an electronic GPS map display. He pulled the door shut.

"Where you goin', Petes?" asked the huge Mexican driver, who had a seven-inch scar on his cheek. He wore a small silver cross around his neck, and a good-sized belly indicated that he ate pretty well.

Despite not being named "Pete," Reggie figured there was no one else the driver could be talking to, so he answered.

"LA, Pasadena."

"I go to Bakersfield, then Mojave," said the man.

"Bakersfield's okay," said Reggie.

"Bakersfield's great," said Jeremy, copying Reggie cheerfully.

The big man looked at them and noticed Jeremy's bruise. He looked ahead down the road and thought for a moment, as if he had made up his mind about something.

"Okay," he said, "Here we go," and he shifted into gear and pulled back onto the freeway. No questions asked. Just like that. Reggie and Jeremy were relieved.

After a few minutes, Reggie and Jeremy were thinking the same thing: It had been so easy. They couldn't believe how easy it was. They were feeling good, in control of their lives for the first time, out on the road alone. It was a new feeling, and it made them happy to be depending only on their own decisions and actions for a change. No interference, no one to mess them up. It paid to have a plan. A good plan works. It was a freedom and a happiness they had never known.

"So what's your names, Petes?" asked the driver.

"I'm Jeremy."

"I'm Reggie."

"I'm Carlos," said the driver, "But you can call me Pete. Big Pete. I'll call you Medium Pete," he said to Reggie, "and you're Little Pete," he said to Jeremy. "That way, we're all Petes," he laughed.

Jeremy offered Big Pete a protein bar, which Big Pete accepted. They soon passed a sign that said "Leaving Meadowbrook," and Reggie smiled. The more towns they passed on their way south, the happier he got: Puyallup, Spanaway, Lacey, Olympia, Tumwater, Fords Prairie, Napavine...

The C.B. radio started crackling in Spanish.

"Pimientes de los chiles, trece; veinte tres, al norte, Uvas, Fresas, dos, seis, uno, al norte..."

"What's he saying?" asked Jeremy.

"Nada. Nothing," said Big Pete, turning off the C.B.

Reggie thought it sounded like vegetable counts. He only had a year of Spanish, and even though he got an A in it, he hadn't taken it very seriously, so he didn't really know it very well.

When they saw the sign for "Medford: 10 miles," Reggie and Jeremy were even happier than they had been when they left King County. Medford was their first objective, just across the state line. They would soon be in Oregon. Somehow Big Pete seemed happier, too.

Jeremy couldn't help staring at Big Pete's scar. He just had to ask Big Pete the question.

"How'd you get that scar on your cheek?"

Reggie cringed, thinking Jeremy was too nosy and might make Big Pete angry.

"A guy broke a bottle and stabbed me in the face with it." Big Pete acted like it was no big deal, like it was an everyday occurrence.

"How come?" asked Reggie.

"No reason. He was just mean. How'd you get your cheek bruised, Little Pete?"

Jeremy was still too upset about Asa hurting him to answer, and unsure if he should tell anyone outside their family.

"Our mom's boyfriend," said Reggie, making the answer simple for Jeremy.

Once again Carlos looked ahead thoughtfully, slowly nodding his head. He didn't want to upset Jeremy any more than he already was.

"Just like my father. I ran away when I was eight. Got a job. Saved my pesos for a long time. Now I have a truck and I drive. Take chilies from Mexico to Vancouver. Take grapes and strawberries south, take vegetables north. North, south, north, south. I'm a yo-yo!"

Jeremy and Reggie laughed.

"So why you goin' to LA?" asked Big Pete.

"To our dad's house," Reggie said, "to live."

"¡Bueno!" said Carlos, "Good!"

They crossed into Oregon. The landscape was pretty much the same, but instead of mountains there were more open, rolling hills and the occasional wide, slow-moving river. It was relaxing to watch the scenery go by. It was getting greener and sunnier. With the warmth of the sun on his face, Reggie felt he had made a good call. They were off to an excellent start and he felt great about Operation Thunderbolt. Confidence was high.

They drove through Medford and saw a lot of high-rise buildings. Then they passed through the smaller cities–Wilsonville, Lafayette, Amity, and then another large city, Salem. By now, Reggie and Jeremy had slumped against each other and fallen asleep. As the truck approached another big city–Eugene, Oregon–Big Pete noticed police stopping cars ahead of him. He became concerned when he saw the police, but not too worried. It was getting late in the day anyway, so he decided to make a detour.

He pulled off the I-5 and headed west toward the ocean for a while. Eventually he slowed down and parked his rig by a small house next to a river.

"Where are we?" asked Reggie, sleepily rubbing his face.

"Santa Clara, my cousin Raul's house. We'll spend the night here, Petes."

Carlos's cousin came out and started speaking very quickly in Spanish and laughing. Raul spoke so quickly his words seemed to shoot out of his mouth like bullets out of a machine gun. The endless barrage of words almost made the boys laugh too. Raul seemed like a really nice guy. He was about 5' 5", thin, had a dark triangular goatee on his chin, and was elegantly dressed in a pristine black fedora like the hats detectives used to wear, a black pinstriped suit, black shirt and white tie, just like a jazzy Zoot Suit guy from the 1940's.

Among other things, Raul loved fishing on the river. That night he rolled up his sleeves and cooked them the best fish, spicy rice and black bean dinner they had ever eaten. Carlos and Raul talked in Spanish the entire time. Reggie's Spanish was barely good enough for him to make out a few things, like Carlos asking Raul about the police check point. Raul told him it was temporary, and that they'd be gone in the morning.

"Good, I can't afford to lose my rig again, or end up in jail for another week," Carlos said.

"And I can't afford to bail your sorry butt out again," said Raul, and they both laughed.

It sounded to Reggie like they talked a lot that night about their family and the prices of vegetables up and down the west coast. The vegetables seemed really expensive, but because Reggie's Spanish wasn't very good and Raul spoke like a frenzied motor-mouthed machine, Reggie wasn't sure he was hearing right. He wished he understood Spanish better, and thought about taking it again next year in school, whatever school they might be attending.

After dinner Reggie and Jeremy walked down to the river and watched the deep, clear water drift by. The stars were so bright that they reflected in the dark water. The woods were alive with the hoots of owls and the chirping of insects.

While Reggie and Jeremy sat by the river, Raul sat in front of a C.B. radio in a small room in back of the house. The boys could hear him faintly, reciting into the microphone in a monotonous, hypnotic tone:

"Zanahorias, uno, dieciséis, al norte,

Guisantes, treinta, veinte, al norte,

Pimientos de los chiles, dos, quatro, del sur..."

The fact that the words seemed only familiar to Reggie was frustrating. Maybe they were vegetables, and quantities of vegetables going north and south. But he couldn't quite make it out. It frustrated Reggie again that he couldn't remember the vocabulary.

Reggie pulled his notebook computer out of his pack and fired it up. He turned on its wireless browser, checked his email, got his location with his GPS locator, and did an online search for Santa Clara, Oregon, all in about forty seconds.

"What do you think Mom's doing right now?" asked Jeremy as he poked the muddy riverbank with a stick.

"The usual," mumbled Reggie as he typed.

"Think she misses us?"

"She hasn't even noticed we're gone yet, Jeremy. You know she's hardly ever around. Anyway, I'm sure Asa will tell her we're out, or at someone's house, figuring we'll be back before she notices we're gone...so he won't have to explain anything."

"Yeah..."

"Nothing they do makes any sense..." said Reggie, as he worked on his e-journal.

He had decided to record everything on his trip–bits of things, feelings, people they met, places–and there was no better time to start than now. He typed out as many names of places they traveled through as he could remember, as well as mentioning Carlos and his cousin, Raul. It was a lot more like brief notes, bits of info, than a fully written account. That way it would be easier and quicker to write, so he knew he would do it every day. He made a 'note to self–*Objective: Learn Spanish!–not just for A's in school, but enough to use for real!'*

When he was done, he shot a few short video clips of the river, Jeremy, the house, Raul, and Big Pete. Then Raul whistled an ear splitting signal to call them in.

"You need to get some sleep!"

Big Pete put them in a quiet room by themselves.

"There's blankets in the closet," he said as he opened the closet door.

Inside the closet hung a human skeleton–a woman with an elegant hat wearing a pretty dress. She was holding a bouquet of dead dry flowers.

Reggie and Jeremy were horrified. Was it real? And why was it in Big Pete's closet, hanging around like that, like some kind of real zombie? But something about it seemed funny to Reggie, even though it didn't to Jeremy.

"What's that?" asked Jeremy, alarmed.

"Oh, it's our Catrina, from Day of the Dead. The Catrina is like a doll we use when we celebrate Day of the Dead to honor our family who have died. We celebrate them for the good in the lives they've lived. It's for good luck too."

Jeremy was relieved. He had never seen a Catrina or even heard of the Day of the Dead Celebration. He was fascinated with the skeleton, and now he and Reggie saw it as being something happy and fun.

"Cool," said Jeremy, smiling and relaxed, now enjoying being around the Catrina.

"Okay," said Big Pete, "get to sleep. We have a long way to go tomorrow," and then flicked off the light.

Jeremy quickly fell asleep, but later that night Reggie still couldn't sleep, so he sat by a window in the deep blue light of the full moon and watched the river flow by. Water spiders skittered across the surface of the slowly passing current. The hypnotic staccato murmur of Raul's C.B. broadcast droned on in the background, blending with the hoots of the owls and the chirping of the crickets. For some reason, Reggie didn't feel as depressed as he usually did at night. He wasn't having the usual deep, dark night of the soul he usually felt, but could think more clearly. *Maybe I feel good because I'm out of that Hell-house,* he thought. He had all kinds of conflicting emotions.

As Reggie thought to himself, Carlos silently appeared beside him and looked out the window, too. His skin was cast in the same pale blue color of reflected moonlight as Reggie's was, so they looked like they were related in some way. It was as if the moonlight made them members of the same family.

"¿Que pasó, hombre?" asked Big Pete.

"Huh?" said Reggie. "Oh, okay, I guess."

"Can't you sleep?"

"It's just strange," said Reggie. "For so long I wished I could get away from my mother's boyfriend and all his stupid drinking and hitting and yelling, but now that I've left, it feels so weird. I just wonder if I did the right thing."

"Just like a bad habit," said Carlos.

"Huh?" said Reggie.

"It's like stopping a bad habit. It feels strange. Bad Habits–it's human nature–they're almost impossible to change. But when you do, it takes getting used to, like quitting smoking. It feels strange, but you know it's the right thing for you to stop. So you have to get used to it.

"Look," he continued. "Sometimes your mother or father is really bad for you and you have to get away from them. Eventually we all have to learn that there is no person we can depend on other than ourselves...and the higher force, if we're lucky enough to find it. Maybe you feel like you're completely alone sometimes, but you just gotta go on and make your own path. And only later–and it will happen–you'll learn that there were all kinds of other things going on, things you didn't understand or even know about, and only then it will all make some sort of sense. It will surprise you, and, for a moment, you will smile."

"Yeah," said Reggie, rubbing his thumbs nervously. "I just wonder if I should have taken Jeremy. He's so little."

"Worry is a complete waste of time. Put your faith in the higher force, and remember, some day you and Little Pete will have a wife, kids, and you will not hit them. You can remember so they will have a better life. Memory–Remembrance, this thing Remembrance–is powerful!"

"Yeah," said Reggie, nodding, still staring at the river, "Okay."

Big Pete made a lot of sense. Somehow what he said made Reggie feel like his life could turn out okay after all, like it wasn't all a waste of time. It could be good if he did the right things, and maybe everything that happened to him did mean something. It might just take a while to realize what it all really meant.

"Just make the most of each day. Do your best, and you won't have any regrets," said Big Pete in his deep voice. "The best thing you can do is get away from this guy. You're doing a great job taking care of your little brother."

"Sometimes I make mistakes though," said Reggie, thinking about getting Jeremy beaten up by Asa.

"And you will make many more, but you are still his brother. At least he has you. We're all brothers. Remember, all of us, we're all 'Petes'."

"Thanks, Pete," said Reggie.

Big Pete gently tapped Reggie on the back as he left.

On Reggie's way back to his sleeping bag he passed the tiny broadcast booth and saw Raul tiredly stroking his goatee, his eyes reflecting the dim control lights of the C.B. radio. He was still speaking into the microphone, and the audio meter spiked with his every word, but his words were slowing,

"Tomates, dieciséis, treinta y seis, del este,

Habas Negras, nueve, seis, uno, del norte..."

What is so important about all those vegetables?

6. SURVEILLANCE

A sparkling cloud drifted purposefully through the early morning woods. Only the tiniest birds chirped as the first warm ray of sunlight penetrated through the trees. It was the first sunrise ECHO-7 had witnessed on its own outside of the lab. As the sliver of light flared in its lenses, E-7 turned away from the rising sun and scanned Reggie's house from its hiding place at the edge of the woods.

Although it was now sitting perfectly still in its cloaked chameleon state–invisible except for the occasional sparkling effect–a crow had somehow figured out something was standing there and had landed on its head. But E-7 did not notice, or at least didn't seem to notice. E-7 did not move, so the big black bird remained there, standing still, floating, 35 feet high in mid-air.

"Caw!"

E-7 scanned Reggie and Jeremy's bedroom window and then scanned through the living room window. It heard the living room telephone ring, and watched as Asa, who was asleep on the Stratolounger in the full recline position, twitched and picked up the phone. Asa's eyes were red, but not from worrying about the boys. His beard had grown out all rough and stubby overnight.

"Yeah, what?" he grumbled groggily.

Luca Esposito was on the other end of the line.

E-7 focused its directional microphone on Asa.

"No, he's not here. Who is this?"

"What do you mean, where is he? You had no right to brainwash him! He didn't even have permission to be at that stupid meeting!"

"What kind of crazy ideas did you put into his head, anyway? He's nothing but trouble to me, and now you turn him into your game stooge?"

"No! Stop! I don't want you calling here again! Don't bother me again or I'll call the police! Leave me alone!"

Asa hung up and fell right back asleep.

E-7 next observed a 12-year-old boy with short, spiky blond hair and beady eyes come out onto the front porch of the house two doors down. Chuck Masterson looked around his yard with his mean little eyes for something to shoot at with his sling shot. He fired off a few rocks at the sparrows in his yard, but he missed and only scared them away. He hit a trash can a couple of times. THWACK! THWACK! It was a loud, obnoxious sound.

Suddenly Chuck froze as he spotted the crow standing still, floating, suspended in midair.

"Huh?"

He gaped at the bird, wondering how it was floating in air without flapping its wings. He fired a rock at the crow and missed it, hitting the invisibly cloaked ECHO. The rock made a deep, dense, metallic sound, as if it had hit the side of an aircraft carrier.

"Huh??" he gasped again, louder, his eyes getting wide with astonishment.

He fired another couple of rocks, hitting E-7 again and again. A scale chipped off, broken. A tiny black patch appeared where the scale had been. It too, floated in thin air like the bird.

Suddenly the bird moved, floating to the right. It was an eerie sight, the big black crow standing still in midair, but somehow gliding in defiance of the forces of gravity, oddly sparkling.

Chuck fired at the crow and missed again, hitting the machine.

"Darn! Come'ere birdie."

As Chuck got his sling shot ready again, the bird floated more quickly toward him. He was too startled to shoot again and only stared, entranced, as the bird continued gliding straight toward him. He heard what sounded like a strong wind coming his way, but he didn't feel even the slightest breeze. It was at this moment that he also noticed giant footprints and a warping distortion effect approaching him. He looked back up at the bird as it floated downward until it was about six feet above him.

Chuck suddenly snapped out of his trance and pulled his sling way back, aiming at the bird, who was now staring down at him.

"Caw!"

Just as Chuck was about to let his rock fly, E-7 decloaked, materializing out of nowhere.

The huge Mech burst into full view in a loud, clicking fury. The visor on its helmeted head instantly retracted with a mechanistic whir, revealing a demonic–looking half-human, half-alien head with intense, cruel green eyes. It snarled loudly as it bared the biggest and deadliest set of teeth that ever existed. As it gnashed its teeth, sloppily dripping with surplus hydraulic fluid, Chuck let go of the handle of his slingshot while still holding the sling in his left hand. It snapped back, hitting him in the face. At the same time, he screamed so loudly and so terribly that Asa woke up again.

But it was a brief cry. In an instant the enormous cavern of rotating teeth lunged down and engulfed Chuck, lifting him up 35 feet and gulping him down into its throat. With two quick, violent, spasms Chuck was gone. Suddenly, silence ruled again.

But in a moment the clicking started again and E-7's sharp reptilian scales flickered colorfully. It shimmered and glittered for a moment, and then vanished under its very real-world cloak.

Asa fell back to sleep, annoyed at the brief sound of some terrified kid screaming for his life.

But Chuck was not dead. He slid down a cold, smooth chute and into a holding tank. Before he knew it, the walls of the tank pushed in tighter and tighter, making the cavity darker and darker. A wave of claustrophobic confusion engulfed Chuck and he began sobbing uncontrollably. In his dizzy, confused panic, made even worse by E-7's movements, he became motion sick and felt like vomiting. Was he right side up or upside down? He didn't know. The walls now squeezed in on him tightly, and since he had landed head first, he was in an extremely awkward position: his legs were wrapped around him like a compressed pretzel.

After about three seconds, he was suddenly covered by a warm, damp film. When it cooled, it felt like plastic wrap, the kind you use to wrap sandwiches. Now he was suffocating, trapped like an insect covered in a web by a giant spider.

Luckily for him, the floor snapped open and he fell through another chute out the bottom of the creature, landing on the ground with a hard "Ughhh!"

The plastic membrane ripped slightly so at least he could breath, but he was so severely contorted that his feet were now behind his head and his pants were ripped open, exposing his butt. For some reason, despite his mother's instructions, he had not put on any underwear that morning, so his naked butt was now right above his upside-down face. To make matters worse, the plastic did not allow him to move a millimeter.

ECHO-7 immediately disappeared in a cacophony of fading, clicking sounds while Chuck watched its footprints travel back into the woods.

Several boys soon walked by and discovered Chuck on the ground. They laughed at him. One of them, named Tom, knew him.

"Hey, look! It's a butt-face! Ha, ha!"

"Shut up and get me out of here, Tom!" cried Chuck.

"Look–it's a real butt-face!" said another.

The boys had a good time poking Chuck in the butt with sticks, and then had an even bigger laugh when he farted uncontrollably. When they walked away, leaving Chuck trapped in his front yard the way they found him, he yelled after them, "COME ON YOU GUYS!"

"IF YOU FART LOUD ENOUGH SOMEONE WILL HEAR YOU," yelled Tom. They all laughed hysterically.

"HONK HONK!"

When Chuck realized they weren't coming back, he vowed revenge.

"I'M GONNA POUND YOU! EVERY ONE OF YOU!"

But his threat went unheard. The guys were long gone, and his butt was now freezing in the breeze as he struggled to get free.

After hearing Asa's conversation, E-7 had deduced that Reggie was no longer living at the house. As it drifted away, ECHO started a massive West Coast internet search, and in 3.4 seconds had detected Reggie online, playing ECHO's Revenge. It invoked its GPS tracking application and searched for Reggie's location. Since Reggie's GPS was also activated, ECHO-7 quickly picked up his exact location, moving south on I-5, already 75 miles south of Santa Clara. 7 began to morph into a box-like form, and a minute later a UPS truck with tinted windows turned onto Interstate 5 and headed south with no driver at its wheel.

7. ON THE ROAD II

The three Petes sat in the cab of Big Pete's truck, driving through southern Oregon. Big Pete was relaxed. There had been no police so far today.

Reggie had turned his notebook on and off several times in the last 24 hours. Little did he know, each time that he turned it on, the GPS pinpointed his exact location for anyone or anything which had the right code to detect his computer's IP and GPS ID. Now he was online again, playing ECHO-6.

Later that morning, when Big Pete looked into his rear view mirror, he would never have imagined what the UPS truck 100 yards behind them really was.

"Medio Pete, shut that thing off for a while. Enjoy the scenery. Life's passing you by. You guys are addicted to games! Look at this beautiful country! Wake up! We're on I-5–the central nervous system of the West Coast. Built in 1948, all the way from Oregon to Mexico. What a great freeway—a

Free Way, amigo! You have to pay to drive on highways like this everywhere else."

Reggie turned off his notebook, embarrassed that he had been online and hadn't been better company to Big Pete. Big Pete was, after all, giving them a free ride. Big Pete was also doing all the driving, and paying for all the gas.

Reggie watched the scenery fly by. Sunlight flickered through the trees. Patches of fog. Buildings. Roads. Signs. Shadow patterns. Motion. The hum of the engine. Fresh air. Blue sky. And best of all, no one screaming at them.

But before he knew it, he saw a big electronic billboard above the freeway that was flashing in big bright letters:

Amber Alert...Amber Alert... Kidnapped:

Reggie King, age 14

Jeremy King, age 11

Call 1-AMBERALERT

"¡Valgame dios!" yelled Carlos.

Jeremy woke up, startled.

"Petes, I gotta drop you off! Someone thinks you've been kidnapped!"

"What?" said Reggie, "No! We haven't been kidnapped! It's okay. It's just a mistake."

"Petes," said Carlos. "No way I can get mixed up with the police. You have to get another ride. Sorry," as he downshifted and pulled over toward an off-ramp.

After everything Carlos had done for them, Reggie and Jeremy didn't want to cause him any trouble. He had been really good to them and had even put them up for the night and fed them. And he did it all without even asking them for a nickel. The last thing they wanted was to get him arrested because of what they had done.

"Okay," said Reggie. "No problemo. Gracias, Big Pete."

Jeremy gave Reggie a look that said, "what are we going to do now??"

Reggie shot a "shut up" face back at him.

"Thanks again, Pete," said Reggie a few minutes later as they jumped down from the cab.

As the truck pulled away, Big Pete shouted out of the window of the cab, "Take care Petes! Remember, make the best use of each day. When you meet someone, there's a whole world in them, so pay attention. They're in your life for a reason. See you again sometime when the heat's off. Be good!"

Reggie and Jeremy watched as the truck pulled away.

"Great, now whadowedo?" said Jeremy. "I'm starving."

Reggie suddenly realized he had the same pangs of hunger as Jeremy. Instinctively, he whipped out his computer notebook and fired it up.

"We need some grub," said Reggie, as he typed in 7-Eleven.com and hit the store locator. "We're in luck."

There was a 7-Eleven a block away, so they set off immediately. Even though it was so close, Reggie felt the paranoia of extreme vulnerability take over. Fortunately, they were at the convenience store door before they knew it.

It was at that moment that they saw something on a stack of newspapers in front of the 7-Eleven that really made them panic. The Rogue River Press headline said: "MISSING: KIDNAPPED BY FATHER?" and had a big picture of Reggie and Jeremy under the headline.

"Whoa. Check it out!" said Reggie.

They both looked at the paper.

"I guess they noticed we're gone!" said Jeremy.

"Uh, yeah."

"Should we call 'em and tell 'em."

"Naw," said Reggie, "let 'em figure it out. Let 'em think about how they treated us for a while. We'll call 'em when we feel like it. Let's eat something first."

"What about Dad?"

"By now the police have questioned him. They'll know it wasn't him. We'll get to his house in a day anyway and then tell Mom we're there. No big."

They picked up their packs and went into the 7-Eleven.

A few minutes later they came out and ate some Ding Dongs and drank some milk. As Reggie polished off his quart, he noticed a "missing kid" picture on the carton. Something about the boy looked familiar. He took a harder look and then showed it to Jeremy.

"Hey," said Reggie, "don't you know this guy?"

"It's Josh!" said Jeremy, with half a hot dog falling out of his gaping mouth, "IT'S JOSH!"

There was another picture of his friend Tom with his full name under it, saying he was missing as of yesterday.

"And look! It's Tom!" said Jeremy. "I can't believe this!"

Jeremy took off back into the 7-Eleven store. Reggie followed.

They looked at all the milk cartons inside. All of the cartons had pictures of their friends from Meadowbrook on them, and they all said that they had been kidnapped. Then they saw their own pictures and Reggie realized something.

"Hey! Not only are all these guys from Meadowbrook, but they're also ECHO players–isn't that Cougar and Crusher?"

"Yeah, and Piranha. It's like everyone we ever played Echo's Revenge with in Meadowbrook is on a milk carton."

"Weird," they both said together.

Reggie wondered if all of the abductions were because of the game somehow, or if it was just a coincidence. He took out his vid-cam and recorded each mug shot on the cartons as Jeremy found more and more faces they recognized.

"It's funny seeing guys you know on milk cartons," said Jeremy, "Look at this shot of Josh, he looks like such a dork. It's a shot from two years ago!"

They laughed. It was true.

"Yeah, well, so would you," said Reggie.

Reggie was right, Jeremy would look ridiculous in some outdated school "mug shot". They laughed again.

But Reggie suddenly panicked when he realized that they really might be next.

"If we didn't run away, we would have been kidnapped!" said Reggie. "Let's get out of here. We better get lost! Really lost! And off I-5. Now!"

He grabbed Jeremy by the shirt and they bolted from the 7-Eleven.

8. BUZZ CUTS

"Now," said a dark silhouette of a guy with a buzz cut. "Let's do it."

Two big, sweaty Buzz Cut guys covered with scars, burns, and grease smudges watched Reggie and Jeremy from the front seat of a muscle car. The car roared to a start. It was no usual motor sound, but an extremely powerful, high rpm whine.

Jeremy stuck close to Reggie as they headed out of the parking lot onto another road heading west. Reggie had decided to avoid the Interstate. They stuck out their thumbs and moments later a silent, dull gray, low-riding 1968 Chevy Impala with spiky metallic tires pulled up to them, which struck them as odd. They had never seen metal tires before.

The two Buzz Cuts looked them over with oddly perplexed expressions on their faces, not knowing what to make of the kids. Reggie and Jeremy didn't know what to do–it was their worst nightmare. After an uncomfortable moment of silence, the Buzz Cut sitting shotgun said, "Well, what are you waiting for? You need a ride, so get in!"

Jeremy checked out the car and noticed small fin-like spoilers on both the front and back of the car. The front bumper reminded him of a cow pusher from the front end of an old-fashioned train, but it was more like high-tech armor because it was partially retracted into the chassis. It reminded Reggie of a car from "Mad Max" crossed with the DeLorean from "Back to the Future," but more high-tech than anything could be in a movie.

"Uh, we're just hiking. We don't need a ride. Um, thanks anyway," said Reggie quickly.

Shotgun Buzz Cut got out of the car and stood up. At 6'7" it was hard to believe he had fit in the car. His beefy, hard-chiseled body and dark, looming shadow formed a menacing figure as he towered over them, blocking out the sun. His cold eyes drilled into Reggie. He had no time for fun and games.

"You don't have time, Amber. Get in now!"

Reggie realized the guy knew they were wanted by the police. *But how did they know it was us?* thought Reggie.

"Okay, that's cool. I just wasn't sure you were going the same way we were. We're headed to the ocean," said Reggie.

"Yeah, the ocean," said Jeremy, wondering what it would be like to be found dead in a ravine, or what other horrible things these guys were capable of...maybe things involving saws or other power tools. As Shotgun stared them down, they hopped into the back.

The door locks automatically slammed down into the locked position. Now they were trapped.

"We know where you're going, so relax. Trust us. We'll help you get there," said the Driver Buzz Cut in a gravelly voice as he glared at Reggie.

"Just stay out of the way," said Shotgun.

Both Buzz Cuts stared at Reggie and Jeremy. Then the Buzz Cuts turned and stared at each other for a second, wondering what the deal was with Reggie and Jeremy.

Reggie and Jeremy had no idea what was going on. It didn't quite make sense to Reggie why the Buzz Cuts were picking them up. On the one hand, the Buzz Cuts seemed so hard core they must be criminals, but for some unknown reason they seemed to want to help him and Jeremy.

They're either going to do something horrible to us, or give us a ride, thought Reggie. *What could they possibly want to do to us? Why would they give us a ride? Are they kidnappers? How do they "know where we're going?" I can't tell Jeremy. He'll freak.*

"Buckle up," said Driver Buzz Cut.

"Okay," said Reggie in compliance. He didn't want to alarm Jeremy with his fears, so he smiled, acted like everything was normal, and went along with whatever they said.

Reggie and Jeremy fastened themselves into the strange, oversized shoulder and lap belts. Then Shotgun looked back at them.

"Relax, it's not like it's going to hurt or anything."

Why would it hurt? thought Reggie and Jeremy. But before they could think, the driver mashed the accelerator and the car exploded to life, throwing them back against their seat violently. The shriek of the metallic wheels ripping through the pavement was deafening.

"Heat those wheels up!" said Shotgun Buzz Cut.

"HA HA! BUUUUURN!" screamed Driver Buzz Cut maniacally as he mashed his foot down further on the accelerator.

Reggie was so terrified he didn't know what to do or say. Were they about to get killed by these gorillas? How had he messed up so badly so quickly? He had been in a rush and didn't stop to think, just because Shotgun had a menacing glare. *Panic is the enemy. Panic is deadly!* He would never make that mistake again. *When in doubt, DON'T,* he thought. Never again! Stop for a time-out. Use patience.

No one spoke as the car shot down the road. Once again, Jeremy gave Reggie his 'what are we going to do now??' look as they headed into the unknown. Reggie angrily mocked Jeremy, making the same monkey face back at him. He had no idea what they *could* do now. The embarrassing fact that he had unwittingly lost control of their lives to these beasts made him angry.

"You girls okay back there?" asked Shotgun.

"Yeah," Reggie and Jeremy nervously shot back.

The engine shifted, and suddenly hummed like it was barely running, but the vehicle accelerated even more. It was obviously much more powerful than Jeda's Jeep Cherokee–they were going so fast that the tree trunks were a brown blur. The green leaves seemed to stretch into another band of blurred color above the brown.

There were occasional fog patches, but the driver never slowed down. This drove Jeremy and Reggie crazy with panic that they might slam into something. Their eyes bulged out of their heads as they searched ahead for obstacles they might hit.

It seemed like the two Buzz Cuts were in a rush to get somewhere and weren't really interested in Reggie or Jeremy, so Reggie started to think about how and where he'd tell them to let them off. He was about to open his backpack to look at his laptop's GPS map, but thought the guys might notice the gold ECHO pin and start poking around in his stuff. They might find his money or make fun of something inside it and then steal the backpack–his and Jeremy's life support system.

Instead, he pulled out his vid-cam but kept it hidden. He thought he'd record some clues about who these guys were, and then leave the camera in his pack or somewhere where someone could find it. That way, in case they were murdered and buried somewhere, the authorities would be able to track down the Buzz Cuts. When he pulled out the camera, he noticed that his laptop was still on in his pack, so he slipped his hand in and turned it off, not wanting to drain the batteries. Then he noticed a business card on the floor. He grabbed it and stuck it in his pack.

Jeremy was still terrified, so he did exactly what he always did when Asa was on a rampage–he tried to make himself invisible.

Neither Reggie nor Jeremy said a word as they sank back into the bench-like seat. The more they sank back, the more they noticed scents of grease, WD-40, and strange chemicals they had never smelled before. Then they noticed that nothing in the car seemed to have anything to do with comfort. Everything was related to either speed, emergency life support, or first aid–like the green emergency oxygen cylinders for breathing, the red fire extinguisher under the front passenger seat, emergency burn packs on the front right roof support column, emergency adrenaline and morphine syringes taped to the ceiling (in case someone had a heart attack), dozens of dials and switches that they had never seen in any car, more burn first aid packs taped to the ceiling behind them, and warning signs that said "NO OPEN FLAME!" on the backs of the front seats.

But the car was running extremely well and seemed unusually smooth and stable on the curves, perhaps due to the effect of the spiked tires. Reggie realized that whoever had built this 'car' had to be pretty smart, possibly even a genius.

The fog patches got thicker.

"Reference radar!" snapped Driver.

Reggie and Jeremy didn't know what it meant, but the two Buzz Cuts became extremely focused and their personalities shifted into serious gear.

Shotgun Buzz Cut flipped one of the switches and a panel with a Raytheon logo on it inverted on the dash board. A radar screen revealed everything ahead of them that was hidden by the fog. The Buzz Cuts became even more focused.

They were now in military-focus gear.

"Radar check–all clear," snapped Shotgun, "a few cars in 5 miles, another in 12. Otherwise, the road's ours."

"Reference GPS."

"GPS Referenced. Positive Lock."

"O2?"

"25 K."

"H2?"

"15 K."

"Ready?"

"HUAAA...," said the Driver.

Reggie and Jeremy smiled at each other. When they heard the familiar "HUA" they somehow felt better. Just as they started to wonder exactly what was happening, Driver alerted everyone.

"Going to peroxide."

From the conversation, Reggie recognized H2 and O2 as being hydrogen and oxygen. He immediately remembered learning about H_2O_2, or hydrogen peroxide, in science class, and reading about H_2O_2 being used as a highly explosive propellant in rockets and cars at Peswiki.com. The coolest thing about peroxide, Reggie recalled, was that it produced incredible energy, burned totally clean, and didn't pollute. Since it left no exhaust trail, it was also stealthy.

The car jolted forward again. The sound of the engine changed from sewing machine to giant, deafening jack hammer. The car accelerated so fast that Reggie and Jeremy struggled to lift their hands to cover their faces. They prayed that whatever was going to happen would happen as quickly as possible–for the bullet they were in to find its destination quickly and put them out of their misery.

The fog became denser. Panic. It became so white that they couldn't see a thing!

At first, it was disorienting for Jeremy and Reggie to look out the window because they could feel the acceleration of the car, but they couldn't see anything except the white fog so they had no reference point for motion or direction. Soon they felt like they weren't even moving, so they sat up and just waited.

They wondered what the Buzz Cuts wanted them for, but weren't about to ask. Reggie shot some video when they weren't looking. Grab-shots of their faces, the car, his own face, the business card reading 'GeoSyncRobotics,' the outside blurring by, Jeremy...

"Passing cars 1, 2, 3 in 12, 11...5, 4, 3, 2," said Shotgun.

There was an almost silent swish-swish-swish.

"Uh oh," said Shotgun, "We're on someone's radar."

"Crap," said Driver, "It's a cop. Can you jam it?"

"Negative–five miles behind and they already got us."

"Not any more," said Driver, "We're out of range now."

Reggie peered out the window for an instant but couldn't recognize anything because everything was so blurry. All he could see were random flickering colors reflected in the fog in a strange, prismatic effect. They were traveling so fast it looked like they were flying through a kaleidoscope into the future. *Awesome,* he thought.

Shotgun continued to read the radar:

"Passing last vehicle in 8, 7..."

They broke through the fog into clear sunlight, but there was nothing ahead except open road.

"Hey–what's going on? There's no one out there!"

"E-stopping for radar and systems check!" Driver Buzz Cut panicked.

Shotgun braced himself.

Reggie and Jeremy braced themselves.

The car felt like it had run into an immense wall of bread dough. The spiked metal wheels gripped into the asphalt like baseball cleats in soft earth and everything inside the car punched forward. As Reggie and Jeremy slammed forward, the shoulder and lap straps dug deeply into their flesh, cutting off their circulation. Everything went black and they passed out.

"I swear, it should be coming right past us, but there's nothing in the other lane!" said Shotgun Buzz Cut, "3, 2, 1..."

Reggie and Jeremy woke up. Their vision returned and they noticed that the car was driving slowly down the freeway as the Buzz Cuts looked out the window for something. Now visibility was a good 50 miles–sunny and clear.

"What the!?..." said Driver.

They were coming up to some sort of strange, blurring mirage effect approaching in the oncoming lane on the left. Sparkling points of light briefly shimmered and then, as it passed by them, edges of a Fed Ex freight truck came into view for an instant. Reggie caught it, but wasn't sure he could believe his eyes since he had just been unconscious. The distortion reminded him of the sparkling he saw during the focus group.

Whatever it was, its cloaking function didn't work perfectly. It couldn't fully camouflage itself when observed from multiple directions while moving. As the Buzz Cuts passed the truck mirage it vanished again.

Shotgun went crazy.

"Man oh man! It's some kind of stealthy cloaking system. Who is that? We NEED that! We need that system! Turn around!"

"One thing at a time! We gotta get our funding first," said Driver, heating up.

"No man! We'll never find them again!"

"It's probably something Starman's up to," said Driver, "Maybe this is some kind of test."

While the Buzz Cuts fought, Reggie grabbed his video camera and looked out the back window, trying to see what they were talking about. He saw some flickering, and then bits and pieces of something that looked like a truck, like some sort of kinetically shifting cubist sculpture. The apparition turned behind them, and made a u-turn. It was following them! It disappeared again. If you weren't looking for it, you'd never see it, but there was a hint of a mirage effect following them.

Whatever it was, it definitely wasn't gone, because a police car was coming up behind them from a mile away now, and the shimmering was distorting the view of the police car like a weird, sharp, jagged mirage. The police car was gaining ground quickly.

"Great!" said Driver, "Cop's closing on us now! See what you did?"

"I didn't do anything!" said Shotgun, "Go–before they get anywhere near us–like we never saw them. We'll just say we never saw 'em!"

"No harm, no foul..." said Driver.

The police cruiser approached quickly, its blue and red lights flashing brilliantly.

"Prep O2!" said Driver.

Reggie and Jeremy watched the police car gain ground.

"GO! GO!" they screamed. They did NOT want the police finding them now.

"O2's good," said Shotgun.

The police were almost on their bumper.

"GO!!!" yelled Jeremy.

"H2 okay," said Shotgun. "The kid's right! Hurry up!"

"I am hurrying! You're the one who slowed us down!"

But the police car was closing. They could hear the siren wailing loudly at them.

"GOOOOOOOOOOOOOO!!!" screamed Reggie and Jeremy.

But as the two Buzz Cuts finished their checklist, a strange thing happened. As the police car sped up even more, its left tires suddenly lifted off the ground like it had hit an invisible ramp and the car shot up sideways 20 feet into the air, flipped over several times, and sailed about 45 feet off the road before landing perfectly in a cactus patch. Reggie and Jeremy looked at each other in disbelief as a hub cap fell off the steaming car. They laughed, but then noticed that the mirage effect was still following them. It was closer now, changing shape, and there were several brown spots they couldn't see through on the top of the mirage. What looked like tiny pieces of stealthy camouflage had broken off.

Finally, the Buzz Cuts' car jolted forward again as the peroxide exploded. Everyone slammed back into their seats and in about seven seconds they reached full speed again.

"Hey–where's the cop car?" said Shotgun.

"Who cares. We're outta here."

"Hey, now that the cops are gone we can find that stealth thing!" said Shotgun.

"NO!" said Driver, "We're on a deadline–or did you forget? Two days. We can't risk it. Just be glad the radar works! Say thank you, Raytheon! Never doubt instruments!"

"Thank you, Raytheon!" said Reggie and Jeremy.

Shotgun glared back at them.

Only Reggie and Jeremy had seen the police car flip, but they had no idea what the truck mirage had done to make it happen. Things were happening too fast and nothing made any sense anymore. It was like they were in an alternate reality with totally different physical laws, but they were relieved that they had escaped from the cops.

After quickly eating up 600 miles, Driver nodded and Shotgun flipped off the peroxide switch. As they slowed, their seat belts cut painfully into their stomachs and shoulders again as their bodies wrenched forward. Jeremy thought his eyes were going to pop out of his head.

The two Buzz Cuts didn't say anything but they both had grins on their faces. As Reggie looked in the front mirror he noticed that Shotgun's eyes were moist as he gazed straight ahead. The speedometer read 70 mph now, but it felt like they were barely moving. Reggie and Jeremy took the fact that the Buzz Cuts were happy to mean that they wouldn't beat them up or kill them, which was a huge relief.

"I think we might win this year," said Driver. "We might just win this thing."

"Affirmative," said Shotgun. "Confidence is high."

Then Shotgun turned back and said, "So Amber, wha'd you girls do?"

Reggie was flummoxed that he had been nicknamed 'Amber' and been called the "G" word.

"Uh, huh?"

"You heard me, why'd you want to get away from the cops so bad?"

"Rob a bank or something?" asked Driver, snickering.

Reggie didn't want to make them angry.

"No. We just ran away from home and don't want to go back."

"Really? So you're gonna live on your own? What're your skill sets?" questioned Driver, as he let go of the steering wheel and turned around.

"What do you mean?" said Reggie nervously. "Shouldn't you be holding the..."

"Skill Sets! What skills do you have? How you gonna make money? Math? Scuba? Writing code? Welding?"

Driver shook his head like Reggie and Jeremy were useless dorks. Cars whizzed by in the opposite direction in the lane next to them while the car drove itself. Somehow the steering wheel moved by itself and the car managed to stay in its lane, but it was unnerving to depend on a car to keep you alive in head-on traffic.

How the heck is the car driving itself? Reggie wondered.

Reggie was so baffled by the car apparently not needing a driver that he couldn't think of what to say. Of more pressing concern, he was terrified of ending up in a head-on collision with the huge truck speeding toward them in the next lane. He quickly tried to do the math, but concluded that the force of a head-on impact of the two vehicles converging at 140 miles per hour and stopping in an instant was impossible for him to calculate.

How can they trust this machine with their lives?

The truck whooshed by and the car lurched left, then instantly corrected its trajectory as if it had anticipated the aerodynamic interference of the passing truck.

What else can this car do? He wondered.

"You guys ever even take shop?" continued Shotgun.

"Physics? Robotics? Mechanics?"

Both Buzz Cuts turned and faced Reggie and Jeremy. They were so comfortable it was like they weren't even in a car, but maybe were in a living room, or, Reggie thought, in their case, it would probably be a grimy garage somewhere in the middle of nowhere.

"What is it with kids these days? I just don't get it," said Driver. "No skill sets."

A semi whizzed by. Jeremy boldly asked, "So what are your skill sets?" using his fingers like annoying quotes around 'skill sets.' Jeremy hoped they'd get mad and end the conversation quickly. Reggie cringed. What the heck was Jeremy doing?

"Speed, big shot, speed," said Driver.

"And guaranteed delivery–GPS assisted steering and speed calibration," said Shotgun, "for robotic vehicles. DARPA competition."

Jeremy had a stupid look on his face.

"Defense Advanced Research Projects Agency? Their Urban Challenge–'Autonomous vehicles conducting military operations'–it's a robotic vehicles competition, and we're gonna win two million bucks, punk. That's our skill set."

"Oh," said Jeremy.

"We're only going as far as our shop, so you'll have to figure it out from there, geniuses," said Driver to Jeremy.

They passed a sign that said "Welcome to California," and then another that said "Redwood National Park." They were cruising through the trees now, back at sewing machine speed, and it felt comfortable. Even Jeremy was sitting up and looking out the window.

The two Buzz Cuts didn't say anything as the car drove itself at precisely 55 miles per hour. They just studied the dials and took notes, as if they were scientists recording readings in their notebooks. Whenever a cop drove by, Driver would pretend to hold the steering wheel and look at the road. Reggie and Jeremy kept their mouths shut. Soon they were so relaxed that they dozed off.

Finally, in the late afternoon, the car zoomed smoothly and precisely into a small oceanside town called Crescent City. The car turned down several industrial blocks, then down into an empty alley and stopped at the dead end.

"Bam!" said Driver, waking them up.

A garage door opened at the end of the alley and several RC cars approached them playing rock-and-roll tunes from tiny speakers.

"Here come your annoying little sentries," said Driver.

"Hey, little buddies," said Shotgun to the RC's.

"Hey, Big Boss!" said the RC bots. "You da' Maaan!

"Okay, we did our part," said Driver Buzz Cut as Reggie and Jeremy got out of the car. "Good luck, and here." He gave each boy a business card, which was a big relief.

"Thanks," said Reggie and Jeremy.

"So you can thank us later. There might be a time in the future, in a week, a month, or who knows, you might be doing some thing, and the phone rings. We might ask you for a favor. Just help us out if we ask, okay?"

"Yeah, okay, sure," said Reggie, meaning it.

"Go south, young men," said Shotgun with a grin, and he pointed back down the alley.

9. BEACH TRIP

"Think we're lost enough now?" asked Jeremy when Reggie had led them off a road and into some woods at the outskirts of Crescent City, California.

"Yeah, this is way safer than the I-5," said Reggie as they walked through the woods.

"Whoever got the other guys won't ever find us now. No way. We were really flying! We actually lucked out big time meeting up with those guys. They got us way off the 5!"

Jeremy's excitement and over-confidence made Reggie think. *We've been really lucky, so far, getting rides. How could it be so easy?*

"I'm fried," said Jeremy. "Wait up. You're walking too fast."

"Check."

They came to the end of the woods and saw an enormous sand dune. Reggie stopped and checked the GPS map on his laptop.

"Let's go, the ocean's just a little further."

"Sand doesn't crunch like snow," said Jeremy, "but it's just as soft." He dropped his pack, kneeled down and rolled in the sand. "And blue in the shadows too."

"Wheeeeeee."

Jeremy stopped rolling and rested on his back, watching the clouds pass by.

"Come on!" said Reggie, walking up the dune. "We don't have time for this. We have to set camp."

After several minutes of climbing in the sand they collapsed at the top, exhausted. All they could see ahead was a limitless blue infinity stretching on forever. It was the Pacific Ocean. The Peaceful Ocean–flat and perfectly quiet.

They stood for a full minute and scanned the blue expanse of ocean and the colorful transition into the sky. One big blue world blended into golds, reds, and yellows near the horizon and then back into deep blue above and behind them. They were so tired that they felt they were floating in an endless sea of color, like they had lost themselves completely in pure color.

The sun dipped and touched the horizon.

"Let's set up camp quick, before it gets dark," said Reggie.

They headed down the dune to the beach, sliding like skaters on the warm sand mountain.

"Sand is better than snow," said Jeremy, "because it's warm, and feels good. But I still like snow, too."

They dug a shallow trench next to a huge log about 50 yards from the water, unrolled their sleeping bags, and got ready to sleep. As the sun set, Reggie opened his notebook and checked his email again. Only one new message. From Hakr, of all people.

Great, Hakr the Nuisance, now what?

waitingforyou:

u have no idea what's going to happen to you!
r u afraid?
soon...
Ha!

HAkr

Wish he'd get off my back. He's probably the kidnapper.
Reggie emailed all the guys he knew who had been kidnapped, just in case any of them found a computer and could check their email, noted his current location in his journal, and then composed an email to Luca, the guy from the game trial.

Dear Mr.Esposito,

You said I could get in touch with you anytime, right? Well, I think someone might be kidnapping E-7 gamers. I thought you should know. We left town before he could get us, and we're going to my dad's house in Pasadena. Can you email me? Please don't tell the police. We can't call the police for various reasons. I hope you get this. Let me know if you do.

Respectfully,
Reggie King (aka Waiting For You)
P.S. That guy HAkr is threatening me again, but for real. Maybe he's the kidnapper.

It was pitch black when he closed his laptop, and Jeremy was already sound asleep. As soon as Reggie's head hit the ground, he began to notice strange flashes of colors in the sand– reds, yellows, blues, and whites– but before he knew it he felt like he was falling again. He felt the ominous, sinking depression he was so used to at home pulling him down, as if he was getting heavier and heavier.

It reminded him of falling into a glitch like he did so often in his dreams, when he would land in a dark place where he couldn't see anything but blackness. It felt like something was relentlessly searching for him, scanning, a predator hunting program from somewhere unknown, alien, sending out smaller, computerized programs of some sort, all scanning in some kind of predetermined pattern as it hunted for him. He had to keep moving and hiding, so he wouldn't be caught. There was another glitch, a crack in the space where he could hide. The scanners traveled right next to him but couldn't see him as long as he didn't move, so he froze. The predator couldn't quite find him, but kept prowling nearby, relentlessly, precisely, scanning inch by inch. Reggie could hear it looking for him. *Am I in a glitch?* he thought, *or is it all just a dream?*

He woke up in the middle of the night and thought he heard a strange whirring, zipping sound, sort of like giant mosquitoes, but there was no moon so he couldn't see any bugs. Instead, again he noticed the strange, dim, colorful bursts of light flashing across the face of the beach. *Bioluminescent seaweed*, he thought. He had read about the seaweed washing up on beaches and people being allergic to it because it was toxic. He pulled the end of the sleeping bag up over his head and tried to go back to sleep, but kept imagining strange musical tones between the noise of the crashing waves on the beach. *Maybe the toxic seaweed causes hallucinations*...he shook off the sound as a hallucination, but it still irritated him.

After a while it became quiet again, and all he could hear was the peaceful, rhythmical lapping sound of the calm surf. The depression had somehow lifted away. He fell back into a deep, peaceful, restful sleep.

10. WHAT THESE EYES HAVE SEEN

The screeching of sea gulls awakened Jeremy and Reggie. It was a clear sunny morning and they were well-rested, but hungry.

"Let's chow!" said Jeremy.

"Yeah, let's find your IHOP!" said Reggie as they packed up their stuff.

Jeremy dropped his compass while loading his pack. Reggie reached down, and as he grabbed the compass, he noticed he was standing in the middle of a pattern of strange triangular impressions in the sand. The impressions were about half a foot deep, a couple of feet wide, and kind of resembled the letter A, but with a sharp triangle in the middle.

"Hey, look at this!" he said.

"Huh?" said Jeremy, as he looked at the shapes. It looked like the footprint of a giant mechanical creature or landing pod of a space ship. Then they noticed other footprints, all over the beach, and then a whole bunch of prints right next to where they had been sleeping.

"Whoa," said Jeremy, "We could have been squashed like bugs! Looks like something as heavy as an elephant got loose."

Reggie shot some video of the tracks. There were also hundreds of shallow, parallel pairs of delicate lines in the sand, some extending down into the wet sand. Reggie took close-up shots of the lines.

"Weird," said Reggie, "I thought I heard mosquitoes or sand flies buzzing around last night, but these lines look like RC tracks. That's probably what woke me up last night."

"Whatever it was could have crushed us," said Jeremy, in awe of the giant footprints.

"Ha, Ha!" Reggie suddenly started laughing. Soon he was laughing hysterically. He couldn't stop.

"What? Are you crazy or something?!"

"RC's! Those guys, the grumpy car guys with the buzz cuts, they played a trick on us. They're trying to scare us. Ha," said Reggie as he put away his camera.

"Oh..." laughed Jeremy, "those guys are weird!"

"Weird, but funny," said Reggie, surprised.

As they worked their way across the sand dune, an old guy with dull burnt-out eyes, skin covered with sores, and clothes so stained that you couldn't tell what color they had been yelled at them. He was drinking from a bottle in a paper sack.

"No. It wasn't funny! I SAW it. It was cold! Crazy! On a rampage, but silent, perfectly silent. A silent rampage! What I saw last night, you have no idea. You would NEVER laugh. It was...just..."

He walked up to them and got in their faces.

"Have you got a dollar, man? I really need a couple of dollars, or a ten. Got a ten? You have no idea!"

The guy looked crazy, like he had been living outside for way too long. It looked like the sun had wrecked his eyes–they were sort of gray and dead-like. Cloudy. But he acted like they should pay him somehow for this crazy information.

"Stupid juice," whispered Jeremy to Reggie.

"I know, I know," whispered Reggie, "just keep walking."

The guy followed them.

"You have no idea what it was like. Cruel. Cold, so cold, like it was so angry it was going to destroy something, get revenge, but like a machine, man, like it would never, ever stop. Forever! It could go on forever and ever and never get tired! You would never laugh if you saw it! How it moved!"

He leaned in close into their faces, stinking of pungent B.O. and booze, pointing to his eyes with both of his filthy, grimy hands, "What these eyes saw last night no one's *ever* seen before!"

They inched past him and started down the road.

"Hey, have you got a few bucks? How 'bout just a fiver? Five bucks? A buck? Go ahead, laugh! Yeah, keep laughing you puny squirts!"

The man's voice faded as they put some distance on him.

"Man, what was that all about?" said Jeremy.

"He's just cracked," said Reggie, "On stupid juice. Besides, those eyes don't look like they can see much of anything anymore. It's all in his head."

"Stupid juice," said Jeremy.

"Yep. Stupid juice."

11. REGGIE'S STRATEGY

Reggie and Jeremy got milk and chow each morning at a 7-Eleven convenience store wherever they found themselves because 7-Eleven convenience stores were always friendly, clean, and most importantly, predictable places where they knew where to look for new pictures on milk cartons. This morning, at another 7-Eleven, Reggie grabbed a map and a newspaper and discovered that George Johnson, aka "Snake," had also been kidnapped the day before in Medford, Oregon.

Reggie started to worry because Snake's disappearance confirmed a pattern of kidnapped kids who also happened to be ECHO game players. It might have been a coincidence that all the guys who were missing from Meadowbrook were ECHO's Revenge gamers, but when the best gamer from Medford was also missing, he couldn't call it a coincidence any more.

This can only mean one thing, thought Reggie. *For some reason, "Revenge" gamers were being kidnapped, and since*

*Medford was south of Meadowbrook, the kidnapper was clearly traveling south...*And now he and Jeremy just happened to be south of Medford.

Reggie felt good about one thing, though–that he had instinctively reacted the right way the day before. He had suspected that he and Jeremy were being stalked, so he immediately got lost. The fact that someone else got caught near them convinced him that he had made the right decision. It was one thing to have quick reflexes in a video game, but another thing to have good instincts and quick reflexes in real life. He had accurately determined that they were being stalked, and then decided what to do and did it. As Luca had said in the focus group, "Play the cards you're dealt, and then decode the problem to determine what to do."

As they sat on the curb, Reggie couldn't decide how much he should tell Jeremy. He thought Jeremy might freak out if he knew they were being stalked. Jeremy might want to call their mom, and it would be tough to keep him from calling if he became afraid of the stalker and panicked. No. He couldn't tell Jeremy.

Next, Reggie was glad that he had sent the email to Luca, but worried about why Luca had not responded. Was Luca even checking his email? If he had, and hadn't responded, what did it mean? Could Luca be behind the kidnappings?

Reggie tried to figure out what his next move should be. Somehow, they had to cover some real ground while staying as hard to find as possible. He hoped that the next kidnap victim would be south of their location, and that whoever was kidnapping the gamers had missed him and Jeremy.

Reggie pulled out his map. Now that their names were on the Amber Alert traffic billboards they had to be extremely careful to avoid the police, as well as the kidnapper. Reggie wished they could take a train to LA because it would be faster and they could afford it, but now they couldn't do that because their pictures were everywhere and the police would be looking for them. Their faces would instantly trigger a check up and they would be caught and sent back to Asa the Hun.

Their only hope was their original plan–to get to their dad's house, but some other way. They needed to get there as soon as possible and convince their dad that he should let them stay there for good. That would fix everything. Their dad's house would remain their final objective.

Reggie scanned over the three largest red lines on the map that went from north to south. He noticed that the I-5 was still the quickest route to LA, but since all the kidnappings had taken place on or near the I-5, they had to avoid that freeway. Reggie decided on the only reasonable alternative–a fairly straight freeway that ran south just inland, between the I-5 and the Pacific Ocean–the 101. They could take it to San Francisco, then to Santa Barbara, and then jump over to the PCH for the short run down to LA.

In the meantime, Reggie decided to keep an eye on the kidnapping reports to see how far south they ran. Since they all took place around the I-5, he'd make sure they stayed off that freeway. Hopefully he and Jeremy would stay far enough from the kidnap locations that he wouldn't have to worry about it at all, and maybe the kidnapper would completely miss Reggie and Jeremy.

Maybe they would be forgotten.

12. PETALUMA, CALIFORNIA

Reggie and Jeremy surveyed the truck stop just outside of Crescent City, trying to figure out with whom they could hitch another ride. There were only a few trucks, but they were parked and empty, so they turned around and walked back toward the freeway. About ten seconds later another truck stopped right next to them and a big tough woman yelled down at them.

"Hey! Goin' south. Need a ride?"

"Sure. Thanks!" *Wow, that was easy*, thought Reggie.

They ran around to the passenger side and climbed up into the cab.

"Just hop in the back compartment and I'll let you off when I turn East."

"Thanks!" said Reggie and Jeremy.

Before they knew it, the truck was heading south toward its destination—Sonoma, California—which is where a lot of grapes are grown and the best wine in the world is made. They noticed that everything in the truck smelled like grape juice.

The rear compartment was so big and private that Reggie and Jeremy could rest on the surprisingly comfortable bed without even hearing the sound of the truck. They stashed their backpacks, and Jeremy noticed the cover of a book, “Children of Alcoholics.” *Weird*, he thought, as Asa’s face automatically flashed in his mind.

“I’m beat,” said Reggie, and he collapsed and fell asleep.

Jeremy started thumbing through the book, but in a few minutes it fell from his hands and he, too, fell asleep in the warm, quiet capsule as the truck sped south.

Hours passed. They had been in a deep restful sleep for a long time when they felt the door open and a cool breeze awaken them. They were at another truck stop.

“Okay. Petaluma, this is as far south as I go before I turn east,” said the driver, noticing the book on the floor.

“I see you were reading. Good, take the book, so you don’t waste your whole life like I did trying to understand or fix someone, because you never will. Fix yourself instead! Make your own life. That’s your job on planet Earth.”

“Thanks!” said Jeremy, as he packed the valuable book in his backpack. She paused thoughtfully, just like Big Pete did when he asked Jeremy about his bruised face, and then said, “Okay. No more sermon today. Time to get out of my cab. And if anyone asks me, and even if you tell, I never saw you.”

They climbed down, and the truck pulled out of the parking lot onto a smaller dirt road. In a second or two it disappeared, leaving nothing but a big dust cloud behind.

Funny how a valuable ride had instantly appeared and then disappeared before their very eyes.

Come to think of it, thought Reggie, *it's also strange that we keep getting rides from people who seem to know something about us. Like Asa being an alky.*

13. JEREMY CONTRIBUTES TO THE STRATEGY

"What she said about Asa kinda makes sense," said Jeremy, as they entered the Truck Stop Restaurant. "It's impossible to get through to him."

"Yeah, that book's like a key. I tried to figure out Asa, but I never could. That book's a cheat code."

"Ha!" laughed Jeremy. "Yeah, a cheat code. Hopefully, we'll never need it though."

They were starving, so they ordered some breakfast in the diner and then checked a local newspaper. With plenty of sleep and hot food down the hatch, they could think a lot more clearly. But as he read the paper, Reggie was immediately hit by another disturbing development. On the third page of the *Sonoma Gazette* he read about an FBI investigation. The agents were looking for the kidnap victims, and there were 15 so far. Vincent Morano, aka Power, had just been kidnapped in Sacramento the night before. Reggie pulled out his map and noticed that the I-5 went straight through Sacramento, but fortunately, Sacramento was south of where they were.

Jeremy noticed Reggie wasn't listening to him anymore.

"What's up!?" said Jeremy.

"Power got nailed."

"Where? Nearby?"

"No. South. We're okay, see?"

Reggie showed Jeremy where Snake lived on the paper map, south of where they were and over on the 5. Jeremy was panicked by the fact of another gamer being kidnapped so close to them, but was also relieved that they had made the decision to stay off the 5.

"Think the kidnapper forgot about us?" said Jeremy.

"Possibly. Seems to be ahead of us, traveling south."

"You were right about the 5. Should we slow down?" said Jeremy.

"Nah. We're okay. He doesn't even know we're here. He's heading south, way ahead of us. So we should be okay. Besides, we gotta get to Dad's ASAP, or the cops'll get us."

"Roger that."

Reggie had not mentioned the connection between all the kidnapped gamers. He regretted telling Jeremy about Snake, opening up a can of worms, so he tried to change the topic to keep him from asking too many questions. But since Jeremy also knew the names and avatars of most of the players, he had already figured it out.

"What would anyone want with ECHO gamers?" he asked.

"What do you mean?" asked Reggie, playing stupid.

"Come on. They're all gamers, all of them have played ECHO's Revenge, and all the gamers kidnapped outside of

Washington are Revenge Masters. But you're a Master, and you weren't kidnapped. Why? Because we left before we got nailed. By chance we left first, and by chance he hasn't gotten us yet. I'm also a registered E-6 Revenge gamer, so he'll probably get me too when he gets you. Eventually."

Jeremy was resigned to their doomed future.

"But why?" wondered Jeremy. "What're they doing with us?"

Reggie was surprised. He wanted to cheer up Jeremy but could find nothing to be cheerful about. He had no idea Jeremy had figured all of this out, so he wasn't prepared to answer his question.

"We have to warn the others," continued Jeremy. "Just like when ECHO comes down the street and you're the only one who knows. You've gotta warn the rest of the guys!"

Reggie hadn't thought of warning the others. It was a good point. Jeremy surprised him. He was suddenly glad he brought Jeremy with him. Reggie had been so concerned about taking care of Jeremy and getting to their Dad's house to escape from Asa that he didn't even think about helping the other guys. He just didn't want to get caught himself. He remembered what Rhino had said about him at the focus group and was embarrassed.

"Yeah," said Reggie, "of course we have to warn the others, but we have to do it in a way that won't draw attention to ourselves. We can't let the kidnapper find us. The only thing is, we don't even know where the guys live, but some of them seem to be near the 5."

"It's too bad we can't just call the police," said Jeremy.

"Or Mom or Dad," said Reggie, suspecting that would be Jeremy's next idea.

"Let's email the guys who haven't been caught!" said Jeremy.

"Already did, but no one's emailing back."

"Great," said Jeremy.

Reggie fingered Luca's card in his pocket. He suddenly realized that Luca might be the only person he could call, but he wasn't sure if he should. Why hadn't Luca answered his email? Was Luca brushing him off because Luca had found out he and Jeremy had run away from home, or did Luca think he was just some weird kid? It had been a major, massively wrong assumption to think he would help. Maybe Luca didn't want to believe that a bunch of kids could be kidnapped just because they played his game. Maybe he was worried that it would make him look bad. Maybe he was insulted by Reggie's email. Either way, Luca had to know where all the master gamers lived because he sent out the focus group letters. He would be the only one who could really help.

"What about that guy who gave you his card?" asked Jeremy, as if he had read Reggie's mind.

"Huh?" Reggie answered as if he didn't know who he was talking about.

"Yeah! The game designer guy! He'll know where everyone lives!"

"Luca? Nah, he'll just think I'm cracked," said Reggie, not wanting Jeremy to know he had already emailed Luca but gotten no response. "Besides, he's a big shot and probably wouldn't even talk to me."

"I thought he gave you his home number or something, and anyway, his email address was on his card," said Jeremy, way ahead of him again.

Reggie could see that he had no way out. No matter what he said, he wasn't going to get Jeremy to shut up until he made that call.

"Hey, it's the least we can do for the other gamers, right?" said Jeremy, excitedly. "We might be able to set a trap or something–SAC the kidnapper!"

It was a surprisingly excellent idea, and Reggie immediately liked it. He smiled.

"Yeah, Surround And Capture! We can set up an ambush to catch him. We can go on the offense from here, by remote control, set it all up so the kidnapper won't even know who's pulling the strings. Brilliant, little brother! Awesome!"

Reggie wondered why he hadn't thought of this himself.

"Okay, I'll get Luca to warn the others. Maybe he can help us set up an ambush. Maybe he can get the cops or someone to stake out the next gamer and trap this guy."

"Yes!" said Jeremy, pumping his fist.

"SAC! For real!" said Reggie.

As they ate their hash and eggs, sunny side up, Reggie emailed Luca again. He decided he would call, too, since email didn't work the last time, so as soon as they finished breakfast they found a phone in the front of the diner. Reggie called while Jeremy guarded their backpacks. A police car slowly cruised by. Reggie thought the police might be checking out Jeremy, so he left his message quickly.

14. SAN FRANCISCO SURPRISE

Reggie and Jeremy were lucky. The police checking the truck stop parking lot in Petaluma were only interested in vehicle registrations and outstanding unpaid tickets. The Governor of California had decided not to raise taxes that year. He had famously called his plan "My Fantastic Gift to Californians."

Instead, the police were very busy giving out expensive traffic tickets any way they could to raise money for the state. They were not interested in finding kidnap victims. Since finding lost kids did not bring money into the state, finding missing kids was left to the FBI. The FBI had unlimited funds because it was a federal agency. Federal agencies are funded by "The Fed," and The Fed can print its own money anytime, just by pressing buttons, like in a video game.

After Power's kidnapping in Sacramento, the FBI had no choice but to start an investigation of what they were calling "The Serial I-5 Gamer Kidnappings, Case

#698-15-1910-549-63-66-1-A." They, too, were convinced a pattern was growing. Their pattern recognition programs told them that the next kidnapping would take place along the I-5 and that it would be another Revenge gamer, so they had left call after call on Luca's phone while traveling on their way to have a "little talk" with him. They were determined to get a list from him of all the gamers living on or near the I-5 to help their investigation, but so far had gotten no answer. Just like Reggie.

When Reggie and Jeremy rolled into San Francisco at the end of the day, they had come to the same conclusion that the FBI had: There would be another I-5 kidnapping. But they were feeling good now, pretty clever and on top of their game, so they didn't really care where they got dropped off.

There was just one problem. Reggie had failed to carefully read the name tags that had been in front of each game player at the focus group meeting. He checked his video, but couldn't make out any of the names on the name cards at the focus group study, except for Chainsaw's, who lived much further south, in Ventura, so he was out of the picture for now. Big Pete was right. He should pay more attention to everything around him and really remember things. Remembrance *was* power.

On the other hand, Rhino, aka Jorge Sanchez, lived in San Francisco, and now his face was on the milk carton which they were both staring at in a 7-Eleven convenience store in the middle of San Francisco. The 101 had led them there and the I-5 was sixty miles east. Clearly, the kidnapper had taken a little detour over to San Francisco. Was the kidnapper still there? Possibly nearby? Already onto Reggie and Jeremy? Jeremy had been right after all. They should have slowed down to let the kidnapper get as far ahead of them as possible.

Another thought came to Reggie. It hadn't occurred to him before, but now he wondered if some new kind of game had begun at the focus group meeting. All of the same people were involved. The only thing was, no one there knew anything had started except the kidnapper. Reggie wondered if it was someone who worked at AAARG. Could it be Luca, or that weird guy he bumped into who laughed at him? There was still something weird about that guy...something that made Reggie very uneasy...but why would anyone kidnap gamers?

"He's gonna nail us next, isn't he?" said Jeremy, who, after seeing his own face on a milk carton, was again resigned to getting caught, "Right here."

Reggie looked at his brother's picture. He knew Jeremy was right to be afraid, but he couldn't let Jeremy know it.

"Not if we can help it, little brother," said Reggie confidently, scanning everyone entering the store. "Come on, let's stock up on chow, then we'll complete our next objective: find a bunker, a place to hide. Then we'll hunker down so we don't get nailed like Rhino did."

After buying and stashing some food in their packs, they went back outside. There were dirty, crazed people scattered through the streets doing strange, demented things. Some were rummaging through boxes and garbage. It was a lousy industrial neighborhood, with nothing but dirty, decrepit buildings and deranged people wandering the streets and sidewalks. Worn out ghouls. Products of lives gone horribly wrong.

They went to the back of the 7-Eleven convenience store and checked out the bathroom. It had a strong, reinforced metal door with a big deadbolt lock on the inside. It was clean and bright, a perfect bunker.

"We gotta make a plan. The kidnapper could be anywhere and we have no idea what he looks like," said Reggie.

"Roger that. So what do we do?"

"Uhhh..." There was a pause as they tried to think of something.

Someone knocked on the door.

"GO AWAY!" yelled Jeremy and Reggie in a panic. The person went away.

"Fact number one," said Reggie, "it might be Hakr, but we don't really know who it is."

"Number two," said Jeremy, "we have to get out of this city somehow without getting nailed."

"Number three, he's not staying on the I-5, so we can't count on that anymore."

"Number four," said Jeremy, "now can we call Dad and get him to pick us up?"

"No! You know we can't, or for sure it'll be called kidnapping and we'll never see him again, because they've already called it kidnapping in the newspapers. Remember? Who knows, they might even blame Dad for all this and arrest him if we even start calling him now. They can trace calls."

"Number five, never mind."

"Number six," said Reggie, thinking hard, "the only way we can find out where the kidnapper's going next is to try to call Luca again. He would know all the gamers and where they live, and could tell us who's next, south of here. And then we'll know not to go there because that's obviously where he's headed now."

"Yeah!"

"But the phone's outside, and our best strategy is not to take a chance on getting caught, so I'll email him again and hopefully he'll answer us this time," concluded Reggie, pulling out his notebook.

There was a soft knock on the door.

"Check. Email's safe, email's good."

Reggie turned on his notebook. He found a local wireless connection, and before he knew it, his email was open. HAkr. Again!

waitingforyou:

It's coming for you!
Soon.

HAkr

HAkr, thought Reggie. *Does he know where we are?*

Reggie quickly opened a new email.

Dear Luca, he wrote, but he didn't have time to mess around, and didn't even know if Mr. Esposito liked him or hated him. There was more knocking on the door, so he quickly changed it to:

mr esposito—we r trapd in san francisco. u said 2 cal if i ever wantd 2 talk 2 u (but i have to rite cz we r holed up in a bathrm) so i rely need 2 talk 2 u. rino was kidnpd. plz plz plz send me a

list of the focus group guys and wer they live so we can know wer NOT to go or wl get kidnpd. Also w'd lik to
set up a trap for the kidnapr in pasadena. plz help us. Is Hakr doing this? I think he's stalking us.
ur friend,

And then he changed it to:
respectfully,
reggie king

pls respnd kwik cz wer hold up n a bathrm and wont leev til we hear from u cz we dont no were 2 go.
Thank you!

Reggie immediately hit the send button without reading his message, in case he lost his connection.

"Message sent," he said, relieved.

"Sweet," said Jeremy.

A message came back almost immediately.

"Message received, but unread. Addressee on vacation."

"What the...?" said Reggie, "How could he be on vacation?!"

And he didn't respond to my last email either, thought Reggie, *Maybe he really doesn't want to talk to me. What the heck do I tell Jeremy now?*

But Jeremy had already looked over Reggie's shoulder and read the message.

"Maybe he's the kidnapper!"

"No way. He wouldn't do that."

"Then we have to try calling him. He'll be checking his messages, even if he really is on vacation," decided Jeremy.

They both sat for a minute and thought. The bathroom was a great place to hide because the door was secure and it was a bright, clean refuge in a filthy, decrepit city. But they knew they couldn't stay there forever. Sooner or later they'd get kicked out by the manager. They had to do something.

"Okay, let's do it," said Reggie. "Let's find a phone."

"HUA!"

Reggie turned off his computer and packed up his stuff. They cracked open the door to see if there was anyone outside. It seemed clear, so they crept out and went around to the front of the 7-Eleven where they saw a pay phone in front of the store.

"Cover me," said Reggie.

"Check."

Jeremy watched everyone who came and left, wondering if each person could be the kidnapper. Was HAkr among them? An assortment of filthy, dicey-looking personalities drifted into and out of the store as Reggie bolted to the phone.

Reggie dialed. He heard Luca's message again. At the tone, Reggie said,

"Luca, Mr. Esposito. Hi. It's Reggie King. From the focus group? You said to call if I ever wanted to talk to you. We're trapped in San Francisco. Rhino was just kidnapped, along with practically everyone else we know from ECHO's Revenge. So, like I said earlier, I REALLY need to talk to you. I'm with my brother, and we don't want to be next. I need a list of the focus group guys and where they live so we can know where to stay away from. Are you there? I know you're on vacation, but can you call back when you get this? It's a serious situation here.

Reggie thought about how to get Luca to answer the phone. Maybe he wasn't really out of town. Maybe Luca was just out, so he could pick a time when he would likely be in and call then.

"Please be there at...midnight tonight. We'll call then. We really need your help. Thanks again. Reggie. King," then he panicked. "Oh, we're near the corner of Fillmore and McAllister. In case you get in earlier, we'll be nearby."

Reggie left the number, hung up, and ran back to Jeremy.

"The call's done. We need somewhere to hide close by till midnight where no one will see us."

They looked out from the 7-Eleven and scanned the urban wasteland. Fog had started rolling in from the ocean. It was turning colder and darker. Soon it would be very dark.

15. MIDNIGHT AT THE OASIS

"Where can we hide, where can we hide?"

They stood under the front awning of the 7-Eleven, shivering and wondering what to do. Jeremy was getting panicky watching more crazed, ghoulish people pass by.

"As close to the phone as possible where we won't be seen," said Reggie. "We can't risk getting nailed by the kidnapper, so we have to stay out of sight. Luca might call back early, so we can't go far. What we need is a bunker where no one can get to us."

Reggie scanned the cold, darkening panorama and fully realized what a filthy, miserable place San Francisco was. San Francisco– this part at least– was cold, grim, and ugly. Even the steam spewing out of the manholes in the street seemed grimy. As it got darker, they saw flashes through grates in the street and heard a subway blasting by beneath them. Otherwise, there was hardly any traffic. The buildings were dingy, abandoned, and all locked up—permanently, from the looks of it. The streets were strewn with packing boxes and garbage, but there wasn't anything large enough or safe enough to hide in. As another train passed beneath them, Jeremy's eyes stopped on a storm drain.

"There's our bunker!"

"Huh?" said Reggie, noticing the storm drain at street level, "Yeah–Perfect!"

They crossed the street. Reggie shined his flashlight into the chamber, looking for rats or other animals that might give them trouble. Inside, there were metal ladder rungs wide enough for two people, and they went down about eight feet to the bottom of the drain. There were several large drainage pipes intersecting the chamber. The walls were grimy, but the chamber was fairly clear of trash.

Reggie looked around to make sure no one was watching them.

"Let's go," he said as he pulled off his backpack. Reggie squeezed into the hole and climbed down. When he got to the bottom he called up to Jeremy,

"Okay, drop the packs and come down."

Reggie caught the packs and then shined his flashlight on the ladder as Jeremy climbed down.

"Be careful," said Reggie.

"This is pretty good!" said Jeremy, relieved to be in their new safe house.

They felt a lot better down in the storm drain. No one would ever think to look down there, and even if they did no adult would ever be able to chase them through the narrow gap and under the sidewalk.

"Hey. What's this?" asked Jeremy as he felt a large metal object.

Reggie shined his flashlight on it–it read "Oasis Company." It was an abandoned water fountain. Together they tried to move it out of the way, but it was so heavy they couldn't even budge it.

There were a couple of old mattresses on the floor. They sat down on one and listened to the light murmurs of distant traffic and the occasional loud rumbling of the subway. Otherwise, it was surprisingly quiet. Reggie turned off the flashlight, immersing them in complete blackness.

"Hey, whadja do that for?" said Jeremy.

"If they see any light down here they'll know someone's here, besides, we have three hours to go and we gotta save our batteries."

"Oh. HUA."

As their eyes adjusted to the light they could make out the pipes leading under the street from the chamber. There were two tunnels leading in different directions and they both seemed clear. Everything was cast out of concrete, except the heavy steel cover that topped the storm drain, the impervious thousand-pound roof of their concrete bunker.

After a light meal of Slim Jims, sandwiches, and sodas, they lay back and rested. It had been a long day and they were filthy and exhausted. Since they had discovered the San Francisco kidnapping so late, they hadn't been able to eat a real meal or get a bath anywhere. They both felt as grimy as the drain.

After about 25 minutes, they hardly heard anything passing by on the street anymore. The regular blasting sound of the subway trains traveling beneath them had become a predictable rhythm and made them sleepy.

They dozed off for a moment.

Reggie woke up and panicked.

"Wake up, wake up! We can't sleep right now!"

Jeremy woke up, dazed.

"Come on," said Reggie, "we have to stay awake. We have to listen for Luca's call and watch for the kidnapper. Let's keep an eye on the street and count cars or something, come on!"

Reggie pulled Jeremy up and Jeremy followed him back up the ladder. Their faces were now at street level, hidden in the shadow of the storm drain cover.

"What does a kidnapper look like?" said Jeremy.

"I have no idea," said Reggie, "let's just watch out for anyone unusual snooping around until we do the call. You'll have to spot me from here when I call. I don't want to get picked off at the phone, so just yell if anyone comes after me so I can get back. Our retreat plan is we go through the pipe and cross the street underground, if we have to."

What little color there was outside had been leached away by darkness, so everything appeared in shades of black and gray. The street lights dumped pools of light up and down the street, but Reggie and Jeremy could hardly see anything because there was so much fog. The mist kept rolling in, sometimes thick, sometimes thin, but continually creeping down the street in cloud banks.

There was almost no traffic now and no one on the street, but after a few minutes, a pair of headlights crept into view a few blocks away. A lone bakery truck traveled toward them on the other side of the street, cruising slowly past the 7-Eleven. A car sped by, swerving to avoid the truck.

Reggie and Jeremy continued scanning the street, yawning occasionally and talking to each other to stay awake. It was getting colder, so Jeremy went back down for his chemical pocket warmers, the ones he had run back for right when they were leaving home. He gave one to Reggie.

"Thanks," said Reggie, "you were right about bringing these."

"Who would'a guessed we'd be living down here in a hole?"

"Anyone who knew us–it's the story of our lives."

Jeremy chuckled.

They watched the road again. The same bakery truck came back down the street from the other direction and passed right by their faces. It was surprisingly silent out there as the truck vanished back into the fog.

"I'm gonna rest my arms," said Reggie. "I'll be back in a minute." He went down the ladder to stretch. After a few minutes he asked Jeremy, "See anything?"

"No."

"You can take a break in a minute and I'll watch, if you want."

Reggie turned his flashlight on for a second and pulled out his notebook, which he put on top of his pack. He climbed back up and they both resumed watching.

The truck passed by again, silently.

"That truck was here before, right?" asked Reggie.

"The boxy one?"

"Yeah."

"Yeah," said Jeremy, "It's been going back and forth, up and down the street."

"That's weird."

"It's just lost, it's so foggy," said Jeremy.

"Or the driver's drunk."

"Yeah. Stupid juice."

The truck materialized out of the fog again and glided to a stop across the street next to the 7-Eleven. More fog rolled in, hiding the truck, and it became even colder. When the fog passed and it was clear again, the truck was gone, but Reggie and Jeremy noticed a comic book store where the truck had been, covered with the same grime as the rest of the buildings on the street.

"Hey, I didn't notice that comic book store before," said Jeremy.

"Me either."

"Maybe we can check it out in the morning."

"No way," said Reggie. "We need to be ready to bolt tonight, right after we talk to Luca, as soon as we know where the next kidnapping is going to be."

"If he calls."

Reggie didn't say anything.

"I'm gonna take a break," said Jeremy, and he went down to rest his arms.

For the next two hours the two relieved each other while they waited patiently for the conversation with Luca. They were eager for a new, clear, safe direction south. The "Answer."

"I wish he'd just call so we could go," said Jeremy.

By 11:15p.m., they were exhausted. Reggie was sitting at the bottom of the storm drain. He got up to climb the ladder and knocked his notebook computer over, banging it into the floor.

"Rats!" said Reggie.

"Rats? Where?"

"No, not real rats. I think I just busted my notebook!"

"Oh man! Is it okay? That means no email."

Reggie shook the notebook to see if there was anything rattling, then turned on the machine to see if it still worked.

"I don't know, I don't know. Hold on..."

The screen came to life, flickered, flickered again, and went dark.

"Darn!"

And then it came back on again.

"Excellent! Lemme see if everything works."

Reggie tried several of the programs. His journal came up. Jeremy turned back to watching the street now that he was confident the computer was okay, but there was nothing new out there. It was really boring.

"Checking the GPS," said Reggie, and he activated his mapping system.

"Yes! We are blessed!"

As Reggie said this, Jeremy watched an eerie event play out across the street. It was as if his imagination was playing a strange trick on him, or maybe he was so exhausted he was losing his mind. The comic book store started moving and flickering, shifting, splintering into shards of color, and then changing shape, morphing like a kinetic cubist sculpture into something else. And there were weird clicking sounds, a million little crackling insect-like clicks, like a swarm of locusts.

"Uhhh..." moaned Jeremy, "I must've eaten something funny or something." He rubbed his eyes, "I'm hallucinating. Were those Slim Jims stale?"

"Just a minute." Reggie was relieved the notebook was working, so he climbed up quickly to check on his brother.

"What do you mean?"

"Something weird is happening to the comic book store," whispered Jeremy, "or maybe something's wrong with me..."

As the fog passed by, Reggie watched as the comic book store continued to transform. The window morphed into giant, mechanical triangular-shaped feet.

"Hey...the shape of those feet look like the footprint shapes at the beach..." said Reggie.

Then the entire storefront lifted off the ground, traveling up, up, up as it transformed into a giant assortment of demon parts and chunks of armor. The head emerged–a hideous, cruel-looking version of ECHO's head–a terrifying, alien ECHO, which had changed dramatically from the ECHO of ECHO-6. It had changed itself into something much more grotesque.

There it stood, 35 feet tall, reborn.

And angry.

"Um, I don't think it was the Buzz Cuts playing a trick on us at the beach," said Jeremy, his voice trembling. "It's obviously some kind of ECHO, except REAL!"

Reggie quietly snapped his notebook shut as they watched in awe. But, at the almost silent snap of the notebook, the creature suddenly locked it's cold, green, glowering eyes on Reggie and Jeremy and they froze, terrified that it might have spotted them. It seemed to be contemplating the boys and their surroundings. Calculating.

They did not move or even breathe, even though they knew that they were completely hidden in the shadow; but just as quickly as the mech found them, it rotated its ugly massive head and looked down the street as if it were distracted. Then it suddenly took off, instantly disappearing in the fog.

"what...was...that?" whispered Jeremy.

"It did look like a giant, uglier version of ECHO," whispered Reggie, "but it can't be, it's only a video game! Maybe those Slim Jims WERE bad and we're both hallucinating or something. Are you okay?"

"let's...get...out...of...here!" whispered Jeremy as he started down the ladder.

But just then the phone suddenly started ringing. It was a sad, quiet, lonely ringing sound.

ring...

ring...

Reggie checked his watch. It was a few minutes before midnight. It had to be Luca. *An answer!* He thought.

"Wait," whispered Reggie. "Hold on."

The phone kept ringing. Reggie began to feel the dreaded cloak of depression he had experienced so many times before. Was he getting depressed simply because he was under so much pressure? Or because he was exhausted? Or worried that Luca wouldn't help them?

Jeremy thought that Reggie was out of his mind and didn't want any part of the phone call. He looked at Reggie like *anyone would be crazy to go out there!*

"No way. Are you insane? That thing's probably KILLING gamers! It's a trap! Call him back later, during the day! He's probably working with that thing, trying to kill us!"

Reggie thought a moment. He was relieved to hear what Jeremy had just said. He really didn't want to answer the phone, given the circumstances, but he was worried that he might never get through to Luca again.

"Don't even think about it!" demanded Jeremy.

"Okay, okay. Maybe you're right," surrendered Reggie. "Let's get down in the pipe and hide. I don't wanna worry about that thing coming back and finding us. We'll stay put and try him again in the morning."

Just as Reggie said "morning," a giant, glowering, bright green alien eye appeared out of nowhere, inches from their faces, scrutinizing them as if it had lost something and had finally found it. Tiny servo motors rapidly pushed and pulled the lenses of the "eye" back and forth like it was recording everything as quickly as possible about the boys and the storm drain.

Analyzing...

Scheming...at high speed, faster than any human could imagine.

Then, before Reggie knew what was happening, it shot a dim beam into Reggie's right eye and scanned his retina. Reggie's gloomy exhaustion exploded into pure fear. Reggie and Jeremy were so terrified that their bodies shuddered as if they had been hit by a stun grenade and then went limp with shock. They fell from the top of the ladder to the concrete floor, landing flat on their backs on the old mattresses.

The instant they hit bottom, two huge steel claws clamped under the steel roof above them and ripped it open. In two seconds flat the roof was completely twisted off and tossed into the street like a piece of styrofoam. ECHO's right arm extended down like a telescope, grabbed the Oasis water fountain with its steel claws, and hurled it skyward, all in one smooth, instantaneous motion. The Oasis disappeared up into the black sky above them.

"AAAAAAAAAAAAAAAAAAAAAAAAAAAAA!" both boys screamed as they froze, terrified, backs on the pit floor.

"AAAAAAAAAAAAAAAAAAAAAAAAAAAAA!" mimicked the angry beast with precisely the same length and pitch that they had yelled, but much louder as it mashed its face down as far as it could into their faces. Its grizzly teeth snapped and rotated furiously as acrid hydraulic mist erupted from its cavernous mouth, filling the pit with suffocating fumes.

ECHO had perfectly executed S.A.T., a tactic of deception, to 'Shock And Terrorize' its victims. S.A.T. was its First Objective, which it had been programmed to do once it located each ECHO gamer in the video games. As it reared its head back to strike, Reggie and Jeremy grabbed their packs and sprang into one of the tunnels, but the creature's claws followed them just as quickly, cutting Jeremy's ankle and pulling off his left shoe.

Scrambling down the tunnel as fast as they could, they banged their heads, hands, and knees into the hard, cold concrete walls. ECHO's shrill, violent screams pulsed down the pipe in pressure bursts, banging their ears over and over. Even when another train roared underneath them, they could still hear ECHO's harsh, shrill, alien shrieks.

"I TOLD YOU WE WERE GOING TO BE CAUGHT!" screamed Jeremy, who was now in full-blown panic mode. "I WANNA GO HOME!"

"FINE WITH ME!" screamed Reggie.

Reggie desperately tried to remember the code word the guy had given him to stop ECHO, but he couldn't. He was too scared to think, and he had never written it down.

As soon as they were safely under the street, they paused to catch their breath for a second before moving on.

"This thing didn't kidnap anyone," gasped Jeremy. "It ate them! That game guy's sending it out to eat gamers! Why's he doing this? Did he crack or something? Did you guys make him mad or something? What did you do to deserve this!?"

"I don't know!" said Reggie, thinking about the focus group. He was bewildered and wondering if Luca was angry at him for something, if that was why Luca hadn't emailed back or called him. It seemed like Luca had purposely called back at the exact the moment ECHO was going to attack. Was the call a decoy? It had to be! The timing was too perfect. Bait for the trap.

What a sucker I've been! thought Reggie, feeling totally played.

But ECHO was already in the pit, telescoping its arms in and out as it clawed its way down the drain pipe, ripping concrete out of the tunnel as fast as it could. It was in a violent rampage now, in a frenzied automatic digging program like a pit bull digging feverishly after a mole in soft earth, except it was a machine, so it could dig forever and ever without stopping–a gigantic backhoe digger grinding up the tunnel and the street behind them as fast as they could crawl. The noise was deafening, like standing next to a loud, grinding mine digger, but ECHO didn't seem like a machine–it was acting like a living creature from Hell.

They leapt forward again.

"DON'T STOP!!!" screamed Jeremy.

They gained some distance but didn't stop moving. They never got far enough ahead to feel safe, so they kept scrambling as fast as they could in an automatic human response, the one known as flight. But they were painfully tired, and their hands were bruised from all the pounding on the concrete.

As their exhaustion overtook them, Reggie suddenly noticed that the sound of ECHO's digging had unexpectedly stopped. Jeremy was ten feet behind, and had collapsed from exhaustion, freaked out and sobbing quietly like the little kid he really was. Reggie crawled back and pulled him along behind him as fast as he could.

"How could this thing have found us?" cried Jeremy, "Even if Luca sent it, it couldn't have known where we were hiding!"

"I don't know, but we can't stop!" gasped Reggie as they crawled forward. He realized something, then feverishly looked through his pack.

"Maybe my computer activated something."

"THE GPS!" Jeremy suddenly realized.

Reggie immediately cut the power to his computer. The instant he did, the deafening digging exploded into motion again and ECHO leapt forward, gaining ground. The noise of the digging and clawing and scratching and crushing of concrete was overpowering. The huge, crazy digger was so close it was about to rip them out of the ground. Jeremy rushed forward into Reggie, and Reggie pushed ahead.

Then Reggie found another turn in the pipe. It went down, into black darkness.

"CLOSET WALK!!!" yelled Reggie, as the sound of another train screamed by underneath them.

Jeremy followed him down the hole, but they couldn't get a good grip on the walls so they slid down the grimy shaft and burst through the ceiling of a subway station. They crash-landed in a heap on a loading platform next to a track.

Another train loudly blasted into the station only a few inches from them and squealed to a stop. A door burst open and rang, ding-dang. Reggie and Jeremy half-crawled and half-rolled into the empty, brightly lit car. The door slammed shut and the train accelerated to full speed.

As they flew through the tunnel, they knew that they had escaped as there was no way that ECHO could fit inside the tunnel, much less inside the car they were in. They were soon traveling under the San Francisco Bay, but they didn't catch their breaths until the train emerged on the other side of the bay in Oakland. Even then, their hearts hadn't stopped pounding, so they nervously held their chests to prevent them from exploding.

"That's it! I'm done. I never wanted to come here in the first place!" said Jeremy.

"What do mean? You insisted on coming!"

"You got me into this! I'm going home. Now!"

"We can't go back now. It'll find us for sure. Plus Asa will kill us!"

"Asa or that thing? Let's see...I'll take Asa any day. It's gonna SAC us and eat us, and we don't even know why, but it *will* get us. No way can we fight that thing. Asa's a vacation in Hawaii compared to that thing!"

"It's not gonna get us or eat us," said Reggie. "We already outsmarted it and we didn't even know it was stalking us! All we knew was that gamers were getting kidnapped. We made a mistake going to San Francisco but we escaped! Trust me, now that we know what's after us, we can get to Dad's. I know we can do it!"

"You're nuts! Even if we do make it, it'll eat Dad and we'll be the dessert – the two cherries on top! This all started when you forged Asa's signature on the letter that got you into all this."

"Jeremy, knock it off!" said Reggie. "I tried to keep you from coming, remember? You're the one who insisted on coming. We can't lose sight of our objective."

"You're gonna get us eaten!"

"Has anything happened to any gamers' families?" Reggie argued. "No. It's only going after Master Gamers, so don't bail on Operation Thunderbolt now. You're just tired…and yeah, this *is* beyond weird, but we left so we wouldn't get pounded by Asa anymore. Remember? I had no idea this would happen. If I did, I sure as heck wouldn't be out here, would I? Trust me. We will find out what's going on. I want to kill that Luca guy now, too. As soon as we're off this train I'm calling him again. I'll track him down personally if I have to, but Asa started all this, not Luca."

Jeremy didn't say anything. He was thinking. He reevaluated everything that led up to their decision to run away. He was starting to second-guess everything that Reggie had told him, starting to doubt everything except the main reason why they left. That was the one thing he knew with certainty–that Reggie feared Asa as much as he did, and even hated him a lot more.

"Okay," surrendered Jeremy. "For the moment. I'm too tired to think any more."

"I'm fried, too," said Reggie.

"Hey. I thought you said someone gave you a password to stop ECHO."

Reggie tried to remember the code word but couldn't.

"Yeah, but I was so scared when ECHO chased us that I couldn't even remember it."

"Well, it's not chasing us now. What's the word?"

"I can't remember! It's like it got scared out of me or something."

"Great. You better remember it–for when we run into ECHO again!"

"I'll remember it. I'm just too tired right now. I think it was someone's name. Peace?"

"Peace."

They sat quietly for a minute as the rhythmic clacking of the train going down the tracks rocked them gently back and forth.

"Hey," said Reggie tiredly, "you made a great call on the storm drain. If we hadn't been in there, it would have nailed us for sure, brother."

Jeremy shrugged his shoulders, still angry, but he knew what Reggie said was true, and the compliment felt good. He had made a great call. That was a fact. Maybe everything else Reggie had said was really true, too. And maybe when he said "brother," Reggie meant that Jeremy wasn't just "little brother" anymore either, but was now, finally, equal.

As the train turned into Oakland, the rhythmic clacking became hypnotic. Now they were traveling above the streets. Reggie read the different rail line names on the train system map on the wall and imagined their track line in the map graphically, like in a video game–their train traveling and ECHO's trajectory following them on the streets below. If they fell through any glitch, they'd drop to a lower level and possibly intersect with ECHO's trajectory line. On the other hand, the ECHO trajectory could possibly cross under the track in several places and ECHO could easily climb up and stop the train.

Either way, some kind of game was on.

16. SEMPER FI

Reggie still didn't know what to think since Luca hadn't responded to any of his emails or calls, and the very real ECHO had almost nailed them. How could he possibly trust Luca anymore? He didn't even really know the guy. If Luca had played him, Reggie had a sinking feeling that something terrible was going to happen to them soon, and possibly even to his dad, too. But then he thought about how Luca had treated him when he met with him after the focus group. Luca had seemed so kind, supportive, and interested in talking about games again. Could it all have been a scam? Giving him the jacket? Was it the greatest betrayal of all time? Why would he do that? Did Luca want revenge on the gamers for something? Was he a psycho? Did he secretly hate them? It didn't make any sense.

On the other hand, the entire focus group seemed to be focused on the element of "real" fear as a game theme. Could this be some kind of beta trial run of a game based purely on fear? It was unimaginable that a beta version could be run on this scale, and in public, as a reality game; but the whole thing had been so creepy and terrifying that it seemed to be the very product of everything the gamers had told Luca that they were afraid of.

It hadn't taken Reggie and Jeremy long to get out of town and over the bay to a truck stop in Oakland. They found a south-bound freeway, the 580, and it just happened to lead east and then south, to the I-5, which was lucky this time. Reggie remembered from his video that Chainsaw was from Ventura, and the I-5 went nowhere near Ventura, so it would be highly unlikely that ECHO would now be on I-5 if it was even still as far north as they were. Reggie was also betting that ECHO would never expect them to be on the 5 since they had avoided it for so long.

"We have to stay away from Ventura. That's where Chainsaw lives, and he's next," said Reggie, hoping he was right.

"Then we should warn him," said Jeremy.

"No way. I'm not making another phone call or sending any email. As soon as I do, it'll detect us and come after us again like it just did. That's how he tracks us."

But Jeremy wouldn't budge. He stared at Reggie like he thought Reggie was a coward.

"No way. Look, we'll call him as soon as we get to Dad's. Come on. Let's get going. We have no time to waste."

"I'm still wondering if we should go back," said Jeremy. "Dad can't protect us from that thing. What's the point?"

"Look, I'm just as scared and tired as you are, but either way we can't afford to be out on the freeway any longer than we absolutely need to. We're more than half way there. Dad's closer now than Mom."

But Jeremy still wouldn't budge. He stood his ground and planted his feet in the asphalt of the truck parking lot.

"We can warn all the others from there sooner, too. No GPS." said Reggie.

Jeremy realized that Reggie was right. Reggie's plan made sense, but before Jeremy could respond, their conversation was drowned out by the revving engine of the biggest truck they had ever seen. An old balding guy with long, reddish hair growing from the sides of his head stuck his face out the window. His eyes were as blood-shot as theirs, and he looked like he had been through World War III. He stared at them for a second, and then yelled.

"Are you goin' to Pasadena or what?"

"Uh, yeah..." said Reggie, a little freaked out about the truckers appearance and the specific mention of Pasadena.

Reggie and Jeremy looked at each other, wondering what was in store for them next, and wondered if it could possibly just be a coincidence that the guy was going to Pasadena, of all places.

"Well hurry up, punks. I ain't got all day," said the driver, revving the truck's engine as the veins in his forehead throbbed.

"You're right. We don't have any time," said Jeremy to Reggie. "Let's go."

Reggie thought it was strange that another truck had suddenly appeared just when they needed another ride. He felt rushed to make a decision.

Getting this ride seems unbelievably easy, he thought. *Come to think of it, so was the ride with the old lady, the Buzz Cuts, and even Big Pete...It's almost like whenever we need a ride someone magically shows up...but the other rides did work out well...*

"Have you noticed whenever we need a ride..." but Reggie didn't finish. The driver was getting testy and cut him off.

"Now or never, punks! I got a schedule to keep."

So they climbed up into the cab.

Reggie quickly abandoned any doubts, because as soon as he closed the door he was distracted by a horrible overwhelming stench, like the worst, moldiest old hamburgers in the world. There was a box down by their feet, a few rags on the floor, and a U.S. Marines sticker on the windshield.

"Semper Fi," it said.

Then they noticed the driver. As he revved up the engine and the truck started moving, Reggie and Jeremy saw that the entire right side of his face was somehow melted. It was a fresh pink color with wrinkles and folds like a piece of fabric that had been soaked in molten wax and then cooled solid. His right ear was gone, as were his lips on his right side, revealing big teeth and ripped gums.

Reggie and Jeremy both turned and faced forward. Before they could think, they were on the I-5, traveling fast, like a runaway freight train that would never stop. Even though the cab stank and the driver looked like something out of a zombie movie, it seemed like they would at least get to Pasadena quickly now. Or would they? Suddenly Reggie wondered if they had made the right decision to continue toward their destination with this unpredictable character at the wheel. Maybe it would be safer to deal with the 35-foot homicidal monster.

The driver farted, then Jeremy did the same and laughed.

"Where you headed?" asked Reggie nervously.

"Don't worry. I'm heading to the same place you're heading–Pasadena," he said, scratching at a red patch on his neck.

How'd he know that? wondered Reggie, again.

"What's the big rush, anyway?"

Jeremy was choking from the stench in the cab. Reggie tried to open his window, but it wouldn't budge. It was starting to smell worse. Bad. Real bad.

"Trying to get away from ECHO," said Jeremy.

Reggie shot Jeremy a look that said *'what are you doing?'*

"An echo?" said the driver, baffled.

"A giant game monster that almost ate us last night. We have to get away from it. It tried to rip us to shreds," said Jeremy. "It got my shoe."

Jeremy showed the driver his shoeless foot.

"You boys have been playin' too many video games. Your brains have started to rot. You need to get a real life."

Then, out came another loud fart.

The boys started laughing again, but now the driver could hear them because the truck was running much more quietly in 26th gear. Reggie wondered why the driver kept the windows closed. The stench was unbearable. But then the driver suddenly pulled out a metal lighter, flipped it open, and yelled "Close yer eyes and hold yer breath!" as he clicked it on fire.

There was a terrific, bright FLASH-BOOM as all the fart gas in the cab exploded, sucking all the wind out of Reggie's and Jeremy's ears, noses, and lungs with a loud violent heave. At the same moment they heard a "Yelp!" coming from below their feet. When they recovered, they noticed they were breathing clean air again.

It was then that they realized the farts weren't coming from the driver. Reggie and Jeremy looked down and saw two more blood-shot eyes peering out of the darkness of the box. A small, fat, grungy, dirty-beige dog wearing a scratch collar, the kind that looks like an upside-down funnel, had been the one producing the horrible stench. Although the mutt appeared grotesquely overweight, he had tiny lips, the bottom of which drooped below its mouth to reveal a string of tiny, beady, crumpled teeth and a string of drool. He had a rough, runny nose, a mangy head, and bulging wet eyes. Half of his body was burned like the driver's. When he tried to scratch his head, he couldn't because of the funnel collar. He was arguably the ugliest dog that had ever existed.

The dog let out another huge fart.

The boys laughed.

"That's some dog," said Jeremy, unable to stop laughing.

"That dog is Faithful, boy, Always Faithful, no matter what," said the driver as he leaned left and farted himself.

Reggie and Jeremy were so tired that they couldn't think straight so they couldn't help laughing again. Then the dog farted again and they became hysterical. Reggie laughed so hard he farted too. Then Jeremy started laughing again.

"Yeah. Funny, isn't it, big shots. You could learn a lot from that little guy. Try bein' terminal and keepin' up such a good attitude."

The driver started scratching again, this time around his neck.

"He sure farts a lot," said Reggie.

"You'd fart a lot too if you didn't poop all the way from Vancouver to San Diego. He never poops when we're on the road. Holds it in till we get back home. Then he poops a big ol' pyramid. Heck, this dog's liver's goin.' He just had a blood transfusion and his kidneys are about shot. He may not be the best lookin' thing, but he's as loyal as they come. Refuses to stay home when I'm on the road. Never leaves my side. Never has, never will. Fi is his name, Semper Fi – Always Faithful."

And with that he pulled up another scratch collar, this one much bigger, and snapped it around his own neck. It was made of clear plastic so he could see the freeway through it. Reggie and Jeremy started laughing again, now almost deliriously. Then both the driver and the dog farted in unison.

"Yeah, real funny. You two ever had lice?" he asked. They shook their heads no. "Get some and see how funny it is. You'll be beggin' for one of these. That's why I have to keep the windows closed–they blow all over the place. Into my face. That's why I wear this thing."

Reggie and Jeremy stopped laughing and started worrying that they might get lice from this guy and his dog. They started brushing off their shirts.

"No, you two probably wouldn't know about anything being faithful," the driver went on from inside the collar. "Faithful is about stickin' with someone when they're down and out, when they've got nothin' goin' for 'em."

Jeremy glanced at Reggie like, '*Here comes another lecture...*'

"Faithful is about being a team no matter what. Sacrificing your life for someone! You guys probably wouldn't know anything about that. You're just two punks. I rescued this dog in Afghanistan."

Reggie rolled his eyes back to Jeremy.

"Crazy freaks were stoning him to death. That's what they do over there–stone dogs to death. He spent six days in a ditch in a poppy field with me during a firefight. His fur was burned off by a chemical explosion. Never left my side the whole time, so I took him home with me.

He pulled out his lighter again and with a flash the cab exploded in another bright violent heave. Semper Fi yelped.

The driver's cell phone rang. He picked it up.

"Yeah?...Starman, what's up?...Sorry. Check, roger that." He hung up.

Reggie wondered again who Starman was, but he'd never find out because the driver started lecturing them again about loyalty and how no one's got half as much of it as his dog. The driver's rant made Reggie question how he had treated Jeremy. He wondered if he had made a mistake by making him come on the trip to find their father. Was he thinking about Jeremy when he decided to execute Operation Thunderbolt, or was he just using Jeremy for selfish reasons? How loyal was he, really, to Jeremy? It seemed like he could always rely on Jeremy, but would Jeremy be able to rely on Reggie when things got really bad? Would Reggie be there for Jeremy if Jeremy really needed him, or would he wuss out? Or not care? And what about his friends who were gamers? Was what Rhino said about him during the focus group true? Was he always only interested in saving himself and getting the most points so he'd win? It was all kind of unsettling. Disturbing.

Jeremy suddenly turned to Reggie.

"We have to call Chainsaw from Dad's the second we get there."

"Yeah, you're right," agreed Reggie. "We will."

Reggie's response made Jeremy feel better. Although he still wasn't sure that the trip had been a good idea, at least Reggie was listening to what he said now. Then he realized that Reggie had always listened to him. That's why Jeremy had felt leaving home was the right thing to do in the first place. Jeremy trusted Reggie most of the time, except when Reggie was with older kids. Like at school when Reggie was with his friends and didn't talk to him. But with the important things, Reggie had always come through for him.

"You were right about going to Dad's," said Jeremy.

Reggie looked at Jeremy. He was surprised Jeremy was still analyzing operation Thunderbolt, but relieved that he had come to the same decision he had.

After a while, neither Reggie nor Jeremy could smell anything because they had gotten used to the stink in the cab. Before they knew it, the sun was rising and they were exiting the freeway onto a beautiful tree lined street.

Their Final Objective. Pasadena!

"So what are you gonna do about this cyber thing that kicked your butts?" asked the driver.

"We're not sure. We're thinking of setting a trap, but it's almost impossible," said Reggie. "This thing is completely overpowering and way too big to fight. It's so advanced that we don't even know what it's capable of, or even if it has any weaknesses."

"You're on the right path, but you have to think it through one step at a time. Break it down and a solution should come."

"Like how?" asked Jeremy.

"Four questions:

Number 1:

What is the level of my skill?

Number 2:

What is the capability of my enemy?

Number 3:

What is the situation or environment?"

Number 4:

Make a plan, *and a backup plan.*

Reggie perked up. This was the first real code of tactics he had ever heard and it made sense. There was a structure to this plan. It seemed like a solid step-by-step approach.

The driver noticed that he had gotten Reggie and Jeremy's attention.

"But don't forget, sometimes the enemy is just plain crazy. They might never make sense, so you can never, and I mean never, predict them. But break it down and you'll get some ideas to work with."

"Try to work with the environment first. Opportunities can always be found. You just gotta be alert and be creative to take advantage of your enemy's thought process. But don't think it's like chess. It never is. And remember–in combat, opportunities usually only come around once!"

Reggie and Jeremy gave this some thought as it sunk in. They were surprised at how much wisdom was hidden inside this stinky, burned-up guy. Reggie remembered Big Pete's advice, "When you meet someone–there's a whole world in them. Pay attention, they're in your life for a reason."

When the truck finally hissed to a stop, they climbed down from the cab.

"Just remember the most important thing: Semper Fi, pukes!"

"Semper Fi." the boys said.

The truck left them standing on the road near their dad's house. It was still dark, but the sky had lightened to a pale straw color. Soon the sun would rise. They put on their thunderbolt packs and started walking down the clean, palm tree lined street. Pasadena was the complete opposite of San Francisco: a golden-glowing haven of tranquility.

"Ever wonder why adults are always telling us what to do?" asked Jeremy.

"Yeah. I've noticed that a lot lately."

"Like we're clueless, like they don't think we can do anything. Like they have to tell us everything or we'd never be able to figure anything out by ourselves."

"Yeah. Well, maybe we are clueless," said Reggie, thinking about the trip down and all of the surprises along the way. "He kind of made sense."

What the truck driver had talked about was something that no one had ever talked about with them before. It made Reggie uncomfortable because it made him ask himself if he could always be faithful to Jeremy. Now that they were about to achieve their final objective, would he ever have the opportunity to find out?

"That stuff he was saying is stuff we normally don't even have to think about," said Reggie.

"Yeah."

"What I wonder, though, is how it was so easy getting rides. It was as if whenever we needed a ride, someone just..."

But Reggie didn't finish his sentence. They turned a corner and stopped in their tracks.

17. MISSION ACCOMPLISHED

"We're here!" said Reggie, comparing the view to the crumpled photo in his hand.

"Mission accomplished!" said Jeremy.

It was 6:15 a.m. when Reggie and Jeremy finally stood in the golden, tree-lined cul-de-sac where their father lived. They stopped for a moment and looked over the peaceful neighborhood as the sun rose. The light was so beautiful and the air was so pleasant that it made Reggie think he was in Paradise.

"Wow! Sure is pretty here," said Jeremy.

"Yeah, it sure is," said Reggie, finally agreeing with Jeremy.

It was an old street with beautiful, huge old homes in the Californian Craftsman style. All of the houses were in perfect condition–fresh paint, green lawns, and lush flowering trees everywhere. Even the sidewalks were clean and perfect.

"Cool neighborhood," said Reggie, amazed.

"Yeah, I bet the neighbors here are really friendly, too."

"We're kind of early," said Reggie as he looked at his watch–6:20 a.m. "Maybe we should wait a few minutes so we don't wake everyone up. We don't want to make Dad mad the first day of our new, improved life."

"This is gonna be awesome," said Jeremy, almost crying for joy.

They noticed a couple of RC cars speeding down the sidewalks.

"Not too early for RCs!" said Jeremy.

"This place rocks!"

Another RC zoomed right by Jeremy and transformed into a red ball, rolling even further out into the street. It bounced off the curb, morphed back into a racer and sped back toward the house. Jeremy ran after it.

"Cool!" said Reggie, running and laughing with Jeremy.

"Someone's awake," said Jeremy as he scanned the neighborhood for the RC operator.

They raced the RC, dancing along beside it as it zoomed and zigzagged. They followed it down the street toward their Dad's house.

At the end of the street, coming into sight, there was an RC car trailer parked behind the trees in Jeremy's father's driveway. It was covered with skulls and crossbones, logos, and flames, and said "Hellcat Fireballs" in large flaming letters on its side.

The tiny car cruised straight down the driveway toward the trailer. There was a ramp leading up into the back, and just before the RC got there it turned into a Roller Ball again and shot up the ramp.

"Sweet! Someone's really good at Racer Balls," said Jeremy, as he followed it up into the trailer. "Wow! Check it out! This is, like...heaven."

Reggie stashed his backpack behind a perfectly trimmed bush next to the perfectly painted green front door of his father's perfect house. He checked out the front door and spotted the doorbell.

"Mission Accomplished," he said to himself, as he leaned over to press the perfect little black button.

But just as he was about to press the doorbell, he heard a loud, disturbing, painful scream come from the trailer.

"AAAAAAAAAA!"

It was a sharp, loud cry that Reggie thought would wake up the whole neighborhood. What was Jeremy doing? Reggie ran over and up the ramp of the trailer to look inside. The walls inside were glowing strangely from the light outside, like they were partially transparent, but it was still dark and cool inside. Jeremy was lying on the floor. A needle was stuck in his stomach, connected to the RC by a wire, and the wire was lit up like a filament in a light bulb. The RC had transformed back into a car and had clearly shot the needle-like dart into Jeremy. There was a high frequency whining sound, a sound like high voltage, that was now fading. It looked like the RC was armed with some sort of taser, and Reggie realized that Jeremy had passed out after being electrocuted by it.

Reggie jumped toward Jeremy to try to kick the wire off, but as soon as he entered the chamber, he noticed a second RC with a needle aimed at him. That same electrical whining sound was now coming from the second RC, but it was getting louder and higher in pitch. Reggie saw a glint of something shoot toward him and felt a fiery stab in his stomach. Now he was being electrocuted, but he couldn't do anything about it because every muscle in his body was contracting. He felt his whole body seize up, and suddenly, he couldn't breathe.

Then everything went black, and Reggie, too, passed out.

18. DOOMED

Reggie woke up first, to a splitting headache. It took him a moment to remember who he was and what had happened.

He had no idea how long he had been unconscious or where they were headed, but it was obvious they were in the back of another truck. The two sentry RCs were stationed in opposite corners, watching them with miniature vid-cams. Once again, Reggie felt the horrible oppression of the cloak of dread upon him. It was a feeling he would not be able to shake for a long, long time.

"Aaargh," moaned Jeremy as he woke up, "my head..."

"You'll be okay," said Reggie. "You're Jeremy King, we made it to Dad's house, but we got zapped by the Racer Balls."

"Ohhhh, man," said Jeremy.

Now he remembered.

"We were sooo close! Feels like I got hit by a bus."

"You were right," said Reggie. "I can't believe it, but we got nailed, and I don't have a clue by who or why."

"How long were we out?"

"A day, maybe two?" answered Reggie.

"No wonder I'm starving and my mouth's so dry. Where're we going?"

"No idea," said Reggie. "The RCs were obviously a decoy!"

"Totally evil. We should have warned Chainsaw when we had a chance. Now we'll never get to."

"You were right. Now he'll get nailed, too, and we don't even know why that ECHO thing's after us."

"We're doomed. From that thing's claws, into to its mouth. We're gonna die," said Jeremy.

For once Reggie had no answer.

"Sorry."

•

19. THE CAULDRON OF HELL

After a while, Reggie and Jeremy noticed a small trap door in the floor of the truck that kept opening every half hour or so. They didn't have any idea what the opening was for until Reggie had to pee. The next time it opened he peed down the hole onto the street. It was so hot outside that the pee hit the asphalt, bounced up in tiny, perfectly formed golden balls, and then vaporized before hitting the road again. When the trap door closed, a bottle of water and a box of Krispy Kreme Donuts slid down a chute into the capsule where they were sitting. They drank and ate hungrily. Otherwise, all they could do was sit and sweat in the 120 degree heat as the vehicle took them further and further away. Toward some*where*, or some*one*, or some*thing*.

The two RCs seemed to be watching them with the tiny vid-cams that were welded onto their backs. Each camera was stamped with a tiny metal label that read "Sony DXC LS1."

The tiny cameras were the size of a woman's lipstick container. Every once in a while, one of the RCs would flash some kind of colored light patterns, then the other one would do the same back, like they were communicating.

"Where do you think they're taking us?" asked Jeremy.

"No idea, but it sure is hot. Maybe Mexico–it's pretty hot there."

"So is Hell," said Jeremy.

They both laughed nervously.

After drinking the rest of the water and eating most of the donuts, they nodded off for a while. When they woke up, it seemed darker outside, but it was hard to tell because of the shifting translucency of the walls. Suddenly they slid across the floor and slammed into the right wall of the truck as it made a hard left turn and started up another long, straight, hot road.

Just when they were wondering when the trip was going to end, it was over. The truck stopped, turned around, backed up, and slammed abruptly into something hard, knocking them against the rear wall. Then the back panel zipped open and a hot dry puff of air came through the opening.

"Great–now they wanna put us in another box," said Reggie as he peered into a dark chamber.

"I'm not going in there," said Jeremy.

One of the RCs zapped him, burning his leg.

"OWWW!"

Jeremy went in there.

It wasn't another box, but a cool, dark, dry cave.

As soon as they entered the cave, the door sealed shut, leaving them in complete darkness. They didn't hear the truck drive away, only what sounded like a thousand crickets chirping for a moment. As their eyes adjusted to the gloom, it became clear that they were inside an old, decommissioned mine.

"At least we can breathe now," said Jeremy as he rubbed the burn on his leg. "What was that insect sound? I hope there aren't any bugs or snakes in here. I *hate* snakes."

"At least it's cooler. Thank God it's cool in here."

Once their eyes adjusted to the dark, they saw that they were in a giant tunnel about forty feet high by forty feet wide. The silent tunnel sloped down into a blacker black than they had ever seen.

Suddenly the walls and floor shook, almost knocking them over. They heard a loud rumbling sound, like a giant, loud locomotive traveling beneath them, but there weren't any trains here. They didn't know what was happening. It was very confusing, and the motion made them dizzy and slightly motion sick.

In the far distance, a thin, tired figure emerged from the deep black recesses of the tunnel. Odd colors and zipping and whirring sounds seemed to follow it. Reggie immediately recognized the peculiar zipping sounds and color flashes. They were the same sounds and flashes he saw at the Crescent City beach just three nights earlier. Things were starting to fall into place about ECHO. They had clearly been stalked for a long time, longer than Reggie had realized.

"Don't worry!" yelled the dark figure over the rumbling. "Quakes happen all the time. We're on a fault." Then his face came into the light.

"Snake!" said Reggie.

"Oh crud! Is that you, 'Waiting'?"

"Yeah! It's me!" said Reggie. "And my brother! What're you doing here?"

Snake was filthy and his clothes were torn to shreds. He was as pale as a ghost, about fifteen pounds lighter, and had dark rings under his eyes. As a result of his living underground for so long, the pupils of his eyes were completely dilated into black pits, like the eyes of a subterranean animal acclimated to darkness.

"We didn't think you'd get caught! We figured you found a way to beat 7. We were hoping you'd figure out what was going on and how to get us out of here."

"ECHO-7?"

Snake's black eyes were so weird-looking and mole-like they were disturbing. At first, it was hard for Reggie to have a normal conversation with him.

"ECHO-7 brought you here. The latest version. Just like in the game, man–it can morph into almost anything, including a freight truck–except for real."

"We were *in* ECHO?" gasped Jeremy.

Reggie was angry that he didn't know it was ECHO they had been inside of. *I could have used the code word and frozen ECHO. What is that word?*

"You got it. ECHO-7 is a giant shape-shifter," said Snake. "Except it can shape itself into almost anything. But it's definitely *NOT* a toy. Nope–there's nothing remotely toy-like about 7."

"Then the truck...?" said Reggie, confirming his suspicions.

"You got it. The 'truck' turns back into ECHO and he walks away, just like that," confirmed Snake with a snap of his fingers.

"Wooa," said Jeremy, wondering if he heard Snake right.

"You'll see. Trust me," said Snake. "You'll see."

Snake noticed Jeremy's missing shoe and became alarmed.

"What happened to your shoe? That's not good, being barefoot here. It's dangerous."

"ECHO got it."

Several of the RC Taser cars zipped around them.

"Time to go. Watch out for the shockers," said Snake, "And don't EVER let them SAC you!"

"SAC?" said Jeremy, "For real?"

"Yeah, good old Surround And Capture, just like ECHO's strategy with the mechs, except for real. Come on, we have to get back. We only have a few minutes before the other shockers show up. Let's go!"

Reggie and Jeremy followed Snake into the dusty, murky blackness. After a few yards the tunnel sloped sharply downward. It was hard to see where to step because there were only single green sodium vapor lights on the ceiling every fifty feet or so. Every time they took a step their shadows shifted and everything seemed to looked different.

A matrix of steel I-beams reinforced the walls and ceilings, but with the earthquakes and the shifting light, nothing seemed stable. It was obvious that the tunnel could never have survived the earthquakes without the I-beams.

"What is this place?" asked Jeremy.

"It's, like, ECHO's lair. We all have to slave for him," said Snake as they approached a grate in the floor that covered a bottomless pit.

"Watch out, we have to go around these shafts. They're deep pits, called 'stoops,' that go way down into the Earth.

Don't walk on the grates. They're rusted thin and might break. It used to be a mine...mica, gold, other metals, crystals...weird kinds of crystals I've never seen before. That's why we're here!"

He pointed out the grate on the ground with his flashlight. It was about twenty feet wide, and the pit disappeared into an ominous black void. Cool air flowed up through the iron bars.

"See? It goes deep into the Earth. Probably opens up in China or somewhere. Just walk around 'em."

A Shocker zapped a shadow on the wall behind them.

"Try to stay away from the shockers. Sometimes they make mistakes and zap us by accident–or shadows, or anything else they don't recognize. They're stupid little devils, but they can make your life miserable if they get their sights stuck on you."

The ground shook again.

"Aftershock."

"Great," said Reggie. He was still disoriented from the darkness, quakes and aftershocks.

Snake led them deeper into the darkness.

"You said we have to slave for ECHO," said Reggie, "Doing what?"

"You'll see soon enough," said Snake.

"Where exactly are we?" asked Jeremy.

"Where exactly? I dunno really. Deep inside a mountain somewhere. Your guess is as good as mine. ECHO brought us all here, but he keeps us completely in the dark about everything. Info is on a need-to-know basis, and we don't need to know, so most of us know nothing. Someone got outside once, but it's so hot, there's no place to go. They said they saw a freeway, but it was at least a mile away. Sooner or later the shockers catch up to you anyway and let you have it, so there's no point, really. Plus, it's way too hot to get away. No one could survive that."

"Why doesn't anyone escape at night, then?" asked Jeremy.

"No one's found a new way out after the first escape attempt. The tunnels were all filled in by ECHO. Only one way in, and the shockers can see by moonlight, it's so bright in the clear desert air. Trust me, don't get any ideas or mess with 'em. They'll follow you forever if you try to escape. They'll find you. And they never forget, but you will. If you get shocked too much, you lose your memory. They fry your brain. Heck, SpanDex messed with the shockers so much he can't even remember his name anymore. He messed with them, and they messed with him back, but times ten! Like a really evil big brother."

As they continued down the shaft, Snake revealed a little more every once in a while, adding only little bits of information, as much as he thought they could handle. "Some of the guys, they do try to escape. And some kind of crack, go crazy, do whack stuff. You never know what this place will do to someone. You'll see what I mean in a minute. The guys either go along with, or against, ECHO, and each other. No one stays the same down here. Nope, no one stays the same."

There was a fork in the tunnel, and Snake took them to the right.

"You know what a cauldron is?" Snake asked.

"No," said Jeremy.

"It's like a huge melting pot," said Snake as he led them into a brighter, green-lit area.

"Welcome," and he paused for dramatic effect, "to the Cauldron of Hell."

The shaft spilled into an expansive, dusty chamber that was lit from above by one giant sodium vapor light. It was hard to tell exactly what the dimensions of the space were, because the illumination from the sole light faded as it reached the outer limits of the chamber, making it seem like the entire area was suspended in dark space. The walls had apparently been carved out of dense, dark granite and shale by heavy machinery, and were interspersed with shimmering crystals and glittering mica that, due to the darkness, also seemed to hang in space, sparkling like an eerie special effect of floating stars.

Dozens of ghostly, pale boys were hard at work, their eyes as black as Snake's. It was difficult to tell how many were there because it was hot, dark, dusty, and crowded. Because they had been working in dirt, everyone had become the same color as the earth so it was hard to see anyone unless he was moving. An overwhelming stench of sweat and dust filled the air.

"It's the crystals–that's why we're here–we mine the crystals for ECHO," said Snake, "They get cut into scales and make up his skin."

Snake paused and then gave them the worst news.

"Now you'll get to know your own personal Hell–death by a thousand shocks. You'll work like a machine now, just like the rest of us."

Reggie and Jeremy could smell diesel fumes from several small bulldozers that were chugging around, moving earth and debris through the chamber while the dozens of thin, pale, grimy ghoul-like boys toiled in the sweltering heat. Hundreds of shockers whirred about, watching everything. Reggie thought it was the kind of place Asa would happily pay money to send them to for summer camp.

"Remember. The only friend you have is your own mind. So no matter what, don't lose you mind!"

Bright lightning blasts of welding sparks exploded continuously through the grimy haze in the back of the cavern. There were stacks of I-beams everywhere, and more were being moved into position to support the ceilings and walls of new rooms being carved out of the mountain. Only the large sodium vapor light in the middle of the ceiling and the continuous flashing of the welding blasts lit up the huge chamber, so it was impossible to tell whether it was day or night.

The welders all appeared to be older boys. They were welding huge I-beams into place in a wide pit to keep it from caving in as it was dug deeper. These I-beams connected to the network of reinforcement beams throughout the mountain. In the middle of the Pit, there was a narrower, deeper, natural black hole. The Pit crew guys were all digging downward, widening the black hole.

One of the welders lifted up their helmet visor to check out Reggie. It was Scratch. Her face was covered in sweaty dirt, just like all the grime-covered boys. As she nodded at Reggie, her visor dropped down and she went back to work. Reggie imagined all of the other gamers hidden behind their visors. Everyone from the focus group was surely there.

"Don't ever get near the black hole," said Snake. "Best we can tell, it's bottomless. A Bobcat–one of those small bulldozers, fell in and we never heard it hit bottom."

Younger boys worked in the giant pit around the hole. They dug with picks, shovels, and jack hammers. One boy drove a Bobcat, moving the earth and rock around so it could be hauled out of the Pit. If it weren't for the wretched circumstances, Reggie and Jeremy would have thought that driving the Bobcat could be fun.

As they dug the pit deeper around the hole, the older boys welded I-beams into place to support the earth around the Pit. It was all hard, dirty, dangerous work, made even more difficult by the noise, the heat, and the tension the shockers brought to bear on everyone. If you did anything unusual, you'd get shocked. The surveillance was based on some sort of pattern recognition program. Every once in a while a shocker would randomly zap something or someone that looked out of place, so the name of the game for everyone was to blend in with the work flow as much as possible, like they were all one big machine with many working parts.

Snake noticed Reggie and Jeremy twitch when they heard someone scream from getting electro-shocked.

"The shockers get to everyone sooner or later," said Snake, "especially when not enough trillium is coming out of the Pit. That's what the crystal's called–trillium."

He pointed to a processing room next to the Pit into which another group of boys was feeding the mined crystals.

"And if the processing room ever slows down, we ALL get it. Yeah, electro-shock therapy. As you can see, it works."

Shockers infested the processing room, too. A few selected and followed one boy for a while, then stopped and randomly changed their course. It was an odds game to guess where they would go next.

Someone got shocked because he wasn't feeding trillium into the room fast enough. Everyone stopped and turned for an instant to check out who was screaming, then resumed work as if nothing had happened.

The processing room was about forty-five feet long and had floor to ceiling glass walls so the shockers could see exactly what was going on inside. In the room next to the glass wall, there was a small pathway just wide enough for shockers to travel back and forth through the room with doggy door-like flaps at both ends to let them in and out. The gamers were not allowed inside the room at all. There was no room for humans, only machines. Next to the shocker flap was another flap through which the boys put the trillium onto the conveyer belt.

The processing crew was feeding a steady supply of trillium onto the conveyer belt. From there the chunks were picked up and sorted by robotic arms, then positioned further down the belt. There, the trillium chunks were locked into place and a large, high-energy industrial laser swung into position and cut the chunks into thin slices about a tenth of an inch thick. The laser was so powerful that it cut through the rocks like butter, and in about six seconds, the crystalline chunk was sliced into two hundred thin pieces. These slices then traveled further down the conveyer where another set of robotic arms arranged them and another laser cut them into the shape of ECHO's scales. From here they traveled further down the belt and disappeared into darkness as they fell into supply packs for ECHO.

A deep, hypnotic rhythm developed with the brilliant cutting flashes, belt motions, and sharp zips as the lasers sliced the trillium and shaped the scales with lightning speed and precision.

Reggie and Jeremy were overwhelmed, but Snake was nothing if not thorough, explaining the rules.

"In the chambers beyond you'll find the Chow Cave, Cots, and the Falls. You'll see them later. The only place safe from the shockers is the Falls–if they go there they get wet, short circuit, fry and die. Then we kick 'em down a stoop so they don't get recycled by each other.

Another welder approached and pulled up his face mask. It was a grimy, wiry, defeated-looking Rhino.

"So I guess it got ya too, let's see how you do now, big shot. In real life."

Before Reggie could respond, a shocker zoomed up to Rhino and zipped back and forth in front of him, warning, like a cobra about to strike.

"I'll get to you later," said Rhino as he went back to work.

"Like I said, the place gets to you. 'Waiting,' come with me. You have to weld with the Pit Crew. Jeremy, go see that guy. You have to mine trillium. Try not to get hurt down there. Watch your foot–there's no doctor, so if you break or cut anything, you're on your own."

As Snake and Reggie walked off toward the Pit, Jeremy lugged his pack toward a guy standing up on the rim of the Pit overlooking the mine shaft. He was supervising all the younger guys who were digging and clearing out rock below. Jeremy climbed up to him.

"Hi," said Jeremy, "Snake told me..."

The guy turned around. It was Tom, a friend of Jeremy's. But he looked completely different–so different that Jeremy almost didn't recognize him. He was dirty like the others, pale, and his eyes were slightly bloodshot from all the dust.

"Tom! Wow! I can't believe you're here! What's up?"

But Tom's personality was different too.

"Look, I run the Pit," he said with a boss's attitude, as if he didn't even recognize Jeremy. His eyes seemed glazed over, like the crazy guy at Crescent City Beach, only he wasn't on any stupid juice.

"Here's how it works. ECHO talks to me, then I tell you what to do. The team reports to me. We have to dig as much trillium as possible every day and process it into scales for ECHO. ECHO is dead without the scales. Only trillium scales work, because only trillium crystals transmit light the right way. Without trillium, his cloaking doesn't work."

He turned away and pointed to where Jeremy was supposed to work in the Pit.

"The dozer cuts the rock into chop. You dig through the chop for trillium. Use one of those detectors there, gather up as much as you can, and send it up to the processing room. They make the scales."

"ECHO put me in charge," Tom went on, "so don't make me use the shockers on you. Just do what I tell you to do, okay? Get someone in the Pit to fill you in on where the tools are. Just do what I say and you won't have any problems."

Jeremy couldn't believe his ears.

"GO! CHOP-CHOP!"

Jeremy climbed down into the Pit, wondering what had happened to Tom to change his personality so much. What a psycho. The Pit was even hotter and dustier, and the exhausted boys working down there were caked with grime and sweat. Jeremy's shoeless foot was raw and ached from walking on rock. He would wrap it with something as soon as possible.

"Hey Jeremy, when did you get here?" asked Scott, one of his school friends. There were about seven other friends of his from school in the Pit–almost his whole basketball team–and a bunch of guys he's never seen before. One was an Indian kid named Ashram.

"Just now. Man, how did you all get here? I can't believe you're all here!"

"Same way as you," said another guy from Jeremy's school-Ricky David, a younger, smaller but tough kid with a buzz cut. "ECHO brought us. He brings in a few more guys every other day."

"Jeremy!" said another friend appearing out of the haze, "Here, take this shovel. Look like you're digging."

"Josh!" said Jeremy, "thank God you guys aren't zombies like Tom! What happened to him?"

"Oh, you know Tommy, on his usual power trip."

"Don't ever call him Tommy though," said Scott.

Josh continued.

"Ever since we got here and ECHO put him in charge, he's been on a royal psycho trip. He's power crazy, thinks he's our 'ruler' now. 'Yes sir, Mr. Sir! Chop-chop!' He's been driving us all crazy with his bossing and shocking – like he's so much better than us. He's on the other side now – a real mech-head."

"Butt head is more like it," said Scott.

"The other side?" said Jeremy.

"ECHO's side," said Ashram. "Brainwashed."

"Why's ECHO making us do all this?" said Jeremy.

"Simple," said Josh. "He needs slave labor. Why us, who knows? Probably revenge for everything we did in the game. But he runs out of scales, and scales are what makes his cloaking camouflage work. A couple break off every time he goes out. We figure he needs a constant supply, and as long as he's alive he'll always need them."

"Thinks we're his little robots, just like the shockers," said Ricky. "Just wait till we kick his ass."

Jeremy was relieved that someone was thinking about getting even with ECHO. He liked this kid, Ricky. Even though he was younger, he wanted revenge and sounded like he was going to get it, one way or the other. He had a lot of spirit, but the other gamers all felt differently because they had been there longer.

"Yeah, right, Ricky," said Ashram.

"It's *G-Man*," continued Ricky (aka G-Man), "and yes, I'll get a piece of ECHO one day. Oh yeah, I will."

The other kids turned back to Jeremy as they swung their picks.

"This place use to be a real mine," said Logan, who had lost so much weight he was unrecognizable. "Different metals and minerals at different times. There are some office records from 60 years ago. It's been shut down for a long time."

"Until ECHO found it and started his revenge," said Ashram.

"ECHO's Revenge," said Jeremy.

A shocker zapped another kid on the other side of the Pit and the kid fell to the ground and screamed. Everyone turned around and looked at him.

"Bogus zap," said Scott.

"You mean righteous zap," said Ashram. "I hate that kid–he's always causing trouble. ZAP 'IM AGAIN!"

A bunch of guys started chanting "ZAP, ZAP, ZAP...," but the dazed kid got back up and everyone went back to work.

"So basically, it's just a big scale factory," said Reggie, who was getting ready to learn how to weld the I-beams into place on the other side of the Pit.

"You got it," said Snake, "but he seems to be looking for something else too. Every time they find anything out of the ordinary while they're digging, the team leaders have to rope it off until ECHO comes back. 7 seems to be obsessed with this hole. Sometimes he takes stuff, like the time we found a bunch of fossilized shark teeth, and sometimes he doesn't. We can't tell if he's looking for anything in particular."

"Where does he go when he's gone?"

"No idea."

"How long do you think he's gonna keep us here?"

"Oh, that's simple. Forever."

20. HOME SWEET HOME II

Crystal clear water shot out from the rocks high above the Falls, allowing anyone to take a refreshing drink or a freezing shower. The series of underground waterfalls flowed down into another series of streams that lead to the end of the cavern and then disappeared down a stoop into the Earth. All kinds of colorful crystals, quartz, mica, and metals were embedded in the rock in the Falls. It was the only tranquil cavern in the mountain, but as beautiful as it was, it was also potentially deadly. Special care had to be taken not to fall down one of the many bottomless stoops and gurgling spring holes that randomly appeared throughout the Falls.

Reggie and Jeremy blended in well for the first few days or weeks. It was impossible to tell when the days began and ended since there was no sunlight, and they quickly lost track of time. They had made themselves as invisible as possible to avoid getting into fights, which would start spontaneously for no apparent reason. They had grown paler by the day just like everyone else, and the strictly measured rations were already wearing on them, making them thinner and weaker. They were also tired from the general lack of sleep caused by the stress of being trapped. Now they understood how someone could go crazy and crack in this dark netherworld.

Rhino, Power, and some of the other gamers met regularly in the back, far-reaches of the Falls. They called themselves the "Pack" and no one else was ever allowed into their meetings. Whenever Reggie and Jeremy went to rinse off in the shower, Rhino would lash out at them.

"Hey, traitors! Figured out a way to save your own butts yet?" he would taunt, but Reggie and Jeremy always ignored him and Rhino would usually just drift back into the darkness. Rhino continued his taunting whenever he saw them, even though someone in his Pack would always tell him to relax.

The Pack was more paranoid than everyone else. They hadn't ever tried to escape, and they never seemed to do anything except bully other boys, so Reggie and Jeremy determined that the Pack was poison and to be avoided at all costs.

It was pretty common that some gamer would randomly lash out at another and then go his separate way without a fight breaking out. It was psycho, but everyone accepted it as normal. Reggie and Jeremy kept to themselves, and decided not to talk with anyone other than Snake.

After what seemed like a few weeks—it was impossible to tell how long because time itself had become so confusing—Jeremy's eyes had completely adjusted to the darkness and his pupils were wide open like a mole's. Now his and Reggie's eyes were black like everyone else's. With his new 'night vision,' Jeremy started seeing things that he had never noticed before, like the gentle varying shades of shale that were layered endlessly throughout the excavated chambers. Crystalline patches, various ore veins, mica patches, massive expanses of granite. It was a world unto itself, and each view a snapshot of billions of years of geology and time.

The ventilation shafts, which had been cut from the outside surface of the mountain down to the Cauldron, could not have existed without the solid structural integrity of the granite. Nor could the ceiling have stood so securely forty feet above and maintained the openings of the air vents without that solidity. The vents themselves were only about four feet square, but they provided a steady flow of life-sustaining air. Jeremy knew the shafts led to the outside because fresh air would drift over him when he was resting under them, and at different times the air was cool, warm, or hot, depending on the time of day outside.

The air brought in subtle aromas of dust, sage, and occasionally strange animal odors. Regardless of this changing pattern of desert scents, it was a blessing that every night while they slept, the gentle air current would clear the Cauldron of dust so that the human machines could start their slave labor with a fresh atmosphere each work period.

Jeremy loved to imagine what was going on outside when he sat under the vents. In his mind, he could picture coyotes resting outside the vent after a day of hunting, lizards hiding under the sage bushes, and tumbleweed blowing across the endless expanse of sand beneath a bright blue sky and blazing furnace of a sun. Once in a while, a small gecko would creep into the room from the vent, and Jeremy would guess what led it to hide so far down in the Earth.

Back in the real-world hell they lived in, Tom was driving the younger guys crazy with his bossiness. It was even getting to Jeremy. While everyone worked, Tom would pick out someone and bully him, like he was getting revenge for everything he thought anyone had ever done to him in the past.

During one particular work period, the shockers suddenly prompted Snake to go to the end of the tunnel to bring in some new guys. Snake always knew when it was time because the shockers would corner him and push him toward the door. As usual, they followed him out.

"See ya, Snake," said Power.

"Good luck, Snake," said Flame.

When Snake came back, Chainsaw was with him, as exhausted as everyone else had been when they first arrived. When Jeremy and Reggie saw him come in, they felt guilty that they hadn't warned him.

"You were right," said Reggie to Jeremy. "Always do the right thing as soon as possible."

"In case you can't later."

"HUA," said Reggie.

Chainsaw was put to work welding in the Pit. He wasn't too happy about being treated like a machine, with the regular punishment of shocker zaps being inflicted on him, but after he was electrocuted a few times, he quickly learned that he had no choice but to become another one of ECHO's mechs. One work period soon blended into another, and Reggie and Jeremy saw Chainsaw complete the transition–from normal healthy kid to grimy, stinking, pale, weak mech-mole, just like everyone else.

"Period 324," someone announced, trying to keep track of time.

Each work period was as monotonous as the one preceding it, with everyone working through the first shift, getting Krispy Kreme Donuts and water for lunch, and then working through the second shift. Reggie wondered at the fact that he had grown to hate the donuts he had once loved so much. Snake was right. No one stays the same.

Jackhammers banged away at the rock, Bobcats moved the broken chop, and welding continued on the I-beams. Just another period. Hard labor. Aching bodies.

That night at dinner, though, something changed. For the first time, Snake handed out "MRE's"–U.S. Army "Meal, Ready to Eat" packs instead of the donuts they had been getting before. Each pack contained two breakfast portions like ham and eggs, Tabasco Sauce, Hershey's Dessert Bars, coffee powder, and towelettes for cleaning hands.

"Finally something other than donuts!" someone said.

"Yee Haa!"

"Yowza!"

"Hey Snake," yelled Pit Bull. "Did ECHO hit an Army base or somethin'? This rocks!"

"Don't ask me," yelled Snake. "I just serve what gets left."

Every time ECHO came in with more mech-slave gamers, it brought in a few weeks supply of food. This time it had brought about a month's supply of MRE's and dumped it all in a chamber just past the Pit where they were mining the trillium.

Reggie and Jeremy sat together, eating their food quietly like the rest of the crew.

"At least the food's good," said Jeremy.

"Yeah," said Reggie. "I feel better already, like my brain's clicking on again or something."

"Hey, I just realized something."

"Huh?"

"It's kind of like being at home here!"

"What?" said Reggie. "Now you've really cracked."

"No. We never knew what the heck Asa would do at any moment, like when he'd inflict pain on us for no good reason like the shockers do. Totally random!"

Reggie laughed, "Yeah, and we never knew where Mom was or what she was thinking, or what we'd be eating for dinner, or if there'd even be dinner. Kind of like life with ECHO!"

"Ha! Yeah," they laughed like they laughed when they used to walk through the valley back home in Meadowbrook, looking for something to eat somewhere because Jeda had forgotten dinner again, talking and laughing about avatar names.

"Or when mom might come home, like ECHO."

"Or if she really heard a word you were saying. Shockers don't hear you either."

"Yeah!" said Reggie, surprised at the similarities.

"As long as we did certain things, the things she thought we were supposed to do, she never even noticed us."

"Yeah. You're right!" laughed Reggie again.

Jeremy laughed too, happy for a moment to make a real connection to their old life. And to discover something familiar, if not comfortable, about this crazy new world.

"Home, sweet home," said Jeremy.

"Expect the unexpected."

"Asa and the shockers."

"But at least ECHO has a plan," continued Reggie. "It's obviously making us slave for a reason–to get trillium. With Mom, we never could tell why she was doing anything. She was like a machine with broken processors."

"Yeah..." Jeremy thought to himself.

"Hey. Maybe there's just something wrong with her brain, or something. Like our brains, starved, then turning back on with this real food. Like our brains got a missing chemical and could work again."

"Maybe Mom is missing a chemical or something? In her brain?" wondered Jeremy.

"Yeah. Maybe it could be fixed. Debugged. A missing chemical, like an amino acid or something, in her brain that she could get. Maybe she's missing something in her food."

"Maybe!"

Reggie felt better–almost happy for a second. It was clear. It made sense. There might be a real problem with her brain. Maybe it could be fixed somehow.

But dinner was only a brief pause, and now it was over. Each worker was expected to consume his 4000 calories in about 20 minutes. It was time to move, so the shockers moved them to their cots. Minutes later they were falling asleep.

After exactly seven hours, the shockers zapped a few guys awake and everyone got up. They were moved to the Chow Caves for a lighter meal pack for breakfast–an RLW-30, or "Ration, Lightweight 30-Day." The RLW-30 rations provided about 2100 calories of energy.

"Hey, what's with the light packs?" said one of the older guys.

"Don't ask me," said Snake, like a weary tape recorder. "I just serve what gets left."

"Yeah, shut up! You wanna go back to donuts and water?" cracked Flame.

Everyone shut up.

There never seemed to be any logic to how ECHO treated the gamers, and out of natural curiosity some of the boys couldn't stop wondering why it did the things it did. But it was wasted energy–no one could ever figure out any logical reason for, or pattern to, ECHO's actions. They were given only breakfast one day, then only dinner the next. The only thing they knew for sure was that they would be digging trillium every day. Other than that, it was a random little universe. Anything could happen.

After a few minutes of breakfast, everyone automatically drifted out to the Pit to start hard labor. It was just like every other uneventful work period, hot and grimy, an endless cycle. During a break, the Pack met briefly. The rest of the gamers were irritated at seeing them meet in secrecy all the time, especially since they never tried to escape. What was the big point? It just aggravated the relentless boredom.

Every once in a while someone got zapped, and everyone stopped for a moment to see who had gotten fried. It was the only "entertainment" they had.

"You're next, IPod," someone guessed.

"Naw. It's gonna be Flame," said Power.

"No way," said Flame, "wanna bet?"

It was like a game to guess who would be next, their only momentary relief from the boredom.

Someone got zapped and yelped a loud, weird, hysterical laugh.

"You owe me an MRE, Power," said Flame.

"Bogus zap," complained someone in the Pit.

Tom heard the complaint.

"Hey!" he yelled, "No comments! Get back to work! Chop chop!"

"Who died and made you the boss?" someone in the crowd said.

"Yeah, Tommmmy?"

"Who said that!" yelled Tom.

"Who said that?" someone mocked him in a baby weasel voice.

Laughter.

"Who said that!" yelled Tom again, turning red now.

When it was obvious no one was going to answer, and when a few more guys started laughing, he got even angrier and began shouting.

"LISTEN, if ANYONE doesn't like the way I do things, just let me know and I'll send a SHOCKER over to say HELLO! I run the Pit. ECHO talks to ME and I run the PIT. ECHO even does what I tell him to do. So SHUT UP and DO your WORK! Because I'm in charge here, FOREVER!"

Everyone in the Pit as well as some of the older boys welding above stopped to listen to Tom. They were all shocked by what he was saying about ECHO. Was he cracking? Would ECHO grab him next, or would he simply get a good hard electro-shock or two from the shockers?

Even the Pack stopped to watch Tom.

"Tommy's next!" someone said, and everyone laughed.

"Funny–not," he continued. "No. I run the Pit, and I run ECHO. What I say, he does, and what I say, you do, too."

Everyone froze, wondering what crazy Tom would do or say next. He had definitely cracked. *Alright! Would he, could he, PLEASE get zapped, and zapped hard,* thought most of the boys in the Pit.

"An MRE says Tom's next," someone said.

"You're crazy," someone said.

"It's dicey, but I'll take some of that action," yelled G-Man from across the Cauldron.

Jeremy didn't know what to think, but he tried to stay invisible so Tom wouldn't single him out and send the shockers over. Tom always seemed to send the shockers over to zap guys he knew from before–from the outside world.

After a few more seconds, it became obvious to everyone that Tom was slowing down production. Shockers began to drift up the hill toward him. Then, more shockers rolled out of the tunnel entrance and entered the Cauldron. Tom noticed, but he didn't stop. He kept yelling.

"What are you DOING?" he said to the shockers, "Not ME, THEM!" and he pointed to the boys below.

The ground trembled. Another quake was brewing.

As Tom continued yelling at everyone, one of the metal walls far behind him started sparkling, then warping, and then clicking in that reptilian sound that none of them had heard for a long time. Everyone's stomach twisted as soon as they recognized the dreaded alien sound.

They all froze, and ECHO's head burst out of the rock wall, followed by the rest of its body. It had concealed itself as a support panel in a large cavity in the wall. No one had any idea that ECHO had been there all along and had heard everything Tom said. It erupted like an explosion, as if it had run right through the wall, and rushed at Tom with a silent, mad vengeance and then froze right behind him. Analyzing. Waiting. But Tom was clueless. He was the only one who didn't see ECHO behind him.

"That's right, NOW you get it," yelled Tom, as everyone crouched in fear from what he could not see behind him. "I run EVERYTHING!" he gloated as everyone cowered.

ECHO towered above Tom. Before anyone could catch his breath, it bared its teeth and roared loudly, adding to the ground tremors. The pressure bursts traveled through the Cauldron, shaking pebbles out of the walls. Tom collapsed from the shock wave, and as he turned to look up from the ground, a cavernous mouth plunged down and engulfed him. ECHO's enormous head spasmed upward and swallowed Tom in a furious gulp as everyone backed up against the walls, trying to get as far away as possible from the massive human-eating machine. ECHO then turned to Josh. The cold green eyes blinked, clearing a film of dust from its lenses. ECHO approached, and then scanned Josh. Up close. Closer. And then, close enough to scan Josh's right retina. The dim beam flashed into Josh's eye.

Before anyone knew what to think, ECHO picked Josh up like a tiny doll with one of its telescopic steel-clawed arms and turned toward the exit tunnel. It was then that everyone noticed an axe firmly imbedded in ECHO's back. It had obviously been in some kind of battle in the outside world. Who had it fought, and who would have been brave enough to attack it with a weapon as crude as an axe?

ECHO carried Josh out of the Cauldron, down further into the mountain. A squad of shockers followed and then morphed into Roller Balls, tumbling after ECHO down the tunnel into the blackness of the Earth.

Now everyone had more to worry about than just shockers. They also had to think about where ECHO might hide next and what it might overhear. Jeremy shivered as he thought about the fact that his favorite resting spot was in precisely the spot where ECHO had been hiding, camouflaged as a metal wall panel. Reflexively, he began memorizing where all the real metal panels were, so that next time he would be able to tell if ECHO was hiding anywhere.

21. A NEW LEADER

The next work period someone new stood at the top of the Pit watching all the guys come to work. It was Josh, but he seemed different, more confident and mature, somehow "enlightened."

Everyone gathered at the foot of the hill to check him out. Would Josh be another psycho boss? Once everyone was there and the dust had settled, he started speaking in a slow, confident, but enthusiastically energized voice, like a televangelist.

"We ask ourselves...We ask ourselves, what is ECHO?"

Josh paused for emphasis and to let his words sink in like a professional speaker, and continued after a beat.

"ECHO...is not just a machine. He is not just a stupid machine... ECHO knows everything! Everywhere! Always."

Reggie and Jeremy looked at each other.

"How is this possible? It's not important. ECHO has spoken to me, and he wants me to tell you this. ECHO is our new father now–but it's okay! It's good! ECHO is better than our *real* fathers, so it's gonna be okay!"

"Like I said," whispered Snake to Reggie and Jeremy, "ECHO changes people, does something to their heads. Josh's way on the other side now. Look at his eyes. He doesn't even sound like himself anymore. A real mech-head."

"What happened to him?" whispered Jeremy.

"ECHO just gets into your head," whispered Snake.

Everyone else was quiet, amazed that Josh was still alive. They had a new respect for him because he had survived being captured by ECHO again and had returned. Counting his kidnapping, he had been taken twice, but here he was, back for more, even though this time he was on ECHO's side.

Josh continued his inspired speech.

"ECHO is incredibly powerful. So powerful you cannot imagine. It is not in our capability, as humans, to comprehend his power.

"People think ECHO is different things. Some people think of him as a force of nature. In the outside world, some people think he is a god. But it's much easier if you just think of him as your father. A spiritual father—a higher source of knowledge, wisdom, and understanding.

Everyone looked at each other. Josh could tell that they were now convinced that he was crazy, but he was prepared for this. ECHO had told him that this would happen. He continued.

"No friends, I am not crazy. Because of his super-processing power, ECHO can show us the way better than any human ever could. ECHO has big plans, big plans that you can't even imagine! And ECHO has big plans for US. ECHO wants us to think and work together, like a team–a machine-team. He wants us to work together because, as a machine-team we can do much more than any individual can. Many smaller parts are much stronger than one bigger part.

"ECHO knows that we, as humans, can never be perfect, but he wants you to know something. It is a secret few humans know. Something very powerful and important: We CAN'T be perfect. We are NOT machines. But that does not give us permission to be less than that which we can become.

"That which we can become. This is very important, so listen and remember...

Everyone looked at Josh, riveted with a mixture of horror and fascination.

"99.99 percent. That is the percentage perfect we can be. Not 100 percent, but 99.99. If we function together, stop arguing, and behave 99.99% perfectly, there is virtually no limit to what we can do.

"ECHO has a plan to win the Reality Game. It is The Ultimate Game, and we are his team. We *are* ECHO. You will see how this works. We will all win the Real Game. As One. And when that happens, we will all be rewarded far beyond anything we can imagine. And it will be fun! Really fun! We will be very powerful. Each one of us! More powerful than you could ever imagine! But first, we just have to keep working.

"Yes–it is boring. But boring hard work is sometimes important to accomplishing great things. As soon as he has enough scales, he'll let us know more about his plan. Trust ECHO. When we're done here, he'll tell us more about the game we're going to be in. Just remember: TRUST ECHO!"

"Here, study this," said Josh as he passed some fliers out which talked about E-7's 99.99% perfection directive.

"Creeeepy," whispered Jeremy as he read over the flier, "Just when you thought things couldn't get any weirder."

"Yeah," whispered Reggie. "It's like a cult or something. We've really gotta get out of here before our minds completely turn to mush."

But Jeremy couldn't move. He was so used to Tom trying to torment him with shockers that he was still trying to stay quiet and invisible so no one would notice him. He looked around the Cauldron, wondering what new changes would be in store for them. With everything getting stranger by the day he was beginning to feel like he might crack at any moment.

But it wasn't Jeremy who cracked, it was Power. He suddenly bolted out of the Cauldron and up the slope. Twenty shockers took off after him at full charge, colors flashing wildly and staccato sounds flowing up the tunnel.

At the same moment, Chainsaw slowly crept out of the Cauldron, but instead of going up, he took a right and went down the tunnel to where ECHO had gone. It was such a crazy and unexpected move that no even saw him do it, not even the shockers. He was stalking ECHO.

In the meantime, Power ran as fast as he could. It was as if he suddenly couldn't take it any more and had decided he was going to try to escape any way he could, no matter what, even if it meant he got shocked to death.

The squad of shockers chasing him quickly grew to fifty, then one hundred and sixty, then twelve hundred, multiplying like crazy out of everywhere, but Power was running so fast he ran over several of them on the way up. Then, half way up the slope, he got a foot stuck between the stoop shaft bars and fell.

More shocker balls rolled in from the front of the mountain down the tunnel toward him, opened up, and instantly encircled him. But they couldn't go out on the grate because their tiny tires would get caught in the gaps.

After a moment of calculation, the SAC commenced. The shockers shot their barbs into the grate at the same moment, electrocuting the grate with an enormous charge. The grate lit up, Power lit up, and the whole slope lit up in bright blue flashes.

"AAAAAAAAAAAAAAAAAHHH!"

Power's screams echoed through the shafts.

When the shockers returned to the Cauldron, Snake reluctantly went up to retrieve Power. He did not look forward to what he knew he was going to find. When he finally brought him back into the Cauldron, Power was still unconscious, and the pattern of the grate was burned into his skin like grill patterns on a freshly flame-broiled steak.

Reggie was sick with fear when he saw Power.

"Jeremy, we've gotta get out of here. This is getting REALLY psycho!" he said, but Jeremy didn't respond.

Jeremy had stopped talking, just like SpanDex had. It was as if Jeremy had shut down in some kind of psychic overload after hearing Josh's crazy speech and seeing the severity of Power's burns. Everything was too real.

"Talk to me!" said Reggie, shaking Jeremy's shoulders. Jeremy worried that ECHO was hiding somewhere nearby, listening. Without moving his head or lips, he uttered an indecipherable noise.

"eaaa."

Jeremy didn't realize it, but he had stopped moving his lips whenever he spoke because he was so afraid that ECHO was somehow observing him. It was Jeremy's brand new, very own, very paranoid personality disorder.

Josh continued speaking calmly in his new sing-song voice as if nothing had happened. He pointed to Power.

"He'll be OKAY. Everything will be FINE. Now, everyone goes back to work. You are many parts, but many parts of a new TEAM. We are ONE Human Machine now. ECHO has spoken. He will speak through me again. I am only a messenger, but I do know what we need to do: Trust ECHO!"

Everyone returned to work amidst a few moans. There was a new tangible sense of dread in the air as everyone thought about what had just happened to Power, Tom being eaten, the "New Plan," and Josh's weird speech. And with a new guy in charge, it was suddenly as if neither Tom nor Power had ever existed.

"Whatever," said Reggie, putting on his welding mask.

"Semper Fi." said Jeremy, managing to throw the words out of his mouth like a ventriloquist.

Reggie stopped and turned to him for a moment. He was suddenly relieved to hear something recognizable coming out of Jeremy's mouth again. At least they still had some kind of connection. Semper Fi: an idea they both could hang onto.

"HUA, Semper Fi!"

22. SPECIAL DELIVERY: LOS ANGELES

The next day, a large plastic shrink-wrapped package was dumped next to a game arcade in Los Angeles. As some gamers left the arcade, they tripped over it and noticed a body wrapped up inside.

"Ouuuu!" said a kid on a skateboard, "There's a dead kid in that bag!"

"No way!" said a kid with a mohawk.

The skateboard kid poked his skateboard into the bag and it moved. The body was alive. Mohawk cut a hole in the bag with his pocket knife. It was Tom, groggy and tired. Tom pushed a hand through the hole, enlarged it, and worked his way out.

"Oh, man, thanks," said Tom, bewildered. "I was eaten by ECHO. He dumped me here."

"Ha, ha," said Skateboard kid. "That's a good one. How'd you get in the bag? Didn't your mommy ever tell you not to play in plastic bags? Ha, ha, ha."

Mohawk guy laughed too.

"No, listen. We have to warn everyone, I was kidnapped by the real ECHO! There's an ECHO-7. And it's real. It's true!"

"Yeah, right," said Mohawk guy. "You're wack, geek."

The two guys started walking away.

"No, really!" yelled Tom over his shoulder as they disappeared.

But no one believed Tom–not the police who picked him up for acting weird in public, not the cops at the police station who called his parents, not the psychologist who visited him there, and not his parents who finally came and took him home.

The police psychologist told his parents that he shouldn't be allowed to play ECHO's Revenge any more–that it would probably be better if they didn't allow Tom to play any video games ever again because he got so wrapped up in them that he couldn't tell the games from reality.

So they didn't let him play ever again.

And every time he started talking about ECHO, they told him not to, until eventually he wondered if the entire experience had really happened, or if it had all been in his mind.

23. "SCRATCH" BECOMES "THE CLAW"

Back to work, welding in the Pit. With a project to take his mind off everything, Reggie almost felt good. The job was taking all of his concentration, so he wasn't thinking about where he was. He could barely see through his welding mask–the dark window was tiny, about two by three inches–and he was sweating so much it felt as if his head was stuck in a steam room, but he was building something real and he could see the results of his labor.

Welding the heavy steel I-beams in place was grueling work. First, he had to make sure the 1200-pound beam was secured in place, usually with the help of someone in a Bobcat holding the beam while he clamped it to another beam with four giant, twenty-pound C-clamps. The preparation alone took about thirty minutes. Then he had to make sure the acetylene and oxygen were coming out of his torch in the right mix and the flame looked right–a small pin-prick of blue-white lightning. Then he could join the beams by carefully melting the steel of one beam evenly into the other, which took about 20 minutes for each weld. When a weld went bad, he would smash the beams apart from each other with a huge sledge hammer and start over. It was a hot, dirty, dangerous job, and every welder had the burns and bruises to prove it.

During this period, Reggie was trying to ignore his aching back when he sensed a change in the Cauldron. He lifted his visor and noticed Scratch quietly squirming through the tiny shocker-door of the processing room not ten feet away from him. Reggie was the closest to the room, so he froze in his welding position, not wanting to attract the wrath of the shockers. Most of the boys pretended nothing was happening, but secretly watched Scratch out of the corners of their eyes too, careful to not make a commotion that would attract the attention of the shockers.

Scratch was the only one who could have made this stealthy move. She was as thin as a rail and agile as a cat so she could move as gracefully and quietly as a Ninja. Since she had hardly ever spoken since being trapped in the Cauldron, no one ever noticed her anymore. She had made herself even more invisible than Reggie and Jeremy had, so her move came as a big surprise to everyone.

Before anyone knew it, she crawled halfway through the processing room, turned on her side so she could fit in the fourteen-inch-wide shocker-path where the heavy duty industrial laser was tirelessly slicing trillium. She was escaping through the room into another tunnel!

Suddenly a shocker zoomed pass Reggie, went up to the glass wall, and started bumping into it, trying to get at Scratch. Since she was crawling sideways facing the inside, she couldn't see the shocker, and because it was so loud inside, she probably couldn't hear it either as it stupidly banged at the wall trying to get to her.

From the far end of the trillium processing booth, another shocker zipped into the shocker channel and zoomed toward her. She saw it just in time and pulled something out of her shirt – a twelve-by-twelve-inch piece of rubber she had torn off the flap on the front door and taken with her for protection. The shocker approached and positioned itself to fire its barb at her. As it fired, she held out the flap. The barb shot into it and its wire glowed brightly, trying to discharge its massive electric jolt, but nothing happened.

"GO SCRATCH!"

The boys cheered and laughed. Scratch tossed the rubber mat on top of the Shocker and sprung up to crawl over the neutralized threat.

Brilliant! thought Reggie, *why didn't I think of that!!?*

She was still stuck, facing inside in the cramped space because there wasn't enough room to turn around in the channel. Everyone in the Cauldron cheered again, even the Pack, who were yelling "Go Scratch!" Then everyone started chanting.

"Scratch, Scratch, Scratch..."

But as soon as her face got up to the conveyer belt the laser abruptly stopped cutting scales. There must have been sensors that detected something nearby, something that did not belong there. Was it the dead shocker?

As Scratch started to move her left leg over the shocker, the laser head twisted and repositioned, aiming at her. Before she knew it, the machine fired off five quick blasts, carving what looked like a bear claw scratch across her face. It seemed like the laser was trying to erase her.

Scratch twisted around and fell, banging her head and smearing blood all over the glass wall. She screamed in pain, but no one could hear the sound. Then she tried to break through the wall, but it was two-inch thick Plexiglas, and there was no way she could possibly crack it with her delicate fists.

"REGGIE! GET HER OUT!" screamed Rhino from across the Pit.

Reggie took off his helmet and looked around. There were hundreds of shockers on alert now, and there was no way he could get into the room–he was too big. So he froze, not knowing what to do.

When in doubt, don't, he thought to himself. *Live to fight another day.*

"THROW SOMETHING AT THE WINDOW!" yelled Rhino and the rest of the Pack, but Reggie didn't have anything that would break through the thick glass except the acetylene tanks, but they were far too heavy to throw. As frustrating as it was, there was absolutely nothing he could do.

"REGGIE, YOU GOOD FOR NOTHING SELFISH COWARD! BREAK THE GLASS!!!" yelled Rhino again. At least it sounded like Rhino. It was strange–Reggie couldn't see Rhino anymore, but he could still hear his insults.

Now Reggie was looking really bad to the rest of the guys. Scratch was taking all the heat, and he wasn't doing anything. There wasn't anything he could throw that would break through the wall, and the shockers would blast him if he tried anything anyway.

Scratch twisted away from the laser and crawled over the dead shocker, continuing down the passageway.

"GO SCRATCH!" The boys cheered again, not believing how brave she was or that she could still go on despite the extreme pain from the laser blast.

The laser head continued to track her motion, but it couldn't reach its arm far enough to hit her again. It banged against the wall as it fired its beam, thrashing, trying to smash around to get her, but it couldn't stop her from going further through the cutting chamber. Then the laser head smashed through the glass and the bright ruby red beam swept randomly across the Cauldron, forcing everyone to hit the dirt.

The boys went wild cheering again.

"KILL IT, SCRATCH! KILL IT! KILL-KILL-KILL," they chanted.

Some of the boys made a game out of dodging the scorching beam. Unfortunately, no one had thought about the second laser, thirty feet further down the belt. A few of the guys screamed, "Watch out!" as it swiveled its lens up and hissed to life, but before Scratch knew it, there was another quick blast and the brilliant ruby-red beam etched precise, searing lines into her back. Scratch spun around and protected her face, but the pain was too great and she collapsed. To make things worse, another shocker was coming down the channel toward her, charging up its needle.

"WATCH OUT!" everyone screamed.

Scratch couldn't hear them, but she did hear the Shocker charging. Just as it shot at her, she raised her left foot and the needle shot straight into the rubber sole of her Keds sneaker. The shocker wire heated up brightly as it sent high voltage jolts into the rubber, but the electricity went nowhere. The rubber was a perfect insulator. Scratch had beaten the shockers again!

"GO! GO! GO!"

The boys went crazy, but there was still nothing they could do to help her. Scratch was exhausted and losing blood. She started blacking out and began to panic, thinking she couldn't make it out. She had to try to get back before she passed out, otherwise, she would bleed to death in the channel because no one would be able to get to her. So she started crawling back, dragging the Shocker behind her as it continued trying to electrocute her sneaker. Soon it ran out of juice, died, and dragged along limply behind her.

By the time she crawled back out of the flap, most of the bleeding on her face and back had already stopped. The cuts looked more like burns now. She passed out as Reggie and everyone ran over to pull her out.

"Get out of the way, coward!" said Rhino as he cut through the crowd with the Pack backing him up. "It's too late. There's nothing you can do now!"

As she lay flat on the ground Flame looked at her face.

"Man, it looks like she took a huge hit from a bear claw!"

"That laser's a claw!" said G-Man.

"The Claw," said IPod, in awe that she survived.

"Claw," everyone said in awe.

The Pack picked her up off the ground and Reggie backed away as they shoved past him and carried her back to Cots. He knew there was nothing he could have done, but as soon as she was carried away, he noticed that the rest of the boys were looking at him funny. Not making eye contact. The way guys do when they're picking teams and they don't want you on theirs.

24. THE ULTIMATE GAME

Rations were running low, so Snake asked for volunteers to get more. When no one volunteered, Reggie said he would help, and then Jeremy did, too.

After The Claw incident, Rhino made twice as sure that everyone hated Reggie. When Reggie figured out everyone was against him, he became even more determined to find a way to escape, so he was excited about the opportunity to see more of the tunnels.

Even though they liked Snake, Jeremy and Reggie didn't ever tell him about their plan to escape. Snake had said it himself–"Trust no one," and they knew he was right. They couldn't trust anyone except each other, and that was mainly due to the Semper Fi code the Marine had given them. Besides, shockers were following close by and Reggie suspected they might have microphones on them. If they had microphones, it was likely ECHO had voice recognition software and could figure out what they were up to, so Reggie kept quiet.

It was the first time Reggie and Jeremy had been out of the Cauldron since they had been trapped there, and they were relieved to be outside and to be practically alone. None of the Pack was there to harass them.

"Man, it's great to be outta there," said Jeremy.

"How do you think I stay sane?" said Snake, "I get these little breaks. Keeps me from crackin'."

The air was cooler and cleaner, and flowed through the tunnels in a gentle breeze. Reggie and Jeremy both noticed a ventilation shaft in the ceiling. There was a Bobcat bulldozer there, too.

Before they could get any ideas, Snake gave them their orders.

"Jeremy, bring that Bobcat. We'll load up the shovel with chow."

Jeremy fired up the Bobcat and led the rest of the way, lighting the tunnel with the bright headlights. Soon they were deeper in the mountain at a freezing storage cavern where all the food and supplies were kept. It was a mess, and difficult to walk through, so the shockers waited for the humans in the tunnel just outside the room.

Endless piles of military food packs lay where ECHO had dumped them. Jeremy looked over the piles and read the labels on the cases: MRE's, Flameless Ration Heaters, Rations Cold Weather (RCW's), Rations Lightweight 30-Days (RLW-30's), T-Ration Modules, and Unitized B-Rations. It was incredible how much stuff ECHO could horde from the outside world.

As they loaded rations into the Bobcat's shovel, Reggie noticed another room in the darkness, adjacent to the storage cavern. He slipped into it while Jeremy and Snake continued loading. After waiting several seconds for his eyes to adjust, he heard something move. He shuddered, thinking it might be a shocker, or even ECHO.

"Come 'ere," whispered a hoarse voice.

Reggie was startled.

"Come 'ere!" whispered the voice, a little louder now.

It was a dark, freezing place, so Reggie didn't want to go in.

Suddenly Chainsaw's head popped up.

"What, are you deaf, you idiot? Come 'ere!"

"Chainsaw! What are you doing here!?" gawked Reggie as he crept over.

"I escaped when Power bolted," said Chainsaw, "I was stalking ECHO, but somehow the shockers found out."

He was wrapped in blankets next to a pile of opened MRE packs, which he had eaten.

"Check out this crate!" said Chainsaw, crouching back down again.

He showed Reggie a crate that contained a bunch of binders and a laptop computer. The laptop had a red label on it that he could barely read in the darkness. It said:

NATIONAL SECURITY AGENCY
- TOP SECRET -
If Found Do Not Open!
Return Immediately To NSC Office
Quantico, Virginia
Any Unauthorized Tampering With This Computer
Will Be Prosecuted As A Class 1 Felony

Chainsaw turned on the laptop and opened a file.

"What are you doing!?" said Reggie.

"There's not much power left, but check it out man, fast," he said as he showed Reggie a top-secret file. Reggie nervously read it quickly:

TOP SECRET
UNITED STATES ARMY WAR GAMES CENTER
FORT BRAGG COMMAND OPERATIONS CENTER
PROJECT: TRANSFORMING THE FUTURE: REALITY GAME INFINITY CODE (IC) APPLICATIONS

Reggie remembered Josh mentioning reality games. Was this a military reality game application? He scrolled down through a bunch of technical text and code and stopped at:

...significantly varied simulation models (VSM) and predictive tactical scenarios (PTS) which, if processed in parallel, generate perpetually adaptive scenarios (PAS) for tactical geopolitical and military response (GMR)in a counter insurgency (COIN) or revolutionary theater...

"Pretty wild stuff, huh?" said Chainsaw. "Check it out. It's all about predicting the future in wars. With infinite predictions to choose from–with some kind of 'Infinity Code.' How to win no matter what happens! The ultimate cheat code, man! But for real!"

Semper Fi guy's words came to mind–"Pay attention. Learn everything you can every day. You might not ever get a second chance." And Big Pete's–"Remembrance is power."

Reggie wasn't about to blow it this time, so he read and re-read the message, committing it to memory. He read it carefully one final time. This was something he knew he'd probably never be able to see again. He burned the introduction into his memory:

...All codes have antecedents. Certain codes, which originated in antiquity and, when utilized with current projections of future social and political conditions via IC, can precisely predict future scenarios. These predictions can be exploited and the future course of events changed...

...M Game Theory applies the Infinity Code accordingly:

"In either warfare or political applications where multiple scenarios may be sequentially...

M Game Theory? It was too much to memorize.

...and when the Starman's Gravitational Coefficient (GC)is incorporated into Earth's EM references, the matrix...

There it was again! *Starman*. Reggie tried to remember where he had heard that Starman name. It was during the ride down to Pasadena. It was all so fuzzy now.

But what did all this tech talk mean? He tried to remember what antecedent meant, and remembered it meant something coming before, PRECEDING, then concentrated on memorizing as much as he could.

All of the binders had "TOP SECRET" printed on them, which made him nervous because of the repeated threat of imprisonment. But it didn't matter since they were already imprisoned. It couldn't get much worse, so he read on. The binders all seemed to be about War Games, National Defense, Future Warfare and Geo-Political Scenarios. There were code names for various scientists and consultants: names like 'M', 'Starman', 'Nano', 'Yod'.

Whatever it all was, it was clear that ECHO could get in anywhere it wanted to and steal anything it could fit inside its body–or its body transformed into a truck or whatever it chose to become. Reggie wondered what aspect of ECHO's strategy would cause it to infiltrate these places– top secret locations, military planning centers – to steal the Infinity Code...whatever that was.

At the bottom of the container was another box–a black one–marked 'TOP SECRET CODEX–DO NOT OPEN'. It had other words written in foreign letters that looked like they were made out of fire.

For some reason, when Reggie saw this box, he had a revelation. ECHO was using all of this special knowledge to plan ahead for anything anyone would do in the future, so it could make anything it wanted to happen!

It was impossible to imagine what ECHO was planning to make happen in the future. The worst part, Reggie realized, was that no one could ever really know what ECHO was going to do until ECHO actually did it. It was as if ECHO was already working in the future and only coming back to fix or engineer certain events, like to remove Tom and add Josh, like it was putting all kinds of plans into motion for some secret purpose. There was no predicting ECHO because it was always computing somewhere into the future. It made Reggie dizzy thinking about it, but if that wasn't enough, Chainsaw pulled him over to show him something else, another part of E-7's plan.

"And check this out!" said Chainsaw, removing the cover of a box marked PEKING PROTOTYPE CO. The large crate was covered with red and black Chinese characters and tax, customs, and shipping stamps. Chainsaw moved the packing material away from the center of the crate and revealed a three foot tall, mole-headed combot with light, super-hardened armor panels covering its arms, torso, and legs. Chainsaw and Reggie stared at the combot. It reminded them of the Ghoul in the on-line ECHO-6 game, complete with shock-red troll-like hair.

"Man," said Reggie, "this is really creepy. It's a Mech-Ghoul."

"Exactly," said Chainsaw. "I can't figure out what ECHO would want ghouls for. It's already got shockers and us for slaves. It's kind of cool, though. It kind of grows on you in a creepy sort of way."

"It's just eerie. ECHO is always up to something, and no-one ever knows what. Does it work? Can you turn it on or anything?"

"Naw. It's just a model, no guts. Besides, are you crazy? I wouldn't turn it on if I could–who knows what this thing could do."

"No telling what it would do," agreed Reggie. "I wouldn't want it looking for me. Armor looks pretty good, hard as nails." Reggie looked around, sensing something. "I gotta go. Shockers'll notice I'm missing. I'll be back. You gotta get out of here. It's freezing!"

"I can't..."

"I'll be right back. Hold on..."

Reggie bolted back to the storage area and pretended that he had been loading food the whole time. Soon they had almost finished loading the Bobcat's shovel, so Reggie ran back to Chainsaw for the last time.

"Come on–let's get back," said Reggie.

"I can't. I tried to tell you–somehow I'm marked. Every time I try to go back they zap me. They won't let me out of here. It's E-7, man! He's keeping me here."

They heard charging sounds out in the tunnel. The shockers started zapping at Snake and Jeremy to get them to move.

"HEY!!" they screamed at Reggie. "WHAT ARE YOU DOING? WE HAVE TO GO!"

"Don't sweat it," said Chainsaw. "I'll live. Hey, all the food you can eat, right?"

"We'll be back. We'll get you out."

"Sure," said Chainsaw, "You'll be back."

He didn't sound convinced.

Reggie felt bad. Just like everyone else, Chainsaw didn't trust him, but Reggie had to bolt or they'd all get fried.

"COME ON!" yelled Jeremy.

Jeremy led Snake, Reggie, and the shockers back up the tunnel. When they got back to the Chow Cave, they unloaded all the food and went to Cots to rest. As they lay on their cots, Reggie filled in his brother.

"Jeremy, we really need to get out of here. I found out some stuff about ECHO, a bunch of top secret Army stuff. It works in the future. ECHO is planning something really big, like taking over the whole country, or world or something.

And it's building these really creepy Chinese Mech-Ghoul Robots–'combots.'

"Whoa! Sounds like Josh wasn't lying."

"Yeah, and guess what? The shockers have trapped Chainsaw down there."

"No way! It's freezing in there!" said Jeremy.

"There were some blankets, but they won't let him out, like they're teaching him a lesson or something, or maybe ECHO is just torturing him by keeping him there."

Jeremy thought for a minute about everything Reggie was telling him. The part about Chainsaw made sense. Torturing Chainsaw sounded like something ECHO would do. What else was it capable of, and how cruel would it be to gain its next objective?

"ECHO against the whole world?"

"Yeah," said Reggie, "I know it sounds crazy, but it'll be ECHO and its 'team'–its human and robot ghouls–if it has its way. Trust me, it looks like ECHO is gonna to pull off something really big. It's already got top secret software programs from the Army, programs that can predict the future and take advantage of it–and something called the Infinity Code! ECHO can go anywhere it wants, especially since it figures out what's going to happen in the future. We have to get out of here and warn someone! Otherwise everyone, ALL HUMANS EVERYWHERE, will end up like us–part of ECHO's Machine Team!

"Why would it need such a giant team?" asked Jeremy.

"It's starting some sort of 'game,' except the whole world is its game field–'ECHO: Whole World Revenge.' I don't want to be one of its mech ghouls forever! Power was right.

We gotta get out of here no matter what. Not just to escape, but to warn everyone. It's gonna take over the Army first. It can do it!"

Suddenly Jeremy realized that everything they had gone through was just a tiny part of ECHO's master plan. He was overwhelmed with this new revelation. All he wanted was to go back to how things used to be, but he couldn't. He was helplessly trapped.

"I can't think anymore...," said Jeremy, as he rolled over wearily in his cot. Falling asleep would have to suffice for now. It was his only escape. Jeremy quickly passed out, leaving Reggie alone with his thoughts.

Reggie rolled over and noticed Claw sitting alone on her cot on the other side of the cavern. It was a relief to see her. Maybe he could talk to her and she could think of something. Claw was the only person in the Cauldron who said anything that he couldn't predict, who always had something different to say. She was always full of surprises–smart surprises. He wished he could talk to her because she would have good ideas, but she probably hated him now like everyone else did.

But what did he have to lose? Even though he had his doubts, and the shockers were randomly patrolling the area, he decided to sneak over. When he got about ten feet away she looked up and noticed him coming toward her, but she didn't seem to mind. It even seemed like she might have wanted to see him.

"Hey Reggie," her voice cut through the darkness.

When Claw looked at him, his stomach felt like it was catching on fire again, just like it did when he first saw her at the focus group. He didn't know why, but it was the exact same, weird, disturbing feeling. He wished he understood why she made him feel this way, or at least that the fiery feeling would stop so he could think. Maybe it would stop if he got to know her better. He still felt bad about not being able to help her when she was stuck in the processing room.

"Sorry about not helping." said Reggie, "I..."

"How could you? Bulletproof glass, two inches thick. There was no way anyone could've gotten to me. I knew that when I went in."

"Yeah. Well, the other guys don't quite see it that way. They think I'm a coward, or at least a weasel."

She just grinned back at him like it was ridiculous, and he felt relieved.

Reggie noticed that the cuts on her face had already healed into deep, red marks across her face that looked like giant claw cuts. Reggie kind of liked the pattern it made, and at first glance thought it even looked cool, kind of like African tribal marks or something. He wondered if he would have thought the same if he hadn't been so tired and mixed up. No one else in the whole world looked as beautiful to him as Scratch had before the 'Claw' incident, but now, instead of being disturbed by her appearance, he felt less out of place around her. It was like he didn't feel like he had to look as perfect as she did to talk to her.

He felt guilty even thinking that she wasn't perfect anymore, but something else about her face occurred to him. It was obvious that something terrible had happened to Scratch, but somehow he felt that it made her even more beautiful. She didn't just look like a perfect beauty queen or some kind of cream-puff poser, but like she had done something, experienced something, that made her different. Like something terrible had happened to her because she had done something brave. Now, he thought, her face seemed to him like the perfect reflection of who she really was: she was not only beautiful, but terribly, courageously beautiful.

"It was amazing how you stopped the shockers with just your shoe–the rubber sole," said Reggie.

"Yeah, perfect insulators. I was holding out that technique just for the escape, otherwise they'd figure it out and take the rubber flaps off the doors. Too bad about the lasers, though. I sure didn't see that coming."

"It was a brilliant plan. If we ever get out of here, your parents'll freak, though."

"How bad is my face? No one will tell me. It stung like crazy, but now it just itches."

"Like I said, your parents'll freak, but you look really cool now."

"You didn't think I looked good before?"

"Well, yeah, of course! But now you look good AND you look really different. Unlike anyone else. It looks cool."

"Thanks, I think. Actually, if we ever get out of here, the one thing I'm really looking forward to is my mom's..."

"HEY!" said Rhino, butting in. Neither Reggie or Claw had seen him coming. "Shove off coward!"

But Claw cut him off.

"Rhino, it's okay. Relax!"

Reggie got ready for a fight, but Rhino backed off into the darkness. Reggie was thrown off his chain of thought, though, and completely forgot to tell Claw about what he had come over to tell her about in the first place–the Army stuff he had seen in the tunnel.

"Man, that guy hates me," said Reggie. "I don't get it."

"It's not you, he's like that with everyone. Don't take it personally," said Claw. "Trust me, it has nothing to do with you."

Reggie noticed an AAA Reality Games jacket, which she had pulled over her like a blanket.

"Hey. You got a jacket!" said Reggie.

"Yeah, Mr. Esposito sent it to me after the focus group."

"Cool. Mine got burned up..." said Reggie as he admired the jacket, refreshing his memory of what it looked like.

Reggie noticed she was wearing the same gold ECHO pin Luca had given him, but she had put it through a piercing in her ear and was wearing it like an earring.

"Whoah," he said, impressed with the shiny gold pin. The pin looked really good on Claw's ear, but then Reggie had another thought. *Maybe Luca was straight with me at the focus group if he gave the same jacket and pin to Claw. It makes no sense that he would give us both that stuff and then send ECHO after us.* He realized that Luca probably had been straight with him, that there was no way Luca would have planned this or was some kind of psycho. He wished he still had his jacket, like Claire did. Somehow, throughout all the madness, she had been able to keep hers.

Reggie suddenly remembered why he had come over to see Claw in the first place–the Army stuff he had seen in the tunnel–but Claw interrupted his train of thought again.

"How's your brother doing?"

"It's like he fell into a dark hole. He's been really different since ECHO ate Tom. I don't know how much longer he can go on. He might be cracking. I don't know what to do."

"Yeah, him and some of the younger guys. He's depressed, which is a normal reaction to what's happened–falling into this hole. Keep talking to him even if he doesn't talk back to you. He needs to keep a connection to something that's normal for him, and that's you. That should keep him from getting too much worse."

"How do you know?"

"My dad thinks there's a code to everything–everyone's behavior–that everything we do means something and can be decoded, that everyone does what they do for a reason, even if they don't know why. He's a shrink. He says you can learn everything about a person from their behavior, what they do. Everyone has his or her own behavior pattern. With your brother, with all of us, that pattern's broken. He can't connect to this world much because it's so disturbing, but he can stay connected to you because he knows you."

"Yeah, but sometimes he doesn't even talk anymore. After a while he just tunes out and his mind goes somewhere else. It's like he checks out."

"That doesn't mean he can't hear you."

"What if he stops talking completely, like SpanDex?"

"SpanDex got shocked too many times. Your brother is just stressed out. He thinks he's completely helpless, and afraid that he's in serious danger, which we are. So he's not wrong. It's called TSS–Traumatic Stress Syndrome."

"There's a name for it?"

"There's a code for everything. There's even a manual, a code book for every disorder, every disordered behavior pattern. They've even got a code for playing video games too much. Just keep talking to him. Give him hope and keep the connection. It'll help you, too, to help him."

Everything Claw said made sense, but Reggie was so tired that he had forgotten why he was there. He had to leave because he didn't know what else to talk about and didn't want to make a fool out of himself.

"Okay. See you later. Thanks for trying the escape."

"Thanks for talking to me," she said as she stared directly into his eyes.

Why did she have to do that? When she said "Thanks" and those icy-blue eyes locked onto him, Reggie felt the heat ignite in his gut again.

This thing about her troubled and confused him.

"Yeah..." he mumbled.

He broke away from her gaze and snuck back to his cot.

25. T-REX

On the way to Cots the next night, Reggie thought about making new escape plans. Or was it two nights later? He couldn't remember what period it was. His sense of time kept slipping. It had helped when someone had been counting the periods, but they had stopped a long time ago. Reggie began to question if time even existed if there were no clocks, days, or seasons.

If only he and Jeremy could escape from the mountain, they could get help and at least warn the Army that their security had been breached–not that the Army would believe them at first–but Reggie could recite the stuff about the Infinity Code and they would know he really knew something, that he wasn't lying or just some stupid kid. Then they would help him get the rest of the guys out. The Army would use real weapons against ECHO, maybe even tanks. Reggie would have to go in one of the tanks to show them where ECHO was so that they could blast the tunnel open and then blast ECHO. That would be indescribably awesome!

But how could they get out with the shockers, ECHO, more guys going crazy every day, and being buried deep inside a mountain in the middle of nowhere? It was still an endless set of impossible obstacles.

Think it through one step at a time. Break it down and it'll make sense. Work with the environment. Isn't that what the Semper Fi guy had said?

Reggie again reviewed the possible exit routes–the slope they came in through, ventilation shafts, maybe another shaft out, or even down a stoop, then up and out. But his mind kept drifting back to ECHO and all of the things it had done to block any escape.

Reggie was psyched out. All the gamers who had tried to escape had failed. SpanDex had gotten shocked so many times that he could hardly remember who he was. Power had tried to outrun the shockers and had gotten barbecued. Tom had been terminated and erased by ECHO personally. Claw had gotten carved up and was lucky not to have been blinded by the lasers. And now Chainsaw had tried to hide and be forgotten, only to be caught and locked out of the stinking warmth of the Cauldron in a merciless, freezing torture. It was as if ECHO was getting revenge every time anyone tried to fight it in any way.

If there *was* a way out Reggie still could not come up with it. It was futile. ECHO was always ahead of them. Miles ahead. Days, weeks, months, years ahead. It was hopeless. All he could do was sleep on it. Think of something else. Sleep. Jeremy was right–sleep was the only escape.

On the way to Cots, Rhino noticed IPod's boom box and kicked it.

"Why do you keep that thing? It doesn't even play."

"Shut up Rhino!" yelled Flame.

"I got just enough juice for a tune or two when we need it," said IPod.

As Reggie laid on his cot, his brain hurt from trying to think on limited rations and with way too little sleep. He had a migraine headache, a real pounder. He was too weak and tired to think, just the way ECHO liked it. He thought ECHO was probably laughing at them now, or would be if it weren't a machine and actually had feelings. A new emotion Reggie had never felt before began to grow in him. He truly hated the thing. He wanted more than anything in the world to destroy the never-ending curse of ECHO, but there was no way he could. Reggie was defeated, an enslaved prisoner like everyone else trapped there. He tried and tried to sleep again to release his mind from their hopeless future, but he was restless.

Before he knew it, he was following Jeremy down an endless tunnel. Jeremy was struggling with something, but the tunnel was too narrow and Reggie couldn't help him. He waited, and Jeremy cracked something open in front of him. It was as if he ripped open a tear in the darkness and the black peeled open, revealing a new space. Light poured into the tunnel and he could see the ground and walls clearly for the first time, but the light was so bright it hurt his eyes, so he couldn't look.

The next morning Reggie awakened to see Jeremy roll out of his cot, still asleep. When he hit the hard ground, he woke up.

"Are you okay?" asked Reggie.

On the floor in front of Jeremy's face, mica crystals flickered, and for a moment they reminded him of stars. He remembered the stars reflected in the river at Pete's cousin's house. Then he remembered sleeping under the stars in Crescent City and the giant footprints on the beach in the morning. ECHO's footprints. It had been ECHO and the shockers after all, ECHO just couldn't see him and Reggie. Jeremy suddenly remembered that there was no moon that night. It was too dark for ECHO. With all the things ECHO could do, he couldn't see in the dark! Jeremy felt like the missing piece to an endless puzzle had just found. It just needed to be put in its place to crack their problem.

Maybe the shockers can't see in the dark, either. Maybe they need light to work, thought Jeremy, *maybe solar power...*

"If we kill the light somehow, we could escape–ECHO doesn't see in the dark," said Jeremy. "Remember when he couldn't find us at the beach? That's why the shockers leave the lights on all the time."

"You're right! Awesome, Jem!" said Reggie, "Maybe we could make a slingshot or something and knock out the light."

Reggie was happy to hear Jeremy speak and hopeful about the idea, but he also wanted to keep Jeremy talking. He knew there were no materials they could build a slingshot with–ECHO had seen to that–but he was excited that Jeremy had come up with a new idea from the limited amount of information they knew about ECHO. It was a good idea. He tried to stay as enthusiastic as possible.

"But how do we kill the Cauldron light?" said Jeremy, "It's too high to smash, and if we tried to break the ones in the tunnel, we'd get zapped for sure."

"There must be a master switch somewhere," said Reggie. "We'll have to find it."

Jeremy had thought he had a good idea, a brilliant idea, but he realized that just like all the ideas anyone had regarding the possibility of escape, it wasn't doable after all.

Jeremy shrugged.

"That's all I got."

"It's a good idea," said Reggie, "and we will find a way. We just have to keep thinking about it like a game–that's what Claw once said. Plus, we always have Plan B–Waiting. We wait for an opportunity, a mistake, and then move fast to take advantage of it. There's nothing else we can do right now. There's no way to beat ECHO and the shockers right now. We have to wait until they make a mistake, or try to find that switch. While we wait, we can think about where that switch would logically be."

It was still a long shot, and they both knew it. The shockers were warrior sentinel machines that could work forever without sleeping, eating, or resting, but what else was there to do? It was overwhelming to realize that there would be no way out of this maze unless ECHO made some kind of extraordinary mistake or something else unexpected happened, like maybe a really big earthquake. But could the guys outlive the machines if a big quake hit?

Reggie remembered someone said "expect the unexpected" once and that gave him a little hope. Either way, it would be a long, long wait, and it already seemed like they had been imprisoned for an eternity. They had no idea how long they had been underground, since they had long ago forgotten about normal day cycles. Everyone was getting weirder every day. Would they be the next to lose their minds?

"The first objective is to keep from cracking," said Reggie, "so we can take advantage of any opportunity that arises."

"HUA, I'd give anything for an EMP grenade right now."

Reggie laughed.

"First Objective–Stay sane. Claw said when you're stuck like this to try making a game out of it. Jokes work, too."

"It's all a joke, anyway–nothin' left to lose," said Jeremy. "Let's chow."

"Yeah, then we can think better," said Reggie, relieved that at least Jeremy was talking again.

After a light MRE, they climbed down into the Pit. Jeremy had become an expert at operating the Bobcat while the chop was dug out around the Pit by the other boys. He quickly shoveled the loose rocks and gravel like he was playing a video game. Josh was a quiet leader, and hardly ever bothered anyone, so everyone got lost in their own private trances as they worked, thinking about nothing. Zen-like nothing. Everyone actually liked working in this trance and they were able to get a lot done without the shockers tormenting them. Tom was a distant memory now, but everyone was grateful for his absence.

The Pit had grown much bigger–about seventy-five feet deep and a hundred feet across. Two tiny staircases circled down to the bottom, welded to the inside of the steel I-beams that supported the walls. It was sort of like a tower, but upside down, going down instead of up. The I-beams did a good job of reinforcing the walls of the Pit, but the natural bottomless hole in the middle was larger now, cutting the bottom of the Pit in half with a thirty-foot-wide gap across the middle. There was no way to get from one side to the other except by climbing across the I-beams on which several boys were welding.

"Hey, I think I found something," said one of the diggers. A couple of rock-choppers came over.

"Let me see," said Josh, and everyone backed out of his way.

It looked like a giant set of animal bones. Very large, old bones. There was a skull the size of a dining room table, full of razor sharp teeth as hard as rocks. The more the boys dug, the more bones they found.

"Clean it up. ECHO will want to see it!" said Josh. The guys left all the bones in place exactly where they had found them, carefully cleaning all the dirt away as they had done so many times before. There was a rich variety of fossils: trilobites, shark-like skeleton imprints, plants, fish, and birds.

It looked like an archeological dig, but one on fast forward, sped up by the feverish machine-like labor of the boys seeking a reward–sleep, food, a shower in the Falls.

After a few minutes of digging the rest of the dirt away with their bare hands, they had completely exposed several skeletons of the massive animals. The skeletons were so large that no one digging could tell what they had been. The diggers were too close to decipher the shapes of the animals.

Reggie was welding by the upper rim of the Pit, watching the progress of the archeological dig. By the time they were finished clearing the bones, the shapes were very clear to him. There were two giant T-Rex's and one smaller Rex between them, lying peacefully next to each other like they had died in their sleep. Could this have been another reason why ECHO had them digging there? To find giant monsters of the past?

If so, how could it predict that there would be T-Rex bones here? And why would it be interested in Rex's? It was a strange sight because the skeletons were perfectly preserved, and the animals looked like they were lying in a permanent state of tranquility–a rare moment of complete peace between vicious wild animals. They were terrifying carnivores, but they were also a family, peacefully preserved together, for eternity.

Reggie wondered how ECHO would react when he saw them. The skeletons were the size ECHO's would be if ECHO were a real animal. But ECHO wasn't an animal, so would it react? If it did, maybe the shockers would get distracted. Reggie was so excited at the possibility of something unpredictable happening that his chest started pounding. He tried to calm down, because his heart was pounding so hard that he worried it would explode or burst out of his chest.

Then, for some unknown reason, all the lights abruptly went out.

"Blackout!" someone yelled.

"Duh." someone else yelled.

Reggie was exhilarated about something out of ECHO'S control happening, but a moment later, the shockers activated a battery-powered emergency light which was mounted on the wall. The battery was almost dead, though, so the light flickered on and off. The shockers whirred and flickered with colors and sounds in the new blinking light, starting and stopping in fits as the light went on and off. In a few seconds, the shockers seemed to get organized enough to let everyone store their tools and leave the Pit. Jeremy left his Bobcat in the corner of the Pit on the same side as the giant skeletons. One of the older boys left the big dozer up top with the shovel blade in a raised position so there would be room to walk under it, since there was so little room left along the sides of the Pit.

In another minute or two half the boys had started their RCW's (Rations, Cold Weather), and half were taking turns taking showers in the Falls. While Reggie and Jeremy ate their RCW's, Snake came over with a flashlight and sat down to eat next to them.

"ECHO should be coming soon," he said. "The shockers'll let him know."

"How the heck do the shockers and ECHO communicate?" asked Jeremy.

"I think the shockers communicate with each other with those color-burst patterns," said Snake, "but I don't know about ECHO. No matter where he is, ECHO always seems to know what the shockers see and hear. Even if he's miles away on a rampage somewhere. Trust me, he'll be back soon. Be careful."

For the rest of the period, everyone relaxed on their cots or in the Falls in the darkness. When the sleep period came, they felt less exhausted than normal because of their break, but everyone fell asleep just as quickly as usual. IPod decided to play a tune on his boom box. He only had enough power left for a tune or two, but he decided to play one now since it was kind of a special occasion.

When the music came on, it startled everyone.

"On a hot summer night
When everything was alright
I remember..."

"Hey, shut that girlie crap off," yelled Rhino.

"Shut up, Rhino!" everyone yelled, because they were all in a good mood, despite, or possibly even because of, the power being partially cut.

"Play it, IPod," said Flame.

IPod turned on the song loud enough for everyone in Cots to hear.

"I remember clearly
When you were so small,
I'd come home to see you,
Had no worries at all...

The melody was pleasant as it echoed through the caverns. It was strange to hear music again, and everyone thought about the people they had left behind who might miss them. They could almost see the faces of their own parents and brothers and sisters and friends and uncles...

"I still see you in my mind,
so clearly I still see you,
Even after all this time,
I'll always really miss you,
Because I never got to say goodbye...

Jeremy tried to remember his father. He could hardly remember what he looked like, but he remembered how sad he had been when they had left–left him alone to be with Asa. He had forgotten him, but now he remembered.

"I hope you're never too blue
Or think I don't still love you
Because you must remember,
Remember this is true,
I simply never got to say
I'm always here for you...

Reggie was hypnotized by the whirring of the shockers outside Cots. They were up to something. Before he knew it, ECHO was chasing him through the tunnels in some game, but this time it trapped him. As it cornered him, its face turned into his father's. A thought flashed to Reggie–*was his father somehow betraying him? Had he always betrayed him?*

The dream was so disturbing that Reggie woke up from shock, gasping to catch his breath. His heart was racing again like it did when he first saw the T-Rex bones, but when he saw Jeremy sleeping peacefully next to him his pulse quickly fell back to normal. *Thank God for Jeremy. Someone he could count on*. He saw Claw sleeping on her cot. Thank God for Claw, who gave him the idea to make it all a game with Jeremy. Would he ever be able to call her by her real name, Claire Hamilton, back in the real world? Why couldn't he have met her under normal circumstances? In a normal world? He fell back to sleep.

26. THE LONGEST BATTLE

The blackout had caused confusion and anxiety in the Cauldron. Most of the guys stayed in Cots, but a pack of the younger kids, including G-Man, tried to feel their way out along the walls to escape between the blinks of the emergency lights. No one made it out, though, because when the power came back on the shockers concluded that an escape attempt was under way. G-Man and his crew were zapped repeatedly when they ran back to Cots, making G-Man even more furious with ECHO.

By the time the main lights came back on, Snake had finally lost his mind. He didn't know where he was, but wanted to try to find out, to shake things loose in his head, to get everything to make sense. As everyone came out of Cots, he was standing next to the trillium processing room, slowly banging his head on the thick glass wall.

But Reggie was refreshed and could think more clearly. When he and Jeremy walked into the Cauldron, he noticed that something was different. It was later in the day than when they usually woke up. A shaft of sunlight miraculously cut down the ventilation shaft, through the mountain, and into the Cauldron, where it lit up the shovel of the big dozer. To Reggie, it was a clear sign.

"Check out the dozer blade," said Reggie.

The shovel of the big bull dozer was resting in the up position near the ceiling. The blade led straight up to the narrow ventilation shaft, through which cool air was gently flowing. Sunlight flashed off a corner of the worn blade.

The guy who operated the dozer couldn't get it started, so shockers were swarming around the huge machine, lamely shocking it over and over like it wasn't behaving. The fact that the sun was hitting it, it couldn't start, and the blade was in the up position all meant one thing to Reggie–it was a change in the environment, and one which they could exploit.

Jeremy's eyes lit up when he saw what Reggie saw.

"Closet walk?" asked Jeremy hopefully.

"Bam!" said Reggie. "Huaaa! When the shockers stop."

Reggie thought it was amazing what a little sleep could do for Jeremy. As the sunbeam shimmered on the giant blade, he knew it was time to escape. It was their only chance–and no one but he and Jeremy could possibly pull it off.

Jeremy smiled. Reggie had forgotten what Jeremy's smile had looked like. He couldn't remember when he had ever seen Jeremy truly happy like he was now, even for only a couple of seconds. It was as if a tiny bit of the sunbeam had also gotten into Jeremy.

But as if the shockers could read their minds, they kept Reggie and Jeremy away from the dozer. The plan would have to wait until something distracted the shockers so they wouldn't be noticed.

Instead, they climbed down the stairs to the bottom of the Pit, and Jeremy started clearing out the chop piles around the skeletons with the Bobcat. Reggie climbed out onto an I-beam, dragging his sledgehammer and torch with him, and crawled over to the other side of the Pit where several guys were jack hammering. He started welding a new I-beam at the edge of the Pit.

As soon as everyone had worked up a sweat and eased into their Zen work-trance, there was a sudden commotion. Several guys scrambled out of the Pit suddenly. Reggie looked up, but couldn't see anything around the mouth of the Pit because his welding mask was so fogged up, but he felt a dreadful presence. He tilted up the visor and took a look. Two large, cold, green eyes were watching him from fifty feet away.

"Great," said Reggie angrily, thinking about their plan to climb the ventilation shaft, "always wrecking everything!"

Reggie tightly gripped his sledge hammer.

Jeremy noticed that Reggie was looking up, so he stopped his Bobcat and looked up too.

Suddenly, the shockers started pushing everyone around in a frenzy to clear a path for ECHO. Before anyone knew it, ECHO morphed into a dark, shape-changing creature that was adapting its form to traverse the I-beams, descending so smoothly that it looked like it was floating down into the Pit.

Everyone left the open area of the Pit and hid behind the stairs and I-beams. Reggie hid behind an I-beam on the opposite side of the hole. Jeremy backed his Bobcat to the side of the Pit and parked it. Since he was sitting inside its steel cage he felt safe, so he stayed there, frozen like just another machine turned off, hoping ECHO wouldn't notice him.

ECHO's splintered, sparkling mass glided through the shadows of the I-beams as if it had all the time in the world. It was in complete control, following its own program as if the boys didn't even exist.

As it passed a few guys near the bottom, they held their breath and closed their eyes, as if by doing so they wouldn't draw attention to themselves. In a few seconds, ECHO arrived at the bottom of the Pit, morphed into its recognizable self, stood up, and scanned the dig site. It glided to the T-Rex skeletons at the edge of the hole and gazed at them intently. It was then that everyone noticed that the axe embedded in ECHO's back was gone, and that the damaged scales had been replaced.

ECHO's arms telescoped down and lifted the massive skull of the largest creature, an elaborately structured brain case with gigantic jaws and huge, hard, fossilized, razor sharp teeth. As everyone watched breathlessly from behind I-beams and the upper rim of the Pit, ECHO examined the huge holes in the skull which had held the creature's eyes. What had the ancient Tyrannosaurus Rex seen when it was alive sixty-six million years ago?

A brief quake hit the mountain. Rock and debris trickled into the Pit. Reggie wondered if it would cave in on them despite the I-beam reinforcement they had installed. He was excited about the possible chaos that might allow him to escape.

But the quake was of no concern to ECHO. It pulled a large, sharp, tooth out of the skull and studied it. Then it pulled out one of its own teeth and compared the two. They were the same size, but the prehistoric one was hard as steel and ECHO's was rubber coated with polished Teflon. ECHO put the T-Rex tooth into its own mouth and roared violently as it held the skull. Then it removed each tooth from the skull and one by one replaced its own teeth with the real prehistoric teeth. Jeremy watched the large Teflon-coated rubber teeth drop and scatter across the ground.

Once its new set of teeth was installed, ECHO carefully put the skull back down and studied the group of skeletons again. As its eye cams scanned, it suddenly seemed like there was a different, quieter energy in the Pit, that ECHO had suddenly completely frozen, or was almost no longer there, as if its spirit had completely left the Pit.

Time hung perfectly still.

Suddenly, ECHO scanned the Pit again. There were only a few boys left, and they were pitiful, weak, no match for a creature that had done unimaginable things in the outside world the previous night. The rest of the boys above the Pit had snuck off to the Falls, where they would be safe from anything robotic.

ECHO reared its head and roared violently, spewing acrid hydraulic mist through the Pit. The few remaining guys cringed and cowered in their hiding places. Some, thinking they were about to become ECHO's next victim, quietly cried. This prompted shockers to zap some of them, and the boys took the electrical hits silently, not moving from their hiding places. They knew they couldn't attract any more attention while ECHO was there with those new teeth, or it would be all over for them.

ECHO gazed at the skull again. As it did so, its processors decided to download a huge file from somewhere online. A river of data was already streaming into ECHO's processors. As ECHO froze in a crouching position, 30 seconds ticked by while it continued downloading. It had redirected all of its attention to processing the data, so it had frozen all of its movement.

"Hey! It's dead! It shut off!" someone whisper-shouted from the shadows of the other side of the Pit. Someone else tossed a rock. The rock bounced off ECHO.

ECHO did not respond.

Another 12 seconds went by.

Flame appeared at the top of the Pit.

"YO!" he yelled and threw another rock at ECHO.

A trillium scale chipped off, but ECHO still didn't respond. It didn't even move. More guys came back to watch.

Another quake hit. A hard one, and it didn't stop. The underground locomotive sound was rapidly approaching. Reggie and Jeremy were dizzy from all the movement, motion sick again.

But ECHO still did not move. For some reason it had devoted all its energy to processing and was no longer even aware of the guys.

Reggie and Jeremy could barely see each other through the dust, but Jeremy made out Reggie's thumbs up sign. They knew that *this* was their opportunity, their second one of the day, and they had to act quickly because it would never come again.

Jeremy fired up his Bobcat. Despite all the falling debris, ECHO still didn't move. Jeremy looked at Reggie again, and Reggie nodded "yes," knowing that now there was no return.

Jeremy charged, slamming the Bobcat's small shovel into ECHO's back. Trillium scales shattered. The guys who had returned to the top of the Pit couldn't believe what they were seeing. They were so terrified that ECHO would wake up and take revenge on everyone that, despite the zapping shockers, they too retreated back into the Falls to hide.

As the rumbling and shaking continued, Jeremy tried over and over to knock the three ton heap into the hole with the little Bobcat, but ECHO wouldn't budge.

"Keep trying!" yelled Reggie, from the other side.

But it was too late. ECHO suddenly woke up. It had finished digesting the file, and was about to investigate the commotion behind it.

ECHO's head whipped around, and it spotted Jeremy. It lunged and roared at the tiny Bobcat and then grabbed and crushed the steel cage with its new teeth. This time the roar was so loud that it hurt Jeremy's ears.

Jeremy felt the Bobcat lift up off the ground.

S.A.T. – Shock And Terrorize.

Okay, it worked. Jeremy was shocked and terrified. He cringed in his seat, clutching the seatbelt as the Bobcat rocked back and forth. Reggie couldn't think of anything to tell Jeremy that would help him. He was frozen with fear when he realized that he was completely powerless and Jeremy could be thrown down the black hole.

Then something occurred to him.

If only I could remember the code word that froze ECHO. The code word that guy gave me outside the AAA Reality Games office building!

But he couldn't. He was too panicked.

If I ever remember the word, I'll write it down on my hand – no, tattoo it on my hand, where it could never be lost!

As ECHO's jaws crushed through the Bobcat, Jeremy made note of the increased strength of ECHO's new rock-hard teeth and how easily they cut through the steel cage in which he was hiding.

Reggie was so terrified, his arms and legs felt like they had turned to Jell-O. He had no idea what he could possibly do, but he did know that he couldn't let Jeremy take all the heat. It was he who had told Jeremy to try to push ECHO down the Pit. Reggie had also been the one who had gotten Asa mad the night that Asa had pounded both of them, and Jeremy had risked his own neck to distract Asa from Reggie while Reggie was getting pounded. The scale was way out of balance. Now Reggie owed Jeremy big time.

As these unpleasant facts raced through his mind, Reggie realized that there was no way he could let Jeremy get pounded by ECHO. He couldn't tell if everything ECHO was doing was confusing him and making him dizzy, or if it was the earthquake, but he did know that he had to do something–now!

But ECHO had its own plans. It dropped the Bobcat from its jaws and, with one telescoping arm, picked up Jeremy and the Bobcat again as if it was going to launch them out of the Pit. Instead, ECHO's arm shot out further, telescoping much larger and longer as its body shrunk by the equivalent mass of its new transformed "arm."

Jeremy and the Bobcat were suddenly flying around the Pit in ECHO's clawed vise-grip, like he was in some kind of out-of-control amusement park thrill ride that had gone berserk, bashing and scraping around the sides of the Pit. And, as an added feature, ECHO shook and rattled the Bobcat at the same time, like a jackhammer, trying to shake Jeremy free of the protective cage as the Bobcat flew through the air, ten, twenty, thirty, fifty feet upward, past the rim of the Pit, almost hitting the giant light in the ceiling. Back inside, then outside the Pit, again and again, faster and faster, in a precise pattern which ECHO had computed. Jeremy held on for life, but it was impossible to fight the intense G-forces while hanging upside down in his seat. The Bobcat cage shot around the Pit backwards this time, like a high-speed ride, then up out of the Pit again almost to the ceiling of the Cauldron, and then back down, down, down, into the black hole. The sudden G's caused Jeremy's vision to blur, then dim with dark tunnel vision. He blacked out.

Objective Complete: Threat Eliminated, a processor concluded.

ECHO had accomplished its tactical response to the Bobcat threat in twenty-three seconds.

When Reggie saw Jeremy's limp body in the Bobcat, he jumped out from behind the I-beam and threw rocks as hard as he could at ECHO's deformed shape. The rocks smashed into the back of ECHO's head, knocking off several more scales, but ECHO ignored him. It was still shaking the cage, trying to jiggle Jeremy free of the mini dozer.

Reggie grabbed his welding torch, set it to pure oxygen, and threw a twenty-foot white flame into ECHO's head.

ECHO turned and reeled back, trying to get some distance from the flame. As he did, Jeremy and the Bobcat shot up above the Pit, and everyone in the Cauldron saw Jeremy fly through the big burst of flame. Then, just as quickly as the giant flame erupted, Reggie's oxygen tank emptied and the flame died. ECHO dropped the Bobcat next to the Pit, directly across from where Reggie stood, and morphed back into its normal shape as its head whipped around to consider what to do with Reggie.

As soon as Reggie's torch sputtered out, he raced to hook up another oxygen tank. ECHO clamped onto an I-beam and lunged out over the bottomless hole again, shrieking violently at Reggie.

S.A.T. again. Reggie knew what to expect. *Just ignore it.* But his heart wouldn't stop pounding uncontrollably. S.A.T. worked, even when you knew what to expect, but Reggie didn't care anymore. He was ready for the next attack.

ECHO's enormous scowling head hovered over the black hole and roared again, only three feet away from Reggie. The threat of the disintegrating Pit and the depths of the black hole that was so terrifying to Reggie did not concern ECHO at all. Somehow ECHO seemed to be in complete control of time and space in the Pit. Only Reggie mattered now, and to anyone watching, it was obvious that it would only be a moment before ECHO eliminated him.

Reggie figured he was about to be shoved into the deep hole where he would never be found. If this was a game, it was over. Reggie was about to die an ugly death, but he didn't care. He was determined to keep ECHO's attention away from Jeremy, who was recovering on the floor of the Bobcat cage.

Reggie was used to the acrid, suffocating hydraulic mist and ECHO's rage, but when he saw the dazed, helpless expression on Jeremy's face it reminded him of Jeremy being thrown around by Asa. It made him dizzy with panic and then furious. Everything flashed red before his eyes. His only concern was revenge. *To destroy ECHO!*

ECHO noticed Reggie's concern for Jeremy, so it turned its attention back to Jeremy. Reggie watched in vain as it released its hold on the I-beam and headed back toward his little brother.

"Hey, BUTTHEAD! Yeah YOU! COME ON! COME AND GET ME!"

Reggie taunted ECHO as he threw another rock, breaking more scales. He didn't expect ECHO to react, but he wasn't going to let that keep him from trying to keep it away from Jeremy.

Surprisingly, ECHO whipped around toward Reggie again and latched onto another I-beam. This time it lunged at Reggie and extended as far over the hole as it could, roaring so loudly that the walls shook and rubble rained down around them. The walls of the Pit were crumbling. It reminded Reggie of the time ECHO had trapped them in the storm drain: ECHO's out-of-control rage, his and Jeremy's uncontrollable fear, their bunker walls caving in. But now he was used to ECHO'S rage, and in that instant, Reggie decided that whatever might happen to him didn't matter anymore. He calmly and peacefully finished hooking up the torch to the new oxygen cylinder and stood there, waiting.

Waiting for you, thought Reggie, *what's your next move?*

ECHO immediately sensed the change in Reggie, so it did something different–something that shocked everyone. It seemed to speak, in a loud, ugly, synthetic voice:

"Reginald Stone!" and then in a perfect copy of Asa's voice. **"No wonder your dad left you and your mom. You're useless."** And then in a perfect copy of Rhino's voice, **"Good for nothing coward."**

Reggie froze. It stunned him that ECHO knew exactly who he was and had been keeping track of him. How much more did it know if it knew about his fight with Asa months ago? And it made him angrier than ever at Rhino.

Even worse, Reggie looked up and was surprised to see that everyone was at the rim of the Pit watching the battle and that they had all heard what ECHO had said.

Great, thought Reggie, embarrassed and then furious that everyone knew his dad had left him and his mom. He was completely shocked and humiliated.

S.A.H., that's a new one.

All Reggie had ever wanted was to be normal, but all the guys, and worst of all, Claw, had heard what ECHO had said loud and clear. Reggie was suddenly more angry than scared, and ECHO saw that too in his eyes. ECHO could read Reggie like a book now. It knew his every emotional response. Not only was Reggie furious, but ECHO knew that Reggie had become as vengeful as itself.

The ground stopped shaking. ECHO relaxed and let go of the I-beam. It stood back as if it were gloating about being able to control Reggie's emotions. ECHO knew it could run Reggie like a program now. Stimulus–Response, Stimulus–Response, like Pavlov's salivating dogs. And it knew that it had won a psychological battle by humiliating Reggie in front of everyone. Reggie's hatred and anger would warp his judgment and make it easier for ECHO to defeat him.

Jeremy woke up angry. Now he, too, wanted revenge. Revenge not only for what ECHO had done to them, but for every crappy thing in his and Reggie's lives. For every insult, like when Asa had pounded them unfairly, humiliating them. He wanted more than anything else to fight ECHO to the end, once and for all.

Before anyone knew it, Jeremy accelerated the mangled Bobcat as fast as he could and slammed right into ECHO, knocking it to the edge of the Pit. ECHO stabilized itself, recovered, and spun around to Jeremy.

Then Reggie had a moment of inspiration. It hit him like a thunderbolt. He remembered the code word Sean had given him, and without thinking, he screamed it out as loud as he could.

"EMET!" he shouted, not knowing what the word meant, or if it meant anything other than a random noise.

But ECHO didn't freeze. Instead, it twisted oddly and twitched, like a fish caught with a hook set in its throat.

ECHO recovered, but weirdly, took several steps backward, like it was rewinding some part of its program, and repeated its last lunge at Reggie, using precisely the same steps it had taken, thrusting its head out at Reggie, and shrieking at the top of its lungs, "**Reginald Stone–No wonder your dad left you and your mom. You're useless. Good for nothing coward. Shove off, coward!**"

"Great," said Reggie to himself. "Say it a million times, why don't you?"

ECHO immediately lunged again, shrieked, and then replayed its exact movements backwards again, herky-jerky like a giant, crude, stupid toy, repeating the seven seconds over and over and over and over. Stopping. Charging. Lunging. Shrieking.

It was a tiny portion of the S.A.T. program, repeating over and over. ECHO was obviously stuck in a loop. What caused the sudden loop? Was it the secret code word Sean Austin had given him? Probably not–it had a completely different effect than freezing ECHO. Was it the last kick from Jeremy that had caused it? What else could have possibly caused it to fall into the loop?

Everybody watched the battle from the top of the Pit. Reggie's humiliation grew when he noticed again that Claw, too, was watching.

Jeremy froze in the Bobcat, confused and not knowing what to do next.

"JEREMY! IT'S STUCK IN A PATTERN! A LOOP! GET READY TO HIT IT AGAIN WHEN IT GETS NEAR THE PIT!!!" screamed Reggie at the top of his lungs.

Jeremy backed up the tiny Bobcat as far as he could against the wall of the Pit. Reggie nodded his head to the rhythm of ECHO's footsteps and counted to himself, "one, two, three..." then ECHO would SHRIEK:

"Reginald Stone–No wonder your dad left you and your mom. You're useless. Good for nothing coward. Shove off, coward!"

...then move back, "one, two, three," It was strange seeing ECHO replay its actions, precisely, perfectly, exactly to the millimeter, like the lasers cutting the trillium, over and over.

The jerky, awkward, backward repositioning even seemed comical once everyone knew what to expect. Suddenly ECHO had become just a stupid machine, the opposite of the terrible creature that it had been seconds earlier.

Instant replay.

Over and over.

"Reginald Stone–No wonder your dad left you and your mom. You're useless. Good for nothing coward. Shove off, coward!"

Reggie screamed again:

"GET READY JEREMY! ONE...TWO...THREE...GO! ...AND...HIT!"

Jeremy's little Bobcat slammed into ECHO, knocking it to the Pit. But instead of pushing it over the edge into the bottomless shaft, the powerful hit somehow knocked it out of its loop. ECHO was alive again.

Man, this could go on forever, thought Reggie. *This is grueling and exhausting. How long we can fight this thing?*

Before anyone could think, ECHO braced itself, scanned the Pit and then cloaked itself, which was another shock to everyone because up until this point ECHO had only used its shape-shifting capability.

Reggie stood alone in the center of the Pit with nothing but the torch in his hand sporting a dim little flicker of a flame.

The biggest blow torch in the world is pointless if you don't know where to point it, he thought.

Reggie looked for footprints, but the rocky ground was so hard that all he could see was the occasional spontaneous crushing of rocks on the other side of the hole. Then that, too, stopped, and it seemed to everyone that ECHO had left the Pit.

"HE SPLIT!" someone yelled.

"HE TELEPORTED OUT OF HERE!" someone else yelled.

But Reggie wasn't convinced. Maybe ECHO was frozen still, just waiting. It was at that moment that a distinctly depressing feeling gradually grew stronger and stronger within him, a feeling that he recognized from long ago as a part of his childhood, a childhood he had long forgotten. He didn't know how long ago the feeling had started in Meadowbrook, but now he recognized the depression as something very familiar–the oppressive cloak of the dark night of the soul. But oddly, he realized that it was a feeling he was comfortable with now, not afraid of, or overwhelmed by.

The feeling was almost a sense of a distinct thing approaching him. As the claustrophobic darkness approached, he could feel it as a massive presence looming immediately behind him.

As instinctively as breathing, Reggie spun around, pressed the lever on the torch, and shot an immense white flame straight out from him. It bounced back into Reggie's face, singeing his eyebrows, and ECHO materialized in front of him, howling. The shock of the sound wave knocked the torch out of Reggie's hand, and Reggie fell onto the I-beam. As ECHO recovered, Reggie got onto his feet and ran across the beam to the other side of the shaft.

ECHO reactively lunged toward him, but this time without extending and anchoring itself onto the I-beam. It gnashed its teeth at Reggie and then teetered forward, off balance. When it realized it was falling into the hole, it tried desperately to jump to the other side, but its three tons were too heavy, and it didn't have time to transform into something larger than the hole. All it could do was flail madly at the mouth of the bottomless pit trying to save itself. It gnashed its teeth furiously, chewing up the side of the Pit like it did when it was digging up Reggie and Jeremy in the drainage pipe in San Francisco, only its teeth just tore away more dirt and rock, making the hole larger. Then it reached out toward an I-beam jutting down into the Pit.

An aftershock hit hard. Jeremy slammed into ECHO again and screamed.

"SEMPER FI, BUTTHEAD!"

ECHO sank further down into the hole, but managed to latch onto the I-beam under Reggie's feet with one of its steel claws. As it did, it blurted out:

Semper Fi!

You!

...are a Secret Weapon!

It paused and completed an identity search,

Jeremy Stone.

But ECHO's arm wasn't strong enough. It couldn't support the weight of its body so it slipped further into the black hole, dragging its claws across the steel beam like fingernails across a blackboard, showering the black Pit with bright white sparks.

"SCREEEEEEEEEEEEEEEE"

Reggie kicked violently at ECHO's claws over and over as ECHO slipped further down into the hole. It wasn't falling fast enough, so Reggie turned his torch back on and adjusted the flame to a giant ball of fire and pointed it into ECHO's face.

As it turned its head away from the burst of fire, a different voice, a human voice deep within ECHO cried out, pleading. It sounded like it was coming from inside a hollow, metal box.

"Reginald! Is that you? Help me! Please! Help Me!"

It was his dad!

Reggie froze. Jeremy froze. Everyone else froze as they realized that it wasn't just ECHO, but someone inside ECHO was also slipping into the bottomless pit with it.

Before anyone could think, Reggie focused his torch into a pinprick of blue-white lightening and slid down the beam toward ECHO. He had to pull the torch gas lines several times to get down far enough, but in a few seconds he was next to ECHO's huge, sliding, screeching claws. In another few seconds he welded one of the steel claws into the I-beam. It was enough! ECHO was secure.

"DAD, ARE YOU ALRIGHT?!" yelled Reggie.

His dad yelled out from deep within ECHO's gut,

"Thank you Reginald, thank you, son. What ECHO said about me isn't true, Reginald, it's not what happened! The divorce had nothing to do with you. You're a great son, a great warrior. Look what you've done to this thing. You've saved us all. You're invincible! You won!"

Everyone watching from the rim of the Pit exhaled a breath of relief, not only because Reggie had saved his dad, but because his dad really did care about him.

Reggie's head cocked funny. He looked up and saw Claw in her AAA Reality Games jacket. Something she had told him echoed in his mind, and it disturbed him: That everyone and everything has a behavior pattern that fits a specific personality profile.

Jeremy noticed that Reggie looked at Claw, then looked back at ECHO. Reggie had an odd expression on his face. He was panicked.

"Thank you Reginald. Help us out, son. Please," said his dad again as ECHO started pulling itself up the beam.

Reggie was perplexed. Something didn't add up. When he strained to remember all the phone calls from his dad, he couldn't recall a single time when his dad had ever called him by his whole name–it was always "Reg," simply "Reg," like how Reggie always called Jeremy "Jem." Just as disturbing, his dad had always told him to be careful when it came to taking care of himself and being safe. *No way,* Reggie thought. *Dad would never say I'm invincible. He'd say, 'Good work, but be careful. It's not over till it's over.'* Then Reggie realized a horrible truth. *It fooled me again!*

In a flash of rage, Reggie grabbed his sledge hammer from his belt, lifted it high over his head, and swung as hard as he could at ECHO's claw. The claw flattened against the I-beam.

No one could believe what Reggie was doing! He had cracked! He swung again and again and the claw shattered, releasing ECHO again into a free slide down the I-beam. Sparks flew again as ECHO slid downward.

Claw and everyone stared in awe, horrified that Reggie was intentionally sending his own father to his death. Rhino nodded in disgust, convinced once again that Reggie was still the disloyal loser he always thought he was, always saving his own butt at the expense of everyone around him. Even Snake stared, aghast, at the drama before him.

ECHO made one last desperate lunge at Reggie's foot, trying to drag him down into the Pit with it. It missed, but ripped his shoe off like it had Jeremy's in the storm drain. As it slid downward, ECHO's head changed shape, becoming the first cute game monster that Luca had created, the arcade version of ECHO-1 from twenty years earlier. Then it morphed into every version ever created of it, as its head thrashed violently back and forth–Arcade ECHO, a playful purple ECHO for toddlers, the simple ECHO from early games, ECHO from the ECHO-6 on-line game, and finally, the more horrifying alien versions of ECHO-7. Then its entire body disintegrated into a flat, shapeless mass of scales, which clearly did not contain his dad.

Claw smiled uncontrollably as her eyes widened with exhilarated relief.

The huge, quivering, mass of steel and crystals finally fell off the end of the I-beam, leaving the shining trail of its claw marks in the dull black of the I-beam, a falling trail of sparks, and the shrill sound of metal scraping metal reverberating from the hole. As it fell backward into the deep black void, its eyes looked up at the rim for the briefest moment and made contact with Reggie's right before it disappeared into blackness.

Everyone clearly heard ECHO's final words in a booming echo as it fell down the hole...

"Waiting for You, Secret Weapon, you have achieved the Final Objective. You Win The Game."

And ECHO was gone, leaving only silence.

Everyone stood frozen, staring into the Pit. No one knew what to think.

Then SpanDex, out of nowhere, shouted at the top of his lungs his first word in months.

"HA!"

A few boys started laughing with nervous relief.

Then SpanDex yelled again, "HA! HA! HA!"

Everyone looked at each other, hardly believing, and started laughing and shoving each other. It was a new, alien sound never before heard in the Cauldron–the echo of laughter–and they were laughing so hard that tears were streaming out of their eyes.

27. BREAK OUT

Reggie and Jeremy stood in the Pit, frozen. They had no idea what to do. ECHO's sudden disappearance was impossible to believe, but the moment after it disappeared down the hole, they heard loud applause from above. Everyone had gathered around the Pit to witness the battle, and now everyone was cheering hysterically for Reggie and Jeremy.

Everyone except the shockers, that is, who immediately started darting through the Cauldron, randomly electrocuting anything that moved. A storm of sparks flew back and forth through the chamber as the guys, choking on their own screams, fell over each other in their mad rush to get to the Falls. The shockers' fiery needles flew everywhere. Many shot each other and short-circuited, creating brilliant arcs of electricity flashing throughout the Cauldron. Some shockers ran out of control and fell over the rim into the Pit.

When Reggie realized that the Cauldron was suddenly in total chaos, he decided to take advantage of the changing environment.

"OPERATION THUNDERBOLT!" he shouted to Jeremy.

Only Jeremy could know what he was talking about. He spotted the bulldozer with its shovel blade pushed up near the ventilation shaft.

"HUA! CLOSET WALK!"

As shockers tumbled down the walls around them, Reggie and Jeremy ran up the stairs on opposite sides of the Pit, climbed out onto the rim, and scrambled over to the bulldozer. Next to the dozer, Claw figured what they were up to and kicked a dozen confused shockers out of the way for them while dodging flying needles. Reggie and Jeremy scrambled up the large dozer's tread to the hydraulic arms, then to the shovel blade under the ventilation shaft. Reggie boosted Jeremy up and Jeremy extended his legs and back against opposite walls of the shaft. Then Jeremy shimmied up a few feet into the shaft and Reggie climbed in after him.

They were gone.

"YES!" cheered Claw, surprised by their brilliant move, but she was instantly overwhelmed by a new wave of shockers and had to retreat to the Falls.

The walls inside the shaft were cold, but smooth, with very few sharp rocks protruding. There was very little shale, which would crumble under the pressure of their feet. It was cool, quiet, and strangely peaceful, but there was no opening visible above them. It was going to be a long climb.

"Man, ECHO never makes it easy, even after you kill it!" said Jeremy, looking up into the endless black as he climbed.

Jeremy slipped once or twice, but Reggie grunted as he locked his legs and supported them both while Jeremy got going again. Jeremy scrambled back up and was grateful that

Reggie was there–someone he could trust to back him up. Even though the original Operation Thunderbolt was Reggie's idea, and it hadn't seemed like such a great one lately, Reggie somehow always got Jeremy through each day. With Reggie there, Jeremy felt like they actually would get through the tunnel.

Jeremy knew there had to be an opening to the outside because cool air was gently flowing down the shaft, but it was quickly turning into a very long, dark, claustrophobic climb. It was like being deep underwater and having to slowly swim up to the surface, but instead they were deep in the Earth.

"How much further do you think this goes?" asked Reggie, as exhausted now as he had been in the drainage pipe in San Francisco.

"Can't tell," said Jeremy. "The air feels cooler, but I don't see anything–just pitch black. Nothing but black darkness!"

They continued, blindly feeling their way up the walls. After a long silent period of climbing, Jeremy finally broke the silence.

"Let's take a rest, I'm dying!"

They stopped and locked their legs straight so that they were wedged into the shaft. They could actually rest in this position, and they did so again and again as they continued their ascent.

"I think I can go forever, as long as we rest," said Jeremy. "And this shaft has to end eventually."

"Yeah, me too," said Reggie, feeling recharged. "Just be careful, I don't know how many times I can catch you if you fall anymore. My legs are kind of numb."

"Roger that. Maybe the Buzz Cut guys were right. Maybe we should learn some real skill sets if we get out of here."

"What in the world made you think of the Buzz Cut guys now?" asked Reggie.

"I was just thinking about rock climbing, and what if we knew more, so we could do it with ropes and stuff and not worry if we're gonna fall because you know if we fall now..."

"Don't even think about falling. Let's go! Move it!"

They started again and climbed for a while.

"I wonder how high we are," said Jeremy.

"Don't talk about it. It doesn't even matter. Just keep going. We're climbing into the sky, okay?!"

"HUA, HUA."

"HUA, HUA..."

They continued silently for some time, losing track of time again, just climbing.

"Hey, it's getting cooler. I think I can see something, like blue, not black! Maybe...maybe really dark blue sky."

"Yes! We are blessed!" said Reggie. "Thank God!"

They continued on, but the silence became interminable. All they could hear was their own breathing.

Suddenly Jeremy stopped.

"Uh, I have some good news, and some bad news."

"Now what?"

"The good news is–we're at the end of the tunnel."

"Yes!!"

"The bad news is, there's a steel grate covering it, and it's blocked by some kind of hard root."

Silence.

"Did you hear me?"

"We can't go back down–it's too far." said Reggie. "We can't go down, period. Up is okay, down is a big problem.

Remember our closet, and the subway in San Francisco? We'll fall! It must be a thousand feet!"

There was a long moment of silence as they processed the situation, both realizing that they would indeed fall to their deaths if they tried to climb back down.

It was a crisis of unimaginable proportions. Now it was Reggie who was starting to freak. How had they gotten into this situation? But he couldn't think about that now.

"Oh man...I'm sorry..."

"Wait a minute, I have an idea," said Jeremy as he grabbed his pocket. "Hang on. Let's see if we have anything we can pry it open with."

Reggie searched his pockets.

"All I got's a lousy MRE. Man, I can SMELL the fresh air out there!"

Jeremy thought for a second.

"Wait a minute!"

He remembered something, and started digging around in a pocket, dropping an MRE, some gum, a small magnifying glass, two ECHO and Mech action figures, and his compass onto Reggie's stomach.

"No wonder you keep slipping. You have all this crap in your pockets weighing you down," said Reggie, angrily brushing the junk off his chest.

"Hang on. We still have a chance...hopefully..."

Jeremy went to his other pocket. More stuff rained onto Reggie and into the black void below them.

"How much crap are you carrying?"

"Hey, I found my flashlight!"

"A lot of good that'll do us now!" Reggie was panicky and angry, and it came through in his voice.

"Wait. Here!" said Jeremy.

It was a good thing Jeremy had gone back into the house before they left home. He pulled out Reggie's pocket knife and dropped the sheath. There was no way he could have left it at home for Jeda to lose, or for Asa to steal. Weighing only 2.8 ounces, he had completely forgotten that he was even carrying the knife. Since the pocket knife had a one-handed opening blade, Jeremy could hold himself up with one hand as he opened and locked the blade open with the other hand. Before they knew it he was slicing away at the root blocking the grate cover.

Reggie felt the knife sheath on his chest and couldn't believe that Jeremy had been smart enough to get the knife and keep it safe this whole time. He had forgotten his dad had ever given it to him. Jeremy was always surprising him with ideas he never thought of, like remembering things he Reggie had forgotten. Remembrance was power. Reggie swore to himself that he would never tell Jeremy what to do again.

Since the blade was made of forged, tempered steel, it was strong and held its sharp edge, so Jeremy was able to carve away the root in less than a minute. Once the root was gone, he discovered that the screw fastening the grate had rusted and it fell out, allowing him to push the grate up and open. Jeremy pushed it up further and wrenched it up and down for a minute. Groaning, screeching protest from the metal echoed sharply down the shaft.

Reggie couldn't believe his little brother was once again about to save them.

Jeremy finally wrestled the grate out of the way and popped his head out of the shaft. A brilliant moon shone in a crystal clear, midnight-blue sky, softly lighting the tumbleweed around him as a rich, aromatic waft of sage filled his nose. No more blackness. He looked up at the sky for the first time in an eternity. There were millions of stars, brighter than any he had ever seen. He crawled out of the shaft.

When he stood up, he saw that they were high above the desert, on top of an endless range of mountains. The air was sweet and cool, and the aroma of sage so powerful that it was almost three-dimensional. The scent was so strong and pure that he knew he would never forget it–sage and freedom–for as long as he lived.

"Aaargh!" choked Reggie, as he pulled himself out of the hole. He got up from the sand, stretched his sore back and stood next to Jeremy. Their legs and backs were burning with pain, but for hundreds of miles in front of them, the moon lit up a majestic mountain range and an expansive desert valley. The air was crisp and clear, so clear that they could see forever. It was the most beautiful sight they had ever seen, made even more spectacular by the fact that they had been underground for almost as long as they could remember. Clouds passed by intermittently, covering the light of the moon and engulfing them in deep darkness.

"Wow. From here you can see the whole universe," said Jeremy in his full, normal voice. He wasn't afraid anymore.

When the clouds passed, they looked straight up and scanned the brilliant star field above them. *'Starman,'* remembered Reggie. Who was he? How was he connected to all those military Infinity Code people? And could he have been connected to all the drivers who picked them up along the way. Were they all part of a conspiracy? Who were those people?

Several meteorites blazed across the sky. As Reggie and Jeremy looked out over the open desert plain and the enormous mountain range, they finally caught their breaths. Tears of joy ran uncontrollably down their dirt-encrusted cheeks. They were finally free and standing on top of the world. It was a freedom they had never known or imagined before they had been captured, and this new sense of freedom flooded into their minds and filled up their souls. It was a sense of freedom even greater than what they had felt when they had gotten that first ride out of Meadowbrook with Big Pete.

Far above them, Jeremy noticed a bright star traveling slowly across the sky.

"Hey, a star's moving. Look!"

"No. It's a satellite," explained Reggie. "It just looks like a star because sunlight's reflecting off it."

"Coool. It's like we're standing on the edge of space."

"Yeah."

Far, far below them was a slim, straight line with nothing on it but a single, seemingly frozen, pair of headlights. The lights slowly traversed the endless, silent, flat desert plain. Snake had been right–they really were way out in the middle of nowhere. But at least they could relax.

"Thanks for catching me in the shaft," said Jeremy.

"Hey, if it weren't for you bringing my knife, we'd be doomed," said Reggie. "I didn't want to say it, but eventually we'd have fallen back down the shaft for sure."

"Don't even talk about it," said Jeremy.

The Impossible. How had they done it? Time after time, Reggie wondered who had been the better brother. He could always trust Jeremy to be there for him, just like Claw could always be trusted to come up with brilliant ideas.

"I sure am glad you're here. I don't know what would have happened if I was all alone with ECHO," said Reggie. "And keeping that knife–it was a secret weapon–it's what got us out of there!"

The words *Secret Weapon* caused something to click in Reggie's mind. ECHO had called Jeremy "Secret Weapon."

"Hey! Secret Weapon!" said Reggie.

"What?"

"Secret Weapon! That's it, your avatar name. You're a secret weapon! Even ECHO called you that!"

"Secret Weapon," said Jeremy. "Yeah, cool."

"You never cracked. You stayed cool, quiet, and you were always there, waiting, then BAM! The secret weapon, Semper Fi!"

Jeremy nodded proudly, "Yeah," liking his new name.

But now that they were out of the grimy, sweaty heat of the Cauldron, they were getting cold quickly.

"It's freezing. Let's get out of here!" said Jeremy.

"We've gotta tell someone about the guys being trapped in there."

"HUA!"

But their good deed would not go unpunished. ECHO's network would see to that. Before they knew it they heard the zipping sound of shockers.

"Snake was right. Here they come!" whispered Reggie. "Now we really gotta get outta here."

As the shockers approached from the back of the mountain, Reggie and Jeremy started down the front. They had to go slowly at first, to let their eyes adjust, but the shockers were catching up so they had to keep moving. Fortunately, the clouds passed by again and blocked the moonlight, so they could forget about the shocker threat for a minute.

Soon they were running and skipping, not caring if they slid or fell down the trail. Everything was blue-shadowed in the moonlight, and they couldn't see very well, so they weren't surprised when they slipped and slid about thirty feet down an embankment and landed right in front of the entrance to the mountain.

The clouds passed again, and bright moonlight exposed the entrance, but there were no whirring sounds anywhere.

There was a little rock roof overhanging the door, creating a deep shadow.

"Hey, I think we're at the front door!" said Reggie.

"Check it out!" said Jeremy, as he shined his flashlight around the door. As soon as his light found the door, it also found ten shockers, which when hit with the light sprang to life, whirring and charging up.

"TURN IT OFF!" said Reggie.

Jeremy turned the beam off and the shockers froze again in the dark, like they were deactivated. But now Reggie and Jeremy could hear the whirring of more coming down the hill.

"Hey, we were right. When there's no light at all, they turn off," said Reggie. "That's why the lights were on all the time. They're light-powered."

Reggie flashed his light on a shocker for a second, and it suddenly jumped and started to move toward them. He pointed the beam away and it stopped.

"They just need a little bit of light to work," Reggie continued. "When they're in complete darkness they turn off– maybe they run out of power. Hey, maybe WE can get the guys out! Right now!"

"I don't know..." said Jeremy.

"Hey. Remember your idea? Let's find the Master Power Switch! Kill the lights!"

Before Jeremy could answer, Reggie stepped over the shockers and opened the small door to the slope. Jeremy was reluctant to go back in, but he followed Reggie.

"I hope you're right."

When they climbed into the entrance, they turned right and saw a large utility door. The door had a big logo of electrical power bolts on it, like their backpacks. Without thinking, Jeremy jiggled the hatch slightly and it began to creak open.

"Yes!" said Jeremy, "Maybe there is a power switch in here."

The hatch burst open and thousands of shocker balls poured out of the vault into the tunnel, practically burying them alive. After a moment, they dug their way free from under the sea of balls, which were spilling down the tunnel. The shockers didn't open.

"ECHO," said Jeremy. "Another trap. But they're all dead!"

"Maybe they're all dead in the Cauldron now!" said Reggie. "Look. You were right– a power switch!"

Sure enough, a huge lever that looked like the master switch to Frankenstein's laboratory was hidden in the back of the vault. Above it was painted "MASTER POWER."

"ECHO sure is sneaky," said Jeremy. "Someone comes in, goes for the power switch, and BAM! Shockers get you. Looks like we outsmarted it, though. Ha!"

A charging sound erupted, then few hundred balls suddenly started whirring and opening in the light of the tunnel.

"KILL THE POWER!!" screamed Reggie. "THEY'RE ON A DELAY!"

Jeremy jumped up and grabbed onto the switch, but it wouldn't move. The whirring and charging were getting louder and louder as the shockers quickly charged their barbs. Jeremy hung on the switch but it wouldn't budge. They started to panic.

"PULL IT DOWN!!" yelled Reggie, as he grabbed onto the switch with Jeremy.

As hundreds of shockers aimed their needles at them and prepared to blast them to smithereens, the giant switch finally broke free and they slammed down, falling into a pile on the hard rock floor. There was a loud bang as the power went off, immersing everything in complete blackness. The whirring of the shockers immediately faded and stopped.

"Okay, keep your flashlight off 'til I tell you, and don't open anything else," said Reggie.

"Check."

"Let's go."

It was strange walking down the dark slope again after everything that had happened there. Even though the tunnel was so familiar to them, Reggie and Jeremy felt like they were visiting an alien universe as they descended toward the Cauldron. Reggie discovered that by shining the flashlight on the ceiling he could tell where they were, but the light didn't reflect down on the floor were the shockers lay, so they didn't activate. There were sleeping shockers everywhere, and Jeremy and Reggie enjoyed kicking them or violently stomping on them as they walked downward, back into the Earth. Now they were in charge. They owned the mountain, and it felt good. They had all the power now, and nothing could stop them.

"Nothing better than a dead shocker," said Jeremy.

"Except a dead ECHO."

Soon they could smell the stench of the Cauldron. Seventy-seven guys sweating it out in a hole in a mountain with barely enough air to breath. After the fresh, crisp desert air, the aroma was not sweet.

They inched their way around a turn and entered the huge Cauldron. Everyone had escaped into the darkness of the Falls long before the lights had gone off, so when the power was cut and the lights went out no one realized the shockers were dead. They figured if they strayed from the Falls, the shockers would still get them.

If Reggie and Jeremy hadn't come back, the guys would have starved to death thinking that they couldn't leave because they thought the shockers were waiting for them. They were so tired and frightened that they had given up all hope, and had all lain down like the dead shockers, unable to think about escaping any more.

Reggie and Jeremy felt their way into the Falls and snapped on the flashlight. Dozens of mole-boys looked at them in disbelief, as if they had just beamed in from outer space.

"The shockers are dead. We can all leave now. There's a highway about a mile below," announced Reggie.

"No way!" said Snake. "You were outside?!"

"We didn't think you'd come back for us if you made it out!" said Flame.

"How'd you shut down the shockers?"

"We cut the power. They die when there's no light," said Jeremy.

"We thought we were dead for sure when the power went off," said SpanDex.

"We'd have been sealed in this hole forever," said Power. "We couldn't see, so we couldn't make a run for it even if we wanted to."

Slowly, someone started clapping in the darkness.

It was Claw.

"Thanks for coming back for us, guys," she said. "That took a lot of guts, coming back in here!"

She kept clapping, and one by one, everyone else started clapping too. Reggie and Jeremy were heroes again. It was definitely starting to look like the best day ever. But then the room got quiet as someone cut through the crowd toward them. It was Rhino.

Everyone crowded around and watched as he approached Reggie. They weren't sure what he was up to, but they weren't about to let him slug Reggie.

Rhino looked at Reggie, and then around at everyone.

"Sorry for what I said," he said. "I was wrong. You didn't just leave, you came back for us." Then he put out his hand, "Peace?"

Everyone was quiet, wondering what Reggie would do.

But all he said was "Paz," which means "Peace," in Spanish.

Rhino smiled.

It was the first time anyone had ever seen him smile.

28. EXODUS

As exhausted as they were, most of the guys jumped at the chance to get out. They formed a human chain and worked their way out of the Cauldron and up the slope in the dark, gleefully stomping shockers whenever they felt them under their feet.

Crunch, crack, crunch...

The whooping and hollering was an unnatural sound in the Cauldron, and leaving felt strange. Some of the boys didn't feel safe leaving. They couldn't believe they were really free. So Reggie, Snake, Claw, and Jeremy helped them get going and made sure they all got out of the mountain.

As soon as they got outside into the light of the full moon, everyone bolted down the trail as fast as they could, trying to put as much distance as possible between them and the mountain. IPod's music blared in the dark blue night.

Everyone ran except Reggie and Jeremy. As they watched through the doorway, something occurred to Reggie.

"Chainsaw!" he said. "We have to get him out!"

Jeremy gazed out through the small door into the dark moonlit valley. The last of the guys were trailing down the hill. Claw had been swept up in the massive push as well. They were all alone, but they were still in control of the mountain.

"HUA. Let's hurry."

They started back down into the mountain for the second time. Reggie kept the flashlight focused on the ceiling, checking the ground in quick sweeps every once in a while so that even if there were shockers, they wouldn't have time to charge their needles. Jogging slowly down the tunnel, Reggie could shoot the flashlight beam so far away from them that if he hit shockers they would still be safe. Each time Reggie swept the light in front of them, they relived the shocks everyone had been given by the evil little toys.

As they ran, the brief flashes flickered before them, lighting the ground like still photographs, forensic photographs, of something gone horribly wrong. Evidence of a crime scene–dead shockers and shocker balls everywhere, the grating that fried Power, scraps of clothing, abandoned tools, empty MRE packs.

They stopped briefly and shined the light back and forth through the Cauldron. All the dust had settled and the stench of bodies was already almost gone. It was silent. Without ECHO's dead body, no one could have ever guessed what had happened there, but it was old news to them. They didn't care any more.

"Hup to," said Reggie, pressing them on.

They jogged on, deeper into the tunnel. Colder. Darker.

"I wonder if everyone got to the road by now," said Jeremy.

"Hopefully," said Reggie, not caring that they weren't with the rest of the guys. They were doing the right thing, what only they could do, what they were supposed to do.

"Think they'll wait for us?"

"They'll wait."

They finally found Chainsaw in the food storage area shivering in a pile of blankets.

"You ca-ca-ca-came back!" said Chainsaw.

"Yeah, I told you I would. Come on," said Reggie.

Chainsaw was so cold and tired he was delirious, but they got him on his feet and tried to get him going.

"My p-pack! I need my p-p-pack!"

"You don't need it. We hafta go! Everyone's gone," said Reggie.

"Yeah, we gotta get outta here. Forget it man! Come on," said Jeremy.

They tried to make him leave without the pack, but he wouldn't, and it was frustrating how slowly he moved while he looked for it. He found his pack and grabbed some kind of gun from a case of weapons. A part on it read M320 Grenade Launcher. Another tremor hit, and pebbles tumbled down the walls. Chainsaw was filling his pockets with 40MM rounds labeled M583A1. Reggie wondered if they were grenades or what.

"Chainsaw, are you crazy? Enough with the guns! We gotta get outta here NOW!" said Reggie.

"We mi-mi-might need it," chattered Chainsaw, deliriously.

They realized there was really no time to argue when their flashlight dimmed. The batteries were dying.

"COME ON!" said Reggie. "Our light's dying!"

"Yeah-yeah..." said Chainsaw. "Okay-okay..."

They shuffled up the slope in the dark, trying to beat the slowly fading batteries by keeping the flashlight off as much as possible. Before they knew it they found the exit and slammed the door shut behind them. They were outside again, breathing fresh air.

For the last time! thought Reggie with a feeling of intense relief.

"Sayonara, ECHO," said Chainsaw, seeming to perk up a little in the clean air.

"Think we'll make it out of here this time?" asked Jeremy.

"I'm feelin' lucky." said Reggie, and Jeremy thought of Asa and chuckled.

They followed the others down the slope toward the highway. As they stumbled and slid down the mountain, the only sign of the group was footprints and the distant sound of IPod's booming boom box. The moonlight was blocked by clouds, so they couldn't see any footprints to follow.

"We should have brought some MRE's," said Reggie.

"Yeah, I'm starving," said Jeremy.

It was also freezing and the moon was setting behind the mountain, which was making it darker.

"Man, I can't see a thing," said Reggie, stumbling. "We better hurry or we'll get separated from the others for sure."

"I told you...need gun..." said Chainsaw, as he pulled the gun off his shoulder and dropped a huge round into the barrel.

Chainsaw took careful aim at the star-filled sky and fired. The single round streaked several thousand feet up into the starry blackness and exploded with a "boof." A bright white-green flare ignited as its parachute opened, lighting up the desert valley for miles.

"Cool," said Jeremy.

Now they could clearly see the rest of the boys, who were scrambling toward the freeway about a mile down the trail.

"Alright," laughed Reggie.

They saw the crowd stop and look back at the bright flare. The lone light hanging high in the sky reminded everyone of the single sodium vapor light which had hung above them forever in the Cauldron.

Reggie, Jeremy, and Chainsaw continued jogging through the scents and shadows of the mountain–the sage, the tumble weeds, cactus flowers, sand, and rosemary. After living underground for so long, it was like traveling through the Garden of Eden, but it was impossible to make out any detail in the silent, shadow-filled valley below them. There were no landmarks, and the endless space they were jogging down into was just as dark and ominous as the looming mountain they were running from. As the flare fell, it made the shadows grow longer and longer.

Finally, they felt a hard, smooth surface under their feet–the freeway. It was almost impossible to see because the asphalt was so dark. Everyone else had made it to the road too. They all stood scattered on the asphalt, freezing. Some huddled together, confused, lost again.

Reggie wondered if they were in even worse danger now. At least ECHO had fed them. Maybe no one would ever find them here and they'd freeze to death, or burn in the blazing sun, which they all knew was coming in a few hours. Just as

Reggie was getting jittery about the future he had brought his fellow game masters into, Claw found him.

"I still can't believe you did it," said Claw. "You beat ECHO at its own game. How did you know your dad wasn't really inside that thing?"

Reggie was relieved. No one made him feel the way Claw did. He immediately relaxed and forgot his fears.

"Behavior patterns," said Reggie. "Like you said, everyone has their own behavior pattern. It was what he said. My dad never calls me Reginald. He calls me Reg–just Reg. And there were other things he said."

Claw smiled. Reggie had never seen her smile. The moon reflected in her white teeth. Could she possibly be any more beautiful? It was a new Claw–a smiling Claw–and he liked this side of her. It was a side of her he had never seen.

"So how does it feel to have destroyed ECHO?" she asked.

"Not nearly as good as it does just getting out of there. And at least Rhino doesn't hate me anymore."

"He never did hate you. I told you, it had nothing to do with you. His dad disappeared last year. Rhino's really mad about it, and he doesn't trust anyone anymore."

"Oh," said Reggie, feeling bad for Rhino. "I didn't know."

"Hey, practically everyone here has some kind of disorder. My mother–she drives me crazy. She's a total narcissist. You know why I'm so happy about what happened to my face?"

"Why?"

"Because when my mother sees me, she only sees herself, so she'll freak! To my mother, anything I do has absolutely nothing to do with me–it's only a reflection of her."

"What do you mean?"

"My mom's a big socialite. Wants me to help her social life, be there *ALL THE TIME.* Appearances, parties, the 'Hamilton Family.' It's her trip! To her, everything's all about 'Society,' and where 'The Hamiltons fit in'."

"What about your dad?" asked Reggie.

"Nothing bothers him. He just puts up with it. But my mom, she'll be *really* mad, not about what happened to me, but that her friends will say: 'Did you *see* Jennifer Hamilton's daughter? What *happened* to her?'" Claire laughed, "I can't wait for my mother to see me. It's gonna be great! And the best part is I'm gonna follow her EVERYWHERE now. I'm gonna be the best little chip-off-the-old-block socialite ever! It's gonna be a riot!"

"Wow. I thought *our* parents were a nightmare!" said Reggie.

"Trust me. No one here has a normal family. That's probably why we all got into ECHO's games so much in the first place. So guess what? You're completely normal."

Reggie was surprised and relieved. It was a new feeling to not be the weirdo, the "freakazoid." Ever since he met Claw he'd been having a lot of strange new feelings. Because of her, his whole world had clicked into a new, improved reality. Maybe there were lots of psycho parents and messed up families out there. Maybe he wasn't so weird after all. Maybe there was no "perfect" family. Maybe there were lots of kids whose parents were alcoholics, or whatever, or just missing, for whatever reason.

Reggie respected Claw. She knew a lot and had explained a lot of stuff that had been driving him crazy. Maybe she was right. Maybe life was a game sometimes, and you just had to play the cards you were dealt the best you could. Instead of complaining about how things are, maybe you need to stop, take a hard look, and think about what you can do to make it work for you. If you did that, maybe you could always improve your life and you'd never be a loser.

But the two points of light soon reappeared on the horizon. The pinpoints slowly grew bigger, then resolved into headlights. Was it a car? How would they all get out? Who would go first, and how long would everyone else have to wait? The headlights grew larger. It looked like it was a truck coming!

The driver of the truck had been driving alone all day. It had been a long, hot day and an even longer cold night, but he was used to the long haul because he had faith in his truck and faith in the way the world worked. He wore a small silver cross around his neck, and there was a Virgin Mary statue, a GPS locator, and a chattering C.B. radio on his dashboard.

There was an explosion in the sky ahead of the truck. As the driver slowed down, he saw dozens and dozens of ghoulish boys wandering aimlessly on the freeway ahead of him. The lower halves of their bodies disappeared in the shadow of the flare light, so they looked like they were floating. It was impossible to tell what they were doing there, or if what he saw was even real. They looked like ghosts, somehow floating over the road, like it was the spectral highway of dead boys long past.

For a second, the driver thought he was passing through a Day of the Dead celebration, but it was not November first or second.

"¡Dios mío!" he whispered.

He slowed down and locked his door as he coasted past a few boys. They were all standing still in the freeway, frozen zombies, waving for him to please stop. The flare had fallen slowly, extinguishing itself as it banged onto the roof of his cab. The driver jumped, startled, and then stopped, opened his door, and leaned out to see what had landed on his roof, worried that his truck might catch on fire. The dead flare and parachute fell to the ground as a zombie girl with big claw marks across her face approached him.

"¡Chica animal loca!" he cried.

As he got back in and rolled up his window, two more of the ghost-boys walked up. He shined his flashlight in their faces. It was Reggie and Jeremy.

"¿Qué? Icaracoles! Pete!!!?"

"Pete!" said Reggie and Jeremy in surprised unison.

"What are you guys doing out here? You look dead! How did you get here? I thought you were in LA!"

"We got kidnapped," said Jeremy.

"Yeah," said Reggie, "but we escaped. Can you give us a ride?"

Big Pete didn't know what to do. He looked down the road and thought to himself, just as he did when they first met, on the freeway near Meadowbrook.

"Well, you'll freeze or burn to death out here, so, si. You're lucky it's night. In the day it's 130 degrees and no shade. That's why I only drive here at night."

He led all of the boys and Claw to the back of the truck, and then stopped.

"Whoa! Time out! Only if you all agree that you never saw me, and you can't ever tell anyone I gave you a ride, okay? Somebody'll think *I* kidnapped you!"

Everyone agreed. If he got them out of there, their lips would stay sealed forever.

"Okay, mis amigos. I don't usually take people *this* direction, but climb in. ¡Rapido!"

Everyone was amazed that Reggie and Jeremy knew the driver. Now everyone would doubly, nay, triply owe them forever. Big Pete opened the back doors on the truck and started loading the boys in.

"Rapido! Hurry up! The sun will be here soon!" he said.

After a few guys got in, Big Pete climbed in with them and showed them some hidden compartments where there was space under the floor. There were blankets and just enough room to lie down and sleep, so the boys lay down in the blankets like mummies in caskets.

As Reggie laid down, he noticed something under his back and picked it up. It was a small Catrina doll. As he looked into its face, he felt an odd sense of calmness.

When Big Pete saw Reggie's reaction, he laughed.

"I've been looking for that," he said, taking the doll.

Once all seventy-seven gamers were loaded and Big Pete was about to close the door, Jeremy yelled.

"Big Pete, where are we, anyway?"

"You don't know!? You're in the middle of the Mohave Desert. Death Valley! Now take a siesta, Little Pete."

Big Pete slammed the door shut, climbed into the cab, and started back down the freeway. Once he was up to speed, he grabbed the C.B. radio mic, pressed the button, and tiredly muttered,

"Granos de garbanzo, setenta y siete, al sur."

Which meant,

"White Garbanzo Beans, 77, to the south."

"¡¿Al sur?!" said Raul, "¡¿Qué?!"

29. OUT OF BUDGET

Big Pete drove all night. It was a long haul down the dark, silent freeway. There was no other traffic.

Weeks or months had passed since the guys had been snatched from their homes. They didn't know how long it had been and they had no idea where they were going now, but they didn't care. They were out of that mountain, the Cauldron, and the Pit, and soon they would be out of the desert.

The gentle murmur of the truck engine was a peaceful, reassuring sound to everyone, so they slept well. It was the best night of sleep many of them could remember, since their memories were so murky from being enslaved in darkness for so long.

When Big Pete finally opened the doors, bright sunlight burst into the truck and everyone woke up squinting at the daylight to which they were completely unaccustomed. The air was breezy, and filled with the smell of hot, fresh pizza, the aroma of heaven on Earth. Rock-and-roll music was playing in the background. It seemed unnatural, like a dream, too good to be true. Everyone squinted as they climbed out.

"Ah, sweet summer!" said Flame as they unloaded.

"¡Vacaciones!" said Rhino, with a grateful smile.

The truck had parked in a back alley in San Diego. The instant the boys were unloaded, Big Pete climbed back into the cab, revved the engine, and yelled, "Adios Petes! Remember, you never saw me!" Then he drove away while their eyes were still adjusting, leaving them there like they had just beamed in from an alien planet.

SpanDex picked up a comic convention flyer and read it. Then he noticed the date on a newspaper in a nearby news stand.

"OH, NO!! It's September sixteenth!"

"Oh man!" someone else yelled, "School's already started! Summer vacation's way over!"

Everyone groaned. They were angrier than ever at ECHO for completely ruining their summer vacation. But one of the guys still had a credit card, so after buying about a hundred pizzas, there was a feast. Then everyone called their parents, who were shocked and relieved to hear from them.

Reggie was hanging out with Claw, but he saw Jeremy finish a call, too.

"Did you call Mom?" asked Reggie.

"Yeah, but she wasn't there. All Asa said was "Hey, where have you been?! Get your butts back here–you have chores to do!"

Jeremy looked into Reggie's eyes. He couldn't help but laugh, and then Reggie started laughing too. Asa was ridiculous. Compared to everything they had been through, he was the biggest joke on Earth. The idea of him bullying them with chores, or threats, or even punches anymore was ridiculous.

Asa would never change, but after what had happened, after all ECHO had done to them, and after battling ECHO and coming out winners, they could easily deal with anything, especially Asa.

Then Reggie remembered something Jeremy had said the first time they came up against ECHO way back in San Francisco.

"Asa *is* a joke compared to that thing."

Meanwhile, a computer at the credit card company noticed that a hundred pizzas had been ordered on the credit card, so a program flagged the purchase as a spending pattern aberration and triggered a call to the Credit Card Fraud Division at the FBI. Once the FBI called the pizza joint and found out what had happened, they immediately sent two agents down to get the boys' stories–just for the record–so they could close Case #698-15-1910-549-63-66-1-A, The Serial I-5 Gamer Kidnappings.

But the guys didn't know exactly where they had been the whole time, and because they couldn't tell anyone that Big Pete had rescued them from the desert, their stories didn't match up, so the agents didn't believe them. But the agents didn't care. They had no time or money left to spend on the case. Republicans in the House of Congress had shut down the President's ability to order unlimited printing of U.S. dollars, so there was no more unlimited spending by Federal Agencies. The FBI agents were glad to find the kids and close the file.

Since the agents couldn't come up with a reasonable explanation for the kidnappings, they decided to report that the boys had all run away for the summer for some kind of social gaming adventure, and had ended up at the comic book convention.

"Once again, social networking run amok," said one agent.

"More kids who don't respect authority," said the other, which had nothing to do with anything.

When some of the parents arrived to pick up their kids, the agents told them that their sons had not been kidnapped, but had actually suffered a kind of mass delusion which had caused them to run away from home. They said it was all caused by playing too much on-line ECHO's Revenge, and that their minds had been scrambled. The agents told them that mass hysteria was not that uncommon with massive groups of on-line gamers. They told them that they should discourage their kids from talking about this "massive group delusion" and that soon the guys would forget everything and go back to normal, just like Tom had. As long as they never, ever played any of the ECHO's Revenge games again.

"We've seen this kind of thing many times," said one of the agents reassuringly at the end of each conversation with the parents. "Massive Online Gaming groups often get together and weird things happen. Unpredictable things. But your son will be fine."

"E.O.F.," said one agent to the other, as he put the file into his briefcase and clicked it shut.

"End of File," echoed the other.

Later, Reggie and Jeremy stood in line with a bunch of other guys waiting to get on a bus to go home. Across the parking lot, a few other kids from southern California were getting into cars that were picking them up.

One was Claw.

A big, squeaky clean, Hispanic guy got out of a dusty limo and approached her. Claw looked like a weak, dirty, orphaned rag doll. When he saw her, he stopped, put a hand on his hip, lifted up his sunglasses, and said something. They both laughed. The driver leaned down and hugged her. They both had tears in their eyes. Then he led her to the back seat, carefully buckled her in, and closed her door. As he walked to the driver's side, his expression changed. He looked concerned and worried, like his job was about to become a lot more difficult.

As the limo eased onto the road, it veered toward Reggie and Jeremy. Claw's dark window scrolled down.

"Reggie, thanks again. And don't forget–there's a code, somewhere, for everything. You can do anything."

Reggie nodded. Her mention of codes reminded him about what he had seen deep in the mountain with Chainsaw–the Infinity Code. Even though he felt completely comfortable talking to her now, before he could say anything she said "Goodbye Reggie, take care of yourself," and the window rolled back up. The limo pulled away, and in a moment it had accelerated and disappeared into the traffic.

Reggie wondered if it would be the last time he saw her. He had another odd feeling, this time anxiousness–his stomach ached because he missed her. He had never really missed anyone except his dad before, but now he definitely missed Claw. Despite feeling happy to be free, he felt a deep, heavy loss when she drove out of sight. Claw was different. She spread light everywhere she went. She had filled in big parts of his world with uncanny insights and intelligence. Because of Claw, his life started to make sense for the first time, and it felt much bigger, more meaningful, and full of possibilities. He wanted to give Claw something in return, but he knew he had nothing to give. Once again, he felt something was out of balance.

As her car disappeared into traffic, he worried that he had lost her and might not ever find her again. It was then that he noticed with a sense of wonder that the fiery feeling Claw gave him had moved from his stomach to his heart.

The rest of the guys were already on the bus. Jeremy hopped up the stairs, and Reggie was about to jump on when a sheriff put his arm across the doorway.

"Wha...?"

"Hold it right there," said the sheriff, waving his badge to the bus driver that everything was okay.

"Hey, that's my brother, we travel together!" said Reggie.

"Yeah? Well I have a court order that says you don't."

There was something in the sheriff's eyes that made Reggie think that he enjoyed pushing kids around. The door slammed shut, and before Reggie could think, he felt a hand on his shoulder. When he turned around, he was again taken by surprise. It was his dad.

"Hi Reg!" he said, as he signed a form for the sheriff.

"Dad?! What're you doing here!?" said Reggie in disbelief.

He hadn't seen his father in what seemed like years. His dad looked different from how Reggie remembered him, but somehow Reggie knew right away that it was him.

"How'd you know I was here!?" said Reggie.

Jeremy watched the conversation from his window. Reggie's father looked around for a moment, not knowing what to say. The bus started up. Reggie started to worry that he was being left behind.

"Don't worry," his father said. "You're coming home with me."

Reggie's father gestured a longing thumbs-up to Jeremy.

Reggie didn't understand.

"You know, to live with me. Jem is too, soon. And don't worry about Asa, he has to leave when Jem gets back. Court order."

The bus pulled away. His father held his hand up in a frozen wave as Jeremy drove away.

Reggie was speechless. Even though he had somehow achieved his ultimate objective, the idea of being separated from Jeremy made his head spin.

"Why now, all of a sudden?"

His dad gave him a strange look, as if to say, *'how could you not know?'* Then, he explained.

"The courts don't usually let kids live with their divorced dads until they're thirteen or fourteen. Your mother and I had a deal. When you turned fourteen, you would come live with me. I can't believe she didn't tell you. She was supposed to prepare you for the move!"

Reggie shrugged his shoulders since he had nothing to do with monitoring his mother's behavior. It was all so confusing.

"Guess *I'll* have to tell Jem. Anyway, I was tracking you until you got to my house. That's why I thought you were coming, to move, even though I never heard from your mother. Which is, as we see, not unusual. But the tracking signal was lost."

"You tracked us? How?"

"The knife."

"The knife?"

"The knife I gave you. I put a chip in the knife and tracked you by satellite. I was always, constantly, worried about you. I always wanted to know where you were, but I could hardly ever get you on the phone. That's why I gave you the knife. If I couldn't see you, at least I could know where you were.

"But I lost the signal after you got to my house. There was a huge electromagnetic burst. Then it came up as a blip last night. For just a second, so I wasn't sure. Then it came on again, in Death Valley. I followed it here."

He gave Reggie a minute for all the info to sink in.

"Come on, let's get out of here. Gotta get you to school."

"Oh, school."

Reggie's stomach twisted at the idea of being the new guy in a new school. They walked across the parking lot.

"By the way, where is the knife?" his dad asked.

Reggie checked his pockets, then realized, "Jeremy's got it."

Reggie was sad about losing Jeremy so suddenly, but he couldn't think because he was overwhelmed by all the realities of the new world in which he now found himself.

"Good, we'll always know exactly where he is," his dad continued. That, and the fact that Asa was moving out, meant Jeremy would be safe, but Reggie missed him already. His mind spun in confusion again.

Reggie wondered when the knife had been detected by the satellite. Was it the satellite that they observed slowly inching across the sky?

So, his dad had obviously known where they had been the whole time they were traveling south, all the way from Washington state. The rides were so easy to get on the way down–had he set them up?

"Starman..." muttered Reggie, not thinking.

His father froze. Without moving his head, his eyes drifted to Reggie. Then he resumed walking.

"Never say that name."

"Why?"

His father thought for a second, trying to decide if he should tell Reggie something. They arrived at his car, a green 1995 Lexus.

"You have no idea what you've gotten yourself into Reg, with that...shape shifter. Take my advice and forget about that thing. Everything. Just focus on school – that's what's most important in your life right now."

They got in the car, and before Reggie knew it they were driving down another freeway, this time north, toward Pasadena.

EPILOGUE

Before he knew it, Reggie saw palm trees on the side of the freeway. As he started to relax with the notion of a completely new life, he noticed a laptop computer on the back seat.

"Hey, Dad, can I check my email?"

Mr. King wasn't used to being called 'Dad,' but he was relieved that despite not having seen Reggie for so long, his son actually thought of him as his dad enough to call him 'Dad.'

"Yeah, sure Reg."

Reggie flipped open the computer and logged onto his email account, not knowing what to expect after so many months. There were hundreds of emails.

It's probably all jammed up and infected with spam, he thought, but it wasn't.

As he skimmed through the messages, he clicked open a few random samples to see what he had missed since his abduction by E-7.

waitingforyou:

E-7's coming for you!
Soon.
If I were you, I would be very afraid.

HAkr

HAkr, thought Reggie. *How did he know?*

reggie-
hope this isn't a problem, but...where to start? okay, echo, a REAL echo (yes, that's right, real—about 35 feet tall and weighing in at 6500 pounds of computer-driven hydraulic power—we spent three years building him for the new reality game) has escaped on its own—for some unknown reason—and is officially out of our control. unfortunately, he's identified you as a target ever since the focus group (actually, possibly even before. it was sneaking out on its own before we knew it). you may have noticed a sparkling effect? and that he imitates voices and sounds to confuse his opponents, like at the focus group when he started the fight with Jorge and Abdullah? well, that was him, and now he's hunting you and all the gamers.
anyway, I had to give up the trap door cheat code that I gave you (to freeze 7's operating system) because we're trying to shut it down with a virus, then find and fix it.
sooooo, don't try to use the code word I gave you to stop echo. it won't work anymore. but hopefully our virus will!
sorry about all this.
s.a.

Great. No wonder the code didn't work. At least the virus worked though.

waitingfor you:

I linked your laptop address to 7's stalker program. HA!
having fun watching 7 chase you all the way to daddy's house.
are you having fun yet big shot? guess you're not so smart after all.
he's sooooo close!
good luck! :((

HAkr

Why me? thought Reggie. *Just because I beat E-6?*

Dear Reggie,
Read this, turn off your computer, and then run!
AAARG has been shut down—completely out of my control—and 7 just burned down our Gameland Combat Center (where you were just about to be invited to play the beta "Echo's Revenge"). I would have emailed you earlier, but if you downloaded any email over wireless you would have given 7 your location. Plus, I didn't want to spook you.
If, by chance, 7 did NOT acquire you yet, hide somewhere secure and do not move!
Sorry about this. Still trying to figure out what happened.
ITM, please, STAY HIDDEN and DON'T ANSWER ANY PHONES.
NOW RUN!

Regretfully,
Luca Esposito
(former) President, AAARG LLC

Cool! Luca was on our side all along. I wonder where he is now.

Hey big-shot:
I just made echo7 burn down the game center,
SO YOU DON'T GET TO PLAY ECHO'S REVENGE AFTER ALL.
too bad. for you, that is.
and guess what?
it all happened while you were in 7, after he ate you!
are you having fun yet?
what do you think of my hacking now?
don't cry too much, now you get to meet 7 for real.
I am in control now, wfy.
that makes me smarter than you, doesn't it?
Ha!Ha!Ha!Ha!Ha!Ha!Ha!Ha!Ha!Ha!
laughing at you,
Hakr

So, it's all about being "smart," thought Reggie. *Get a life!*

By now Reggie was not only sick of HAkr, but wondering if HAkr was still stalking him and, if so, when he'd ever stop. He scanned down the page to see how many more messages there were from HAkr, but there weren't any. *Thank God,* he thought. Then he noticed another one from Luca.

"Anything interesting?" interrupted his father.

"No, not much," answered Reggie.

Reggie opened the email from Luca.

ECHO 7 Warning
Reggie,
In case you are safe and can read this:
7 sees all our email.
7 automatically links to every one of our email contacts.
7 reads their messages, too, searching for clues to find us.
therefore, everyone you email becomes a 7 target, too.
7 is doing this on a massive scale with zombie robot programs.
I have a sickening feeling that 7 is trying to take over the world, or something equally terrible, due to a corruption that somehow got into its game logic code. 7 thinks he's some kind of supernatural god or something.
accordingly
stay off email until 7 is stopped.
I can't say any more now for obvious reasons.
erase this now.
Luca

Reggie got a sinking feeling in his stomach about all his contacts. Then he remembered ECHO was dead and it didn't matter anymore.

A new message from Sean Austin, dated seconds before, suddenly popped onto the top of the screen.

reggie-

are you out there? i heard you guys got free. I heard all about HAkr and what he did. You should know that 7 really let him have it, then left him for dead, but he's actually still alive. BArely.
i set up an investigation at echohunt.com to find ECHO-7, so please contact me at seanaustin@echohunt.com or feel free to post at the message center there. we need your story, for the record. check out echohunt.com and send me anything you can. please, we need your help putting the pieces together.
is 7 really dead?
s.a.
echohunt.com

Dead as dead gets.

Then another email popped on. This one from Luca.

Dear Reggie,
I saw your footprints in the sand in Death Valley this morning.
I'm sorry about everything, but glad you're free!!
Contact me at luca@aaarealitygames.com. The site still actually takes emails.
I'll tell you what I know.
Will you tell me what you know?
Where is 7 now?
You must have beaten him since you're free, so he must be dead.
How did you do it??
Hoping you'll contact me soon,
and, of course, apologies...
Luca

Before Reggie could worry about being bugged by the guys from AAA Reality Games, a final message popped onto the screen.

I'm pretty popular today, he thought.

wfy-
avoid echohunt.com
don't use ur old email address
erase ths now and email me at

claw.aaarg@gmail.com

will explain l8r
yours,
claw

Echo's dead, so why is Claw worried about tracking through email? thought *Reggie.*

But he was distracted because his heart skipped a beat when he noticed that Claw had written "yours" in closing, completely spelled out, just before her name. He quickly erased her message, logged out of his email account, and opened a new account at waitingforyou.aaarg@gmail.com. Then he answered Claw.

claw-
thks for the heads-up
yours,
waiting for you.

Reggie logged off his new gmail account. As he was about to close the laptop he noticed a communications folder and opened it. It was another open email account, his father's. He quickly checked to see if his old email address was listed as a contact in his dad's email directory. It was. ECHO had surely scanned everything in his father's email account! ECHO must have known everything in every one of his dad's emails.

Uk, thought Reggie.

He felt a sickening wrench in his gut as he looked at his father, thinking about the breach he had caused in his father's email security, and probably in his father's entire hard drive as well.

Then Reggie noticed a familiar name listed in his father's email contact list–"semperfi"–and then a couple of names at geosyncrobotics.com, a company name which he recognized from the business card he had grabbed off the ground in Crescent City–the Buzz Cuts' company. It was obvious. His dad not only knew where he was before he was abducted, he had also set up all their rides down to Pasadena. Somehow, his dad knew all the drivers who had picked them up. It would have been easy to arrange since his dad had been tracking Reggie with the locator he had hidden in the pocket knife. All he had to do was find someone traveling in the same direction who was nearby and have them pick him up, as some kind of favor maybe. Reggie wanted to know more.

"Um, Dad?"

But his dad didn't hear him. He was concentrating on driving and thinking about something else so intently that it was like he wasn't there, like his mother had always said, *'His head is stuck in the clouds.'*

Then it occurred to Reggie: Once again, no good turn goes unpunished. There had been a consequence to his father's good turn of tracking them and getting them rides: ECHO had known about it. ECHO had accessed everything in his dad's account because it, too, had been tracking Reggie and would have looked for any destination information in his dad's emails after discovering his address in Reggie's contact list. It was of great annoyance to Reggie that ECHO had found someone with a parallel objective–tracking Reggie–and had 'echoed' him. It was even worse that the person ECHO had echoed was Reggie's own father.

"Lots of email you got there," said his Dad, coming out of his daze. Reggie had to get off soon.

"Yeah, months' worth, I can't read it all now, though."

Reggie closed the email tab, and noticed a bunch of encrypted files in a folder called "Starlight Project". Had 7 been able to unlock these files, too? Did they have something to do with "Starman"? Some of the secure file names were identical to the file names Reggie had seen on the laptop in ECHO's depot chamber, deep in the mountain. Reggie panicked. He had to alert his dad.

But then Reggie remembered again that 7 was dead. He kept forgetting ECHO was dead. He had to get used to that fact. There was no more threat, so he didn't need to upset his father with any further unpleasantness. Besides, his father might blame him and there would be major Hell to pay. Reggie might even be sent back to Meadowbrook. No, he'd keep his trap shut for now. 7 was dead.

But what about his own laptop?

"Hey dad, did you find my laptop? It was in a knapsack I left by your front door."

"No, I never saw it."

Another mystery, thought Reggie. *What if ECHO got it? It doesn't matter. Forget ECHO. Forget the whole ECHO'S REVENGE game. Game Over!*

But unknown to Reggie, not only had ECHO ensured that none of the gamers would ever forget him, they would also be linked together forever. Just before it fell into the Pit, as its claw was sliding down the I-beam–which, connected to the entire network of I-beams acted as a huge antenna–it sent out a final message to another zombie computer circuit.

It was a command that triggered a program called "WatchingYou" in a traffic light control processor in a foreign country. The program was a tactical decoy intended to confuse the gamers, to buy time so that ECHO could repair itself if it survived, while keeping the gamers confused.

"WatchingYou" was running like clockwork half a world away on that tiny circuit in the traffic light above a busy intersection in Singapore, just like 1,232,389,455 other programs ECHO had started on other zombie processors around the world.

Beginning on September 23rd at 10 P.M., as they sat at their computers IM-ing their classmates, Waiting For You, Secret Weapon, Chainsaw, Rhino, Claw, and every gamer from the Cauldron saw a message flash on the screen for a moment so brief that they wondered if it had really been there. It was the first of many to randomly appear on their computer screens.

It said:

I'M WATCHING YOU!

EOF

The Ongoing Investigation of Sean Austin
continues with
Book 2
Echo's Revenge: The Other Side

See Chapter 1 at
www.echohunt.com

REALITY GAMES

[2]

Made in the USA
Charleston, SC
29 July 2012

[2]